The Rivenhall Weddings

A brand-new trilogy from Carol Arens

The three children of Viscount Rivenhall couldn't be more different: serious Thomas feels the responsibility of his position as heir, while fun-loving William struggles to settle down. But even he hasn't the same capacity for causing scandal as his younger sister, Minerva!

Now it is time for all three to be wed— but will they marry as they are expected to?

Book 1

Inherited as the Gentleman's Bride

When William Grant is told it is time to settle down, he isn't sure that he wants to swap life as a London gentleman for the life of a farmer. Until he meets his prospective bride...

Available now

And look out for Thomas and Minerva's stories, coming soon!

D0711855

Author Note

I appreciate so much that you have picked up a copy of Elizabeth and William's story.

I hope that you will be touched by their tale. They begin as strangers from different worlds but in the end, they find a way to make a happily-ever-after out of it.

You rightly guess that their path will not be a smooth one. Elizabeth is a country girl. William is a viscount's son.

They choose to wed because they are really given no choice in the matter. William is a rascal who needs to settle down and is given Wilton Farm as a place to do it...oh, and a bride comes with the farm. Elizabeth does not want to leave Wilton Farm, the only home she has ever known. The only way to keep it is to wed the stranger who will soon own it.

Worlds clash...worlds meld. Each of them must resolve a question. What will they do for love?

And what, dear reader, would you do for love?

Like Elizabeth and William, I hope you would find your heart's desire.

CAROL ARENS

———

Inherited as the Gentleman's Bride

H HARLEQUIN®
HISTORICAL™

ISBN-13: 978-1-335-40770-2

Inherited as the Gentleman's Bride

Copyright © 2022 by Carol Arens

This edition published by arrangement with Harlequin Books S.A.

For questions and comments about the quality of this book,
please contact us at CustomerService@Harlequin.com.

Harlequin Enterprises ULC
22 Adelaide St. West, 41st Floor
Toronto, Ontario M5H 4E3, Canada
www.Harlequin.com

Printed in U.S.A.

Carol Arens delights in tossing fictional characters into hot water, watching them steam and then giving them a happily-ever-after. When she is not writing, she enjoys spending time with her family, beach camping or lounging about a mountain cabin. At home, she enjoys playing with her grandchildren and gardening. During rare spare moments, you will find her snuggled up with a good book. Carol enjoys hearing from readers at carolarens@yahoo.com or on Facebook.

Books by Carol Arens

Harlequin Historical

The Cowboy's Cinderella
Western Christmas Brides
"A Kiss from the Cowboy"
The Rancher's Inconvenient Bride
A Ranch to Call Home
A Texas Christmas Reunion
The Earl's American Heiress
Rescued by the Viscount's Ring
The Making of Baron Haversmere
The Viscount's Yuletide Bride
To Wed a Wallflower
A Victorian Family Christmas
"A Kiss Under the Mistletoe"
The Viscount's Christmas Proposal
Inherited as the Gentleman's Bride

Visit the Author Profile page
at Harlequin.com for more titles.

Dedicated to Sean DeCuir,
my much-loved son-in-law.

You are a wonderful man and
a blessing to the family.

Prologue

October 1869—London

'I left Dollie on the park bench,' Elizabeth said, tugging on her aunt's sleeve.

When she got no response, she looked up at her uncle and told him the same.

Why had they brought her to London if all they wanted to do was speak to other grown-ups? They chatted happily with two people Elizabeth did not even know and all the while Dollie was abandoned on the bench where she might be snatched away by another child.

Elizabeth could see the bench from where she stood. At eight years old she was capable of fetching her doll by herself.

'I am going to get Dollie,' she said, but because they were so caught up in speaking to the strangers, she doubted her aunt or uncle heard her.

Hurrying towards the bench, she felt a little scared. She was not used to so many people and all of them strangers. Back home at the farm there were only neighbours. She had never really met anyone she had not known all her life.

But she was a brave girl, so when the crowds closed around her she did not hesitate to run along the path towards poor Dollie, all alone on the bench and her rag legs dangling off the edge.

Snatching the doll up, she gave a great sigh of relief. She would be back with Auntie and Uncle before they even knew she had ventured away on her own. But then, glancing about, all she saw was the path crowded with people. She turned in a circle. Whichever way she looked she saw skirts and trousers shifting and blocking her view of where she had been.

But, oh, my…where had she been? Had she come from this way or that? Clutching Dollie to her heart, she walked the way she thought was right, calling for Aunt Mary and Uncle James. Conversations went on above her head and no one paid her any mind.

At first, that was. And then a big, heavy hand clamped down upon her shoulder.

'Uncle James!' In her profound relief she nearly dropped Dollie.

But then she looked up and it was not Uncle James, but a stranger.

'Come with me, little girl. I know where your uncle is, and I will take you to him.'

She might have been only eight years old and never met a proper stranger before, but something told her this one was not to be trusted, that he was not a gentleman with a child's best interests at heart.

It could be the sight of his beak-like nose or his missing teeth that made her distrust him. But he was also missing several buttons on his coat and an odd smell came from his stained shirt.

Staring up, she knew she must run from him, he was a bad man and he did not know her uncle at all. She tried to scream, but her voice made no sound. But she was brave, and she was eight, so she nodded to make the ugly fellow think she was going with him.

When his fingers relaxed a tiny bit, she yanked out of his hold and dashed away. She ran as hard and as fast as she could, then turned down a quiet, narrow alley. There were barrels stacked near a wall, so she ducked behind them, huddled into herself and shivered. Heavy footsteps ran past her hiding place.

'Hey, you!' someone shouted. 'What are you about?'

Everything was quiet for a long time after that. But still, she did not dare to even breathe. The kidnapper might come back and find her. And the man who had shouted at her pursuer might be just as wicked.

She waited, waited and waited, shivering and weeping because she was convinced she was so lost that she was never going to see her aunt and uncle again.

They would think she disappeared, just like her father had. She did not remember her father or her mother. She had been a baby when Mother died and Father vanished a few days later.

Aunt Mary and Uncle James would think she'd simply puffed away the same way as her father had.

She had overheard Aunt Mary speaking to Uncle James about Father one day when they did not realise that she could hear them. Father had been gone for so long and they thought it was time to stop hoping he would return, to accept what the constable had told Aunt Mary years ago, that the man who had been found in the Thames a week after Father disappeared was probably him…but of course no one could be sure.

Even though she did not know her papa, she'd cried and cried when she heard that. Even if he had not fallen in the river, something scary had happened to him.

The alley started to grow dark with evening coming on. Fog crept along the cobbles, making everything look milky. Things that had been solid and ordinary now looked vaporous…and creepy.

Perhaps this was how Papa had disappeared? Perhaps a fog had swallowed him? If it had, where had it taken him? To the river maybe.

Hugging Dollie tight, she wiped her eyes. Perhaps she ought to come out from her hiding place and ask for help. But, no. It was now fully dark and there might be other bad men creeping around. She shivered, wondering if, just like Father, no one would ever know what had happened to her and Dollie, either.

There was a lamppost shinning at the end of the alley. It sent a bit of light to the awful dark, which ought to be a comfort. But in the fog it only looked ghostly…as if the spirits of the disappeared wandered in the mist. Perhaps Papa was in the mist…

She had to clamp her hand over her mouth because, all of a sudden, footsteps sounded on the cobbles, heading her way. The long, watery shadow of a man, or an evil spirit, was cast on the brick wall behind her. The shadow shifted and swayed just over her head.

It moaned. She was certain it did. Oh, it had to be a spirit because how was a man to cast a shadow in the fog?

Her heart was beating too hard…her breathing came in gasps and was far too loud. The creature was bound to hear her. Any instant she would be joining her father in the mist. The thought might be a comfort except that she would not know her papa, even coming face to face with him. Encountering anyone in the fog was too terrifying to consider for even half a second. And yet terrifying images would not let go of her.

Then she heard other footsteps in the ally. A woman laughed in an odd way and then the shadow faded away. As far as she could tell whatever had cast it was walking away with the woman.

Elizabeth started to shake, whether, in relief that the shadow had not been supernatural, or from the cold—she did not know which. Even shivering, she reminded herself she was safe now. Morning would come and her uncle and aunt would find her.

And then she heard a noise…the skitter-scatter of tiny feet. Peeking out from behind the barrels, she saw rats darting across the cobbles. Fog hid and then revealed them. It was impossible to judge how many there were. Dozens, perhaps, and now three of the dirty beasts were exploring the hem of her dress. She threw her doll at them.

To her complete horror, one of them bit Dollie's apron and dragged her off. Four more went after Dollie, their eyes catching the milky lamplight and making them glow red.

She ought to go after her doll, but she was too scared to do anything but watch across the alley while the rats nibbled Dollie's pretty blue-satin shoes. Perhaps…oh, dear, even her thoughts were shivering…but perhaps this was how Father had disappeared…devoured by rats…

Chapter One

March 1886—London

Alone, at last.

William Grant relaxed into the coach cushion, anxious to feel the vehicle begin to move through the foggy night.

It had been a stressful evening at Rivenhall. What a relief it was to get away from home and be on his way to the sanctuary of his club. There, he could count on the company of friends to restore his normally cheerful mood.

He loved his father and his older brother, Thomas, but at times their preoccupation with his conduct wore on him. The lecture he had just received from Father, with Thomas frowning on, had been especially intense.

And all over a rumour that he had stolen a kiss from Lady Penelope Briswell. While it was true that he had kissed her, he had not stolen said kiss. Penelope had offered her lips quite freely and he was not one to cause insult by refusing her lovely offer.

The truth was, he had never stolen a kiss. There was

no need to when ladies so enjoyed offering them. Also true, the occasions of his kisses were not as frequent as gossip liked to portray. It was laughable, really. Did society believe he did nothing else?

It was true that he was not a saint. His reputation did have some merit, but at the same time he was not the scoundrel that some of his contemporaries were. In spite of the talk, at heart he was the gentleman his mother had raised him to be. As such, he had never pressed a flirtatious moment further than that. Still, gossip, deserved and undeserved, tended to get his father's attention.

In the dim interior of the cab, William gave a snort. Attention was attention no matter how one got it, he supposed, but now he was quite in the hot seat, even though he and Penelope had not been caught in the act. But people did enjoy whispering behind their hands. He imagined they might enjoy speaking of a suspected indiscretion more than he enjoyed indulging in one. With only speculation to accuse him and the lady of wrongdoing, her reputation would not suffer past tomorrow.

Sadly, for Father, the same could not be said of William's reputation. Viscount Rivenhall was all too aware of the giggles and whispers surrounding his secondborn. More and more William felt his father's frown resting upon him. This was especially rankling because Father always smiled in pride at Thomas, who was being groomed to take over the title one day.

One would think that having adored Mother as he had, Father would appreciate that William was remarkably like her in appearance and behaviour. Mother had always been a free and happy spirit who'd brought joy to everyone she met.

As far as William was concerned, lively behaviour honoured that wonderful woman's memory. Thirteen years had passed since he'd last seen her smile, but he felt it every day in his heart. He liked to imagine she smiled down upon him and his harmless escapades. When he was small and given a lecture for being caught out in mischief, Father would be stern. Then afterwards Mother would pat him on the head, kiss his cheek and give him a secret wink.

Feeling the coach bump along the cobbles, he could still hear this evening's conversation. He had been impatient to go out and join his friends at the club, but Father had summoned him to his study.

'It has come to my attention that you did not behave respectfully towards a young woman at Lady Hamilton's ball last week.'

'Brought to your attention by whom, Father?' He knew that no one had caught him 'disrespecting' the lady. In his opinion what he had been doing was paying respect to her womanly charms.

'It hardly matters.' Father, seated at his desk, narrowed one eye at William, who stood before him feeling once again like a condemned child. He could only hope that his mother was giving him a wink from the Great Beyond.

'Gossip is all it is.'

'Gossip or not, I heard the whispers. Who knows how many other people did as well? I will not have you besmirching our family name,' Father had announced. 'Your sister will soon make her debut. You must keep that in mind. Anything you do will reflect on her chances of making a good match. But Minerva's best interests aside, it is time and past that you married and settled down.'

'I have yet to fall in love with a woman.'

'As far as I can tell you are in love with them all!'

Not in love—William simply enjoyed their company. Why should he limit himself to enjoying the companionship of only one lady? One day he would wed, recite holy vows. After that he would be so faithful Father would not know who he was. William was his mother's child, after all, and knew there was a time for living in gaiety and afterwards a time to settle down. Father, having been devoted to Mother, ought to understand that.

'I am not ready to settle down. It would break the gossips' hearts if I did. What would people talk about?' he replied flippantly.

Ah, just there, he felt his mother give him a heavenly wink while at the same time his father's fist thudded on the polished desktop.

'You are thirty years old and it is time you grew up.'

'I shall give it some thought,' he said, but only in order to be away from here and on his way to the club.

He was not halfway down the corridor when he felt a tug on the back of his coat. 'Were you eavesdropping, Minerva?'

His eighteen-year-old sister blocked his way towards the stairway. 'How else am I to discover anything?'

'Have you never thought that some things are not meant for you to discover?'

'Nonsense, William. I need to know things in the same way that you need to kiss debutantes.'

'Who says I do that?'

His sister shrugged, giving him a sly smile. 'Nearly everyone.'

'You should not believe gossip.'

His sister, her eyes bright and sparkling with curiosity, cocked her head at him. 'I would believe your confession if you told me.'

'There is nothing to tell. No sin to be confessed.'

'I cannot say what a relief that is, Brother.'

Good, the matter was settled and he was free to get dressed for the evening. He resumed his way towards the stairs, but Minerva hurried ahead and blocked his way.

'Do you want to know why?'

No, he did not. He shook his head to let her know.

'I will make my debut this year and it is a relief to know that kissing a suitor…or two or three…will not be a sin.'

'Minerva Grant! You will do no such thing!'

He was known for liveliness, but his sister was his match in every way. They were both like their mother. Poor Thomas took after Father.

'But you do it.'

'That cannot be proven. But never mind that, you are a proper young lady.'

'The sort you steal kisses from?'

'I have never stolen a kiss in my life and you will not freely give yours away.'

'Do not be a hypocrite, William.'

'I am not—'

Well, perhaps he was. But everyone knew the behaviour requirements for a young lady were different than those for a single gentleman.

Dash it! In addition to being a hypocrite, he was

also a dunce of the first order. Perhaps his behaviour was not as harmless as he thought…not if he was encouraging young ladies to scoff at society's standards.

He stomped up the stairs, hearing Minerva's laughter echo up after him. Quite suddenly flummoxed, the thought of kissing a woman who was bound to be someone's sister made him want to keep his lips to himself. He had told Father he would consider marriage and perhaps he ought to. Many of his companions had wed and did not seem the worse.

The coach took an odd shift, then proceeded away from the house. Perhaps the wheel had encountered a divot. At least the jarring drew him away from thoughts of the conversation with Minerva. It had been unsettling to say the least.

Alone in the dim interior of the cab, he grunted unhappily. What to him had been a delightful distraction to enhance the enjoyment of an evening might be something else altogether to whichever lady was involved. In his mind, it had seemed so innocent until he thought of his sister doing such a thing. The idea of Minerva secreted in an alcove with some young blade made him see red.

The coach stopped in front of the club. The cab shifted with the weight of the driver stepping down.

'You need not wait—' The coach shifted again.

He and the driver glanced at each other in question.

'An earthquake?' the driver suggested.

'In London? I rather doubt it.'

'So would I if I wasn't in Colchester in eighty-four. That quake shook me to the bones, it did.'

'No doubt this jolt had only to do with the horses shifting. Please return for me in two hours.'

'Perhaps I will wait with the coach, just to be sure you will not need me. One never knows when nature might strike again.'

'Thank you, Thompson,' he said, certain the jolt had not been due to an unlikely quake.

With that he went inside to join the company of his friends...the ones who had not yet wed.

Since no one inside claimed to feel a jolt, he put Thompson's concern from his mind in favour of enjoying a spot of whisky with James Murray.

After a moment he wished he had not since his friend would not leave off the topic of him kissing Lady Penelope.

'I did not realise you were such a devotee to gossip, James.'

'Ah, but I know it to be the truth.'

He could not possibly, but— 'How do you know?'

'My cousin Elsa. She knows everything. For some reason people confide in her.'

'I confess to nothing, but none the less Father has lost his patience with me.' He tapped his finger on the glass balanced in his fingers, feeling annoyed at his friend's grin. 'Elsa is a busybody and you know it.'

James arched his fair brows, laughing. 'Indeed she is, but I find I like hearing what she has to say.'

'Because she does not gossip about you.'

'Nor will she, I imagine. I have news. You are the first to know it. I am to be wed to Lady Sarah Greenbriar. I hope you have not kissed her.'

'I do not kiss as many—' Dash it. 'But congratulations! I hope you will be incredibly happy...although

I suppose I will now lose another friend to domestic bliss.'

'I do not intend to spend my nights here with you when I have a beautiful wife at home.'

How long would it be before William was the only one left of his crowd, how long until he was conversing with walls?

Being thirty years old did put him past the age of casual flirtation, he supposed, which did not mean he didn't enjoy the company of ladies. They were sweet and engaging. The sound of their laughter when he coaxed a smile from them made his heart smile.

'Grant!' someone shouted from the corridor. He heard the rustle of shuffling feet as if someone were being dragged against his will.

On occasion a curious fellow did try to invade the club, but there was no reason for his name to be connected to the uproar. Everyone he knew was a respectable member.

'I believe this person belongs to you?'

'Minerva!' He leapt from his chair, watching his sister wriggle and squirm in the doorman's grasp. She was dressed as a boy, but a swathe of dark hair falling from under her cap gave her away as a female to one and all.

He nearly had to rub his eyes to be sure of what he was seeing. He knew his sister was at home safely tucked in her bed…and yet here she was.

'Tell him to release me!' Minerva flailed her arms, kicking her captor's shin.

'Ouch!'

Free of his grasp, she rushed for William, pressing close to his side. 'I thought this was a gentleman's club,' she declared with a loud, indignant sniff.

'Which begs the question, what are you doing here?' He hoped his frown was severe enough to hide the upward quirk of his mouth. Mother must have been very much like Minerva at eighteen.

'I was curious about what you do at your club.'

'How did you get here?' Please let her not have traversed the streets this time of night. That would change his half-indulgent mood in a heartbeat.

'I folded up into the carriage trunk rather neatly.'

So that was the source of the coach jolting upon leaving home and arriving here, Minerva climbing aboard and then disembarking. At least Thompson would be relieved to know it had not been an impending catastrophe.

'Come along.' He snatched her elbow, eager to draw her out of the establishment before she attracted even more attention. The last thing they needed was for this to come to Father's attention. He imagined they would both be in for it, then.

If there was one thing to be grateful for in this situation was that there was no way anyone would discover his sister's mischief. Gentlemen of the club were discreet about what went on within these walls.

Two days later when the summons came to visit Father's study, it was for William, alone.

'What have you done this time?'

'I cannot imagine what you mean.' He could imagine, of course. What he could not imagine was how Father had discovered it.

He had never had a lecture delivered to him with Father looking so angry. The man was nearly always composed. The only time he had seen him not composed was the day they buried Mother.

'It is being said that Minerva followed you to the club.'

How could he possibly know such a thing? And yet he did. Perhaps James Murray had foolishly mentioned it to his cousin.

Poor Minnie was in for it now. Which did not explain why William was the one to be summoned, to be bearing the brunt of Father's anger in her stead.

'You know your daughter, sir. It is not hard to imagine how curiosity got the better of her. No real harm was done and so I hope you will not be too severe with her.'

'Real harm has been done. With stunts like this, her debut will be tainted.'

Or she might appear irresistible to some young man who wanted a wife who was not stuffy. But it would be best to leave that unsaid.

'Gossip will soon focus on someone else and Minerva's adventure will be forgotten, Father. Please do not be too hard on her.'

'Hard on Minerva when it is you I blame for the mess?'

'I did not know she'd stowed away in the trunk. If I had I would have prevented her.'

'Not only did you not prevent her—you did not inform me of what happened. What I blame you for is being a reckless example to her. This must stop.' His father folded his hands together on top of the desk blotter and held his gaze. 'William, son…you have a kind heart and never mean any harm…you know that I see your mother in you and it warms my heart to no end.

However, this last bit involving your sister—such a thing must not happen again.'

'I shall be more diligent in the future to make certain I am not followed.'

'As shall I. I admit that I am also at fault. I do know Minerva and I ought to have been watching her more closely.' Father sighed deeply, his shoulders sagged and he pressed his palms flat on the desk. 'But surely you must now see it is time for you to grow up. Your actions have consequences to the family. Because they do, things must change.'

What things? This seemed ominous.

Father's fingertips turned white against the dark blotter. 'Minerva's prospects must not be damaged by even a hint of scandal. Because of it, I give you one of two choices for your future, William. You may pick the one which suits you best. The first I cannot imagine you will take to…or the second, to be honest, but it is up to you.'

Sweat began to bead on the back of his neck, heat flushed from his skin. He would speak in answer to what he imagined was going to be an outrage had he a voice to do it with.

Father did hold the purse strings of his existence and so he was bound to live according to his wishes. And the last thing he wished was to hurt his sister's marriage prospects, although he feared she was quite capable of doing it on her own.

'You may join the clergy. I have connections, so your reputation will not hinder you there.'

'The clergy!' He nearly choked on the notion. 'Father, you know that I am not cut out for such responsibility.'

'But it is responsibility you must learn.'

Did his father just grin at him? Surely, he could not have. What would his other option be? He was terrified to find out.

'Or you may run one of my holdings in Ambleside. Wilton Farm is a lovely sheep farm.'

'I am to be banished to the country?'

'It is hardly so awful as that. People do live there.'

'I know nothing about sheep.'

Why was Father smiling? Life had just come crashing down on William's head and yet his father was grinning. It was a wonder his heart was not splayed upon the rug.

'No need to worry, my boy.'

No? He was far beyond worry in the moment.

'There is one more thing to it.'

One more thing! This could not get any worse.

'The farm is a wedding gift…to you and your bride.'

That just went to show how wrong one could be. Things had suddenly grown a great deal worse.

'A bride…for me?' He shook his head because he had to have heard wrong.

'I have not seen the lady since she was quite young, but I am assured that she is an agreeable young woman who knows all about sheep.'

'You are jesting, no doubt. In league with Minerva to play a fine joke.' That must be what was happening.

'I do not suppose you recall the little girl who was lost those many years ago?'

He shook his head, his voice being useless for anything but croaking. Even if he did recall her, in the moment he was too stunned to bring up the details.

'Well, her aunt and uncle are my tenants. Wilton

Farm is my holding in the north. Over the years they have become friends as well as tenants and now James wishes to retire to London. His health is not what it was and they have long wished to live here.'

'Why must a wife go along with the sheep farm?' It made no sense that he should need both. Surely the place alone could accomplish what Father wanted him to learn.

'I have not the heart to put her out. Surely you must recall that I was the one to find her when she was lost? Rescuing someone…well, one does feel a certain responsibility for them.'

'One does?' He had never heard that said before.

'I do. And as I said, after what happened, Mr and Mrs Morsely became friends as well as tenants. I do not wish to see the poor girl put out of her home. But the choice is yours.'

Fortunately, there was a chair close at hand. William plonked down hard on it, trying to gather the scattering pieces of his life.

Chapter Two

One week later—Ambleside

'I, for one, do not wish to encounter tourists sleeping in my hedgerows!'

Elizabeth stood up, clapped her hands in staunch agreement with the man who had spoken.

There was a respectable-sized crowd gathered to discuss the proposed rail spur from Windermere to Ambleside. To her relief more of today's attendees were against the spur than for it. There usually were more against than for—however, the ones who were in favour tended to express their opinions rather loudly. It was no wonder, she supposed, since profit and not love for the community was what drove them.

She sat down, hoping the next person to speak would be on the correct side of the debate.

Drat! The next speaker was Bart Miller. He charged to his feet, pumping his fist in the air.

'People are not sleeping in the hedges of Windermere! No, indeed. They are staying at inns, eating at eateries and adding to the town's prosperity.'

Silence sat heavy on the meeting room. Would no

one answer Mr Miller's statement and defend bucolic Ambleside?

No? Very well.

Elizabeth stood up. She would not be the most elegant-looking speaker today since she had mud and grass stains on the hem of her gown from walking through a pasture to get here, but if no one else would speak, she would. Truly, it was not as if she had not done so before…many times.

'Let the tourists have Windermere!' she declared, waving her hands about in passion for her cause. 'We do not wish our beautiful countryside to be dissected by railroad tracks, nor do we wish to have our skies muddied with smoke.'

She felt Samuel Fowler's gaze resting upon her in admiration. She ought to be used to his attention by now since it was far from a rare thing. No doubt people were wondering when she would accept one of his frequent offers of marriage.

Samuel stood up suddenly. 'The spur will attract cottages and inns! What will become of our tranquillity?'

He gave her a nod, holding her gaze with an expression which declared he was on her side.

Other women might consider Samuel an excellent choice as a husband. His homely appearance was quite offset by his steady and sincere temperament.

It was not as if she had never given the matter of marrying him consideration. She had considered and rejected it. She was simply not ready to move away from her beloved Wilton Farm. Marrying would require she do so.

Sitting down again, she listened to arguments for and against the spur.

* * *

As usual, the meeting ended with no one changing sides on the issue. In the end it did not matter since it was not up to the residents of Ambleside to determine, but up to the railway. All they were doing by attending these meetings was to make opinions known... both for and against. Although she could not imagine how anyone could possibly be in favour of ruining the peace and quiet of the village and surrounding farms.

Coming outside into the fresh air and sunshine, she closed her eyes, then smiled at the warmth kissing her face. It was finally spring. The land was bursting with green, the trees were alive with birdsong. The earth was fairly singing with rebirth. And thinking of birth, she had best hurry back to Wilton Farm. Several of her ewes were ready to deliver lambs.

'Miss Morsely!'

Drat... Samuel was striding after her rather quickly and she did not wish to speak with him, but neither did she wish to be rude. More than that, she did not wish to have to craftily steer the conversation away from yet another proposal. No matter how sincere the man was...no matter how pleasant and dependable...it was what she would do.

If she wed...and it was past time she did, she knew that very well...it would mean she would leave Wilton Farm and live somewhere else with her husband. She did not wish to leave her home. Her heart and soul dug into this soil the same as the roots of the trees did.

One day her aunt and uncle would want to leave the farm. Uncle James was growing older, his health and energy not what they had been. It had been their cherished dream to live in London for as long as she could remember.

It was ungrateful of her, she knew, to hope and pray that it would not happen. If that day came, it would break her heart wide open. There truly was no better or safer place in all the world than Wilton Farm.

'You were quite well spoken this morning, Miss Morsely.'

'Hello, Mr Fowler,' she answered. 'It was easy since our cause is a just one.'

He fell into step beside her. Sunlight winked off strands of fair hair poking out from under the brim of his hat. Freckles on his nose wrinkled with his smile. 'Have you any lambs yet?'

'Two, but more due any time now. Have you any yet?'

'Three! And I reckon there will be more by the time I get back to the farm.'

Samuel's farm abutted Wilton Farm, the properties divided by a stream. Even though both farms were large and prosperous, she had no wish to trade living at Wilton Farm for living at Brookside Farm.

'How wonderful!' She walked faster. 'I will not keep you from them!'

'But I was hoping to have a word—'

A word which she would rather avoid. The longer she put off answering his question, the better.

There might come a time when she was forced to accept him. Surely her aunt and uncle could not wait for ever to retire to London. It was unreasonable to hope that, for her sake, they would not. No doubt they had expected her to marry long before now and be living with her husband.

She glanced sidelong at Samuel. Could she do it? Wed him so that Aunt Mary and Uncle James could get on with the life they had always dreamed of?

For all that she owed the people who had loved and raised her since she was a baby, she would never move to London with them. It would take all of her courage to even visit them in that vast, crowded and frightful city.

Pretending she had not heard Samuel, she hurried home.

Elizabeth smiled coming into the kitchen through the back door. She had returned from the meeting and found a new lamb in the pen.

She carried it in her arms, nuzzling its neck and breathing deeply of the scent. What was more precious than a newborn lamb? She could hardly wait to show it off to Aunt Mary and Uncle James.

'What have we here, miss?' Penny, the cook, set aside her stirring spoon with a great smile. Penny loved lambs as much as Elizabeth did. 'Let me see our new beauty.'

'It is only two hours old and I must get it back to its mother, but I wanted to show it off for a bit.'

'And such a pretty baby ought to be shown off. I am grateful you always bring them to meet me first thing. I will return it to the nursery pen for you. Your aunt and uncle are waiting for you in the study.'

'Waiting for me?'

Penny took the lamb from her. 'I believe they have an announcement of some sort to make.'

'Of what sort?' She knew Penny would be aware of what it was. The cook had a keen ear and knew everything that happened at the farm.

'Of the sort I am not at liberty to divulge. Go on with you now, miss. They have been most anxious for you to get home.'

Lamb forgotten, Elizabeth hurried out of the kitchen. On a half-run she dashed down a long corridor and burst into the study where Aunt Mary and Uncle James sat across a large oak desk from each other, speaking quietly.

As soon as they saw her the conversation stopped, their frowns turning into smiles. False ones unless she missed her guess. Having been raised by them, she knew when they were trying to turn something disagreeable into something agreeable.

Given Penny's reticence to speak of the matter, it could only have to do with her. She had to swallow hard to keep her heart where it belonged.

'Please sit down, my dear.' Uncle James indicated a third chair which had been pulled to the desk from its usual spot in the corner.

'We have marvellous news!' Aunt Mary's smile was bright.

That was a relief, to be sure. Still, Elizabeth sat on the edge of the seat, highly curious about what the marvellous news might be.

'Your uncle's joints have been bothering him more of late.' Yes, she knew that. Her uncle was twenty years older than her aunt, who was her late mother's twin sister. For the most part, Uncle was hale and hardy, but at sixty-five years old, he had begun to complain about aches and walked slower than he used to.

'Surely that is not marvellous news.' She was beginning to get a crawling sensation on the back of her neck. No one thought aches were marvellous. She truly hated the thought of this dear man suffering pain and she knew her aunt hated it, too.

'Naturally not. But quite out of the blue a solution has presented itself.'

A solution to the aches? Relief washed through her. This was good news after all.

'We have decided it is time for us to retire to London. The milder weather in the south ought to help your uncle greatly.'

Stunned, she stared at their grinning faces. Heart crushed, she could not manage an answering smile. Really, this should not be such a shock. She had known this was coming. Aunt Mary and Uncle James had every right to quit sheep farming and retire.

Understanding that did not keep her throat from constricting, or tears from welling in her eyes. The home she loved would no longer be her home. New tenants would move in. And where would her home be? With Samuel? In London? Both of those options made her feel sick to her stomach.

'I see that our news has distressed you.' Aunt Mary patted her hand where it had curled into a tense fist on the desktop.

'But it is lambing time…what will become of our sheep?'

She was uttering nonsense and she knew it. The well-being of lambs did not compare to the health of the man who had lovingly raised her. Besides, the new tenant would take over their care. He might not love them the way she did, but they would not perish without her.

Wilton Farm was large, profitable even. It was the envy of Ambleside. What was to become of everyone who called it home? They employed six shepherds and two housemaids, along with Penny, the cook, and Mr Adams, the foreman.

'What will become of the household staff and our herdsmen?' There was no saying that the new resident would want to keep them on.

'Lord Rivenhall has agreed that everyone will keep their positions,' Uncle James said with a quick glance at Aunt Mary.

'Even if the new tenant wishes otherwise?'

'Oh, but…' Aunt Mary wrung her hands, but held her smile. 'He does own Wilton Farm and you will recall how kind he is.'

That was something she would never forget. It had been getting dark on her second day of being lost and she had felt so scared, being certain that the bad man had found her again and was following quite closely while she wandered in the park.

Then she had heard a loud exclamation and Lord Rivenhall galloped towards her very fast on his great tall horse, then leapt down from the saddle. He'd knelt beside her and patted her back, telling her that so many people were looking for her. She'd sobbed into his shirt because he was not a stranger, but her aunt and uncle's landlord. She knew him because they had called upon him at Rivenhall on their first day in London. He had been quite friendly, even though she had half-hidden behind her aunt's skirt upon being introduced to such a lofty person as a viscount.

Aunt Mary and Uncle James had visited Rivenhall a few times since, but she'd steadfastly refused to accompany them. The memory of that time had left its scars which she had no wish to rub raw.

She was grateful that Lord Rivenhall was going to

allow the staff to remain. But what was she to do? Of the two choices she had, neither was acceptable.

She truly did not wish to wed Samuel. At the same time, she genuinely did not want to live in London… doubted that she could even if she tried to.

'When must we be out?' she managed to ask without breaking down in a selfish weeping fit.

She tried to remind herself that she had expected this to happen…only she had expected it to happen in the vague and distant future.

'I realise how hard this is for you,' Uncle James murmured. 'You feel you will be put out of your home. In the end, the choice is yours, Elizabeth. We will not retire to London if you object to it.'

Looking at their dear faces, knowing what was best for them even if it were not for her, how could she object? It would be the worst sort of repayment for all they had done for her. Had not Aunt Mary and Uncle James taken her to their hearts after her mother died, raised her as lovingly as any parents would? With her father gone she might have been left at an orphanage had it not been for her aunt.

The fact that she'd lived a life she loved in a place only a step shy of paradise was because of them. It was only for Elizabeth's sake they had kept the farm as long as they had. Even now they gave her the last word on it all.

'You have my agreement to—' Dash it…why did tears have to be leaking down her cheeks? Her agreement was going to appear as weak as it was.

'But, my dear,' Aunt Mary cooed, 'do you not recall that we said we had good news?'

'You will finally be able to move to London. That is excellent news.'

'For us, yes, but crushing for you.' Uncle James cleared his throat. Aunt Mary gave him an encouraging nod. 'Let me explain the good news. You need not move away from here.'

'The new tenant will employ me in some way?'

No, she could not live at home with it not being home. It would be better to simply…well, she did not know what because her situation was not at all simple.

'If you choose, you may become the wife of the new tenant…or rather the owner.'

'Viscount Rivenhall! Surely not.'

'Hardly that! But the new owner is to be Lord Rivenhall's son. The viscount and I have agreed that if you consent to wed his son, the title to the farm will be in both of your names…in addition, he may not sell it without your permission.'

If she had been stunned to discover the offer, she was now utterly floored to discover the details.

'This makes no sense, Uncle. Why would the viscount's son agree to such a thing? He cannot possibly have an interest in Wilton Farm. I imagine he does not know hay from straw.'

'Well, you see, the boy is a bit of a rascal and the viscount hopes that life on the farm will teach him responsibility.'

This did not sound good. What would she be getting herself into if she agreed? Would she be required to teach a fancy gentleman to be a farmer? Or perhaps he would be content to…well, to do whatever society gentlemen do and let her go on about her life…let her run things as she had been doing these past years.

'Still, I do not understand why Rivenhall would agree to it.'

'William Grant, that's his given name…his older brother will become Rivenhall, of course…but William has been offered a couple of choices for his future. He has decided that this is the better of them.'

'This keeps getting worse, Uncle. What has he turned down to think this is the solution to his problems?'

'I cannot say, but the man is willing.'

She would laugh at the absurdity of it all if her world were not standing on its head. Both she and William Grant had been given an outrageous choice to make.

It did her ego little good knowing the least of his evils had been to wed her. She did not know what the least of her evils was. At least Samuel wanted to wed her because he liked her.

If she chose living in London, she would be free to…to do whatever one did with one's time in the city if one had the nerve to venture outside the front door.

What William Grant offered, or had been forced to offer, was home. All she had to do was put up with his company and she could remain here among the green acres and her dear little lambs, but a husband was the cost of it. One who did not want her any more than she wanted him.

'The choice is yours, my girl. If you do not wish to accept this offer, we will withdraw from it and re-main here.'

Whereupon she would watch Uncle James hobble about on his sore joints, trying to hide his pain with a smile. She could not claim to love the man who was dearer than a father and not do what was best for him. It might look as if she had a choice but, truly, she did not.

And yet... 'Do you mind letting me have the night to think it over?'

Aunt Mary stood, bent to kiss her cheek. 'Whatever your choice, we will be content with it.'

Giving Uncle James a nod, Aunt Mary hurried out of the study.

Her aunt put on a brave face, but that was all it was. Seeing how her husband suffered with daily pain hurt her deeply. At the same time, presenting Elizabeth with such a choice had to also be breaking her heart.

There was no question that her decision would be for them to retire to London...the question was, what would be the outcome for her? Miserable prospects would keep her restless all night.

With the walls of her bedroom feeling like they were pressing upon her, Elizabeth went to the stable, sat down in the clean straw of the lambing pen, then drew a blanket around her shoulders.

It was quiet at this hour, the only sound being the soft bleat of newborn lambs. With Seth Adams, the foreman, retired to his upstairs loft, the area was quite peaceful.

Further out in the pasture, Wilton Farm's shepherds would be gathered around their campfire with the dogs. Some would probably retire to the small shepherd's wagon, but she knew some of them preferred to spend the night keeping watch under the stars, making certain the sheep did not become nervous or frightened within the sheepfolds.

Wilton Farm's shepherds were, in her opinion, quite devoted to the sheep in their care. She would make sure William Grant knew it.

For all the tranquillity surrounding her, there was a storm in her heart. Thinking over the options for her future, she rejected them all. Then she went over them again, looking for a bit of hope she might have missed.

Earlier, after getting the news, she had remained with her uncle for a while, asking him what he knew of the man who would inherit the farm. Nothing recommended him as being content as a farmer or a husband. He was a gentleman of society, quite the blade with the ladies. But he did have an agreeable disposition and he was more of a gentleman than his reputation accounted for. Uncle had faith that Lord Rivenhall would not lie about this, and he knew it first-hand, having met the boy on a few occasions.

Still, William Grant was being sent here to improve his character.

She could marry Samuel, whose character was already fine. She would be guaranteed a quiet, steady life. But if she was honest with herself, and there was no reason to be sitting here if she were not, there was more than one reason she had turned down Samuel's proposals so many times. The thought of sharing any kind of intimacy with him seemed off-putting. If she did not enjoy walking down a quiet road with him… honestly, it did not bode well for the bedroom.

Besides, that, she could not imagine living so close to Wilton Farm and seeing someone else living in her home. She was certain she would never get used to it not being hers. It would take all she had not to simply walk in the front door as she had done thousands of times before.

The last option was to live in London with her aunt and uncle. The very thought of it terrified her.

Even after all this time the thought of the city made her stomach churn. London was vast and noisy. One street looked like another. Lanes and avenues melded together like dirty, frightening snakes twined in a heap...at least that was how it had seemed to a lost child of eight years.

Even now she recalled the rancid scent of the barrels she hid behind that night. And she had been desperately hungry. But the noises had been worse than the hunger. Women laughing and screaming, men shouting, weeping and moaning...and dogs barking madly, announcing unseen threats.

And the rats. A shiver of revulsion prickled her skin. Thankfully Mr Adams and a dozen cats kept them out of the stables.

On the occasions she allowed herself to think back on that time, she knew she ought to have asked for help, admitted to being lost. But she had been far too frightened to do so. Cold and sleepless, she had feared that if her father could just disappear, the same terrifying thing could happen to her. At any moment she could just be...gone.

When daylight finally came, she'd ventured out from behind the barrels. Hands shaking, she'd gathered scraps of Dollie, then she'd wandered about a park, hoping Aunt Mary and Uncle James would spot her. She'd drunk from a pond which made her sick for two days after Lord Rivenhall rescued her. He had called for a physician and then insisted they all remain at his huge home until she felt better.

At least a friendship had sprung from the ordeal.

After returning home, Wilton Farm became her

sanctuary, its peacefulness a salve to her wounded spirit. And now she faced losing it.

Her choices pressed upon her, making her wish to weep all over again. She pressed her fingers to her eyes to keep the tears from falling. Oh, but what was that? A soft velvet-feeling nose nudged her hand. The weight of a lamb settled on her lap. It was the very one she had brought to the house…a hundred years ago, or so it seemed.

'Well, hello, you.'

It bleated softly in answer.

Samuel had lambs, but they were his, not hers.

Were there even lambs in London?

But this one falling asleep in her lap was hers. In the stable that could be hers, on a farm which could be hers…legally hers…with her name on the deed as well as William Grant's, she had been assured of it. If she was willing to pay the cost…

The lamb's little chest rose and fell in slumber under her hand. Her own breathing relaxed, keeping time. And there it was. Her haze of confusion cleared; she saw her answer.

Once faced, she knew there could be no other way for her. At least, sitting here in the security of the stable in the lovely quiet of the night, that was how it seemed. Apparently, she was going to have a man to shepherd as well as her sheep.

Chapter Three

One month later
—on the road from Windermere to Ambleside

It had taken a full week for William to make a decision about his future. A week wherein he spent an hour sitting in the front pew of church, watching the Reverend encourage his flock to good works and kindness. Also, a week wherein he had been cut off from Father's funds and banned from his club.

What he'd learned was that he was not nearly eloquent enough, or noble enough, to preach God's word.

After four days banned from the society of his club…he realised he was not meant for poverty, either.

Which was why he was now riding his favourite horse, Ace of Hearts, along the road between Windermere, where his family resided at an inn while awaiting the probable wedding, and Ambleside.

He could not recall ever rising so early, but since he had been restless and anxious to see what banishment would look like, he found himself watching the sun crest a hill and thinking that perhaps it might be possible to skip the early morning hours that farmers reportedly kept. He had heard of gentleman farmers. Perhaps he could become a farmer of that ilk.

If the woman he was to marry really did love this sort of life, as he had been led to believe, she could perform whatever needed performing while he continued to keep gentleman's hours. Inasmuch as possible, he would like to hold on to his London way of living.

Glancing about, he did not think it likely. But he did have to admit that the land was pretty. Skies were bluer here than in the city and the air filled with scents that did not exist there. If the colour green had a scent, this was it…fresh and crisp. Swathes of pastureland swept all the way to the base of a rough-looking fell. Above the ridge, dark sky was giving place to vivid blue.

Rolling hills seemed to go on and without a soul in sight. That might have to do with the early hour. No one would be outside this early by choice. Except him—he had chosen it, but only because anxiety kept him from sleeping.

He was not an anxious fellow by nature. No doubt that was because, until recently, he had nothing to be anxious about. Now, here he was, looking for the place he was to spend his future.

Wilton Farm…where was it? He had no idea. As far as he could see there were no respectable street markers to point a traveller along the way. He could only hope that as the day went on, he would meet someone who might direct him towards it. Without property markers of any kind, he felt rather lost.

All he wanted at the moment was to see the farm, but from a distance. He needed time to see the lay of it and come to grips with what his new life would be.

Later on, he and his family would go to Wilton Farm together to renew and make acquaintances as well as to finalise the wedding agreement. Somewhere in this vast, green acreage there was a woman he would spend his life with.

Marriage? For him?

The idea was having a hard time finding a place to settle in his brain. Accepting the notion in his heart was even more daunting. He had no great aversion to wedded bliss. His parents had been happy with the arrangement, even though his father and mother had quite different dispositions. Darkness and light, he'd always thought, each one complementing the other.

While he had no aversion to marriage, neither did he feel greatly drawn to it. Marriage was for the responsible son, for Thomas. Living light-hearted was for the son who balanced between respectability and rascality.

What woman would wish to wed a fellow of the sort he presented to society? A dallier who was not committed enough to kiss the same woman twice? If he ever had proposed to a lady, he feared she would simply have slid her gaze to ever-steady Thomas and turned him neatly down.

Better to avoid heartache all together and play at affection. Which, he had to admit if he looked honestly into his heart, was a lonely way to live. Ah, but Father, bless his dear, manipulative heart, had supplied a woman who could not turn him down.

What was the lady doing while he wandered about? All he knew of her was that she was an agreeable sort who loved Wilton Farm and her sheep—at least, it was what he had been led to believe.

An image of Little Bo Peep came to mind…at least

what he imagined such a fluffy, fictitious creature would look like. No doubt his shepherdess bride was somewhat like her...as fair as sunshine and sweet as clover. She would be gently spoken and quick to smile. Frills and lace would be what she wore while she led her docile lambs behind her.

In his mind he watched her stop and pluck a handful of flowers, hold them to her nose and delicately sniff them. The bonnet of yellow silk and lace he had purchased for her as a gift from the finest shop in London would look lovely on her as she meandered country paths with her flock. The vision was a pleasant one. The only thing it needed was a parasol to match the hat. Now that his funds were restored, he would order one.

'Mollie!' A shout shook him from thoughts of his delicate, sunny bride. 'You must get your feet under you! Up, up, up...push!'

Apparently, there were other early risers this morning. One of them seemed desperate to get the other, Mollie, out of some dire situation.

Leading Ace of Hearts over a rise, he spotted a woman kneeling in a gully while forcefully urging a sheep to rise from where it sat in a foot of water and mud.

'Good morning,' he said. 'Perhaps I might be of assistance?'

Even kneeling in mud with her hands caked and dirty, the woman was appealing.

She glanced up from her task. Her eyes went wide, clearly startled to see him. No doubt she had been so involved in trying to get the animal out of the mud she had not heard him approach.

Her deep-brown hair was a lovely contrast to the

clear green of her eyes. Even the fact that she narrowed those eyes at him did not distract from their beauty.

Suddenly his spirit rallied. It would be a pleasurable challenge to extract a smile from those lips, which were pressed together in what he could only think was displeasure. It was not likely to be directed at him since all he had done was to say good morning, to smile and offer to help with the stuck sheep.

It must be the situation making her frown.

He thought it would be pleasant to see her smile and, since he was skilled at making ladies smile, he decided to give it a go.

If her smile was half as lovely as he imagined, it would be worth the effort.

Elizabeth knew who the stranger was as soon as she spotted him.

My word, who else but her probable intended would be riding about the countryside on a horse which was clearly not meant for farm work? Only a fellow from the city would prance about wearing clothes fit for a ballroom.

At least, to her eyes they were fancy enough for it. She had never seen a ballroom with her own eyes, so she had no way of knowing with certainly.

One thing she had to admit, he did have a compelling smile. He was handsome in a way that made her heart flutter as merrily as the butterfly flitting around her hair.

The fellow lavished his manly, congenial smile upon her as if she were the most desirable woman in the world and he had waited his whole life to bestow said smile upon her.

Further proof of who he was, she supposed. William Grant was known to enjoy flirtation.

It was a bit of a shame that she knew this about him because she enjoyed the way he was looking at her. While his attitude ought to be off-putting, his appreciative expression made it difficult to feel that way.

Honestly, his charming expression made her feel as pretty as a daisy in the grass, when what she resembled was a frog in the mud.

No man had ever looked at her that way before. No, indeed! Samuel had never cast her gazes which made her feel admired for her womanly traits.

For just a moment she allowed herself to indulge in William Grant's smile…but only halfway. She did not begin to fool herself into believing his attention was sincere.

Perhaps he did intend it to be sincere. But reasonably, she could not trick herself into believing that it would not be equally as sincere for any woman he happened to come across.

'I hope you do not think it forward of me to say how nice it is to meet such a lovely lady this early in the day?'

'Flattery will not get Mollie out of the mud and it is urgent that she gets to dry ground at once.' She forced her lips into a firm line when all they wanted was to smile back at him. 'I believe you did offer to help.'

He bounded off his tall horse in one strong, graceful-looking leap. Oh, my word. No wonder he had such success entertaining ladies.

Against her good judgement, he was keeping her entertained even while she was in a desperate situation with Mollie.

'Tell me what needs doing, miss.' He placed his hand over his heart. 'I am at your disposal.'

'Come down here and help me pull her out of the water before she gives birth.'

'Before she—' The gentleman from London blushed from his pressed white collar to the roots of his dark hair. 'Yes…indeed.'

To his credit William Grant dashed down the bank, seeming oblivious to the damage being done to his polished boots.

When he went to his knees beside her, he did not wince at the mud caking those fine wool trousers.

'Move aside, miss, I've got her.'

Placing his hands under Mollie's hindquarters, he lifted her without appearing to strain. Again, Elizabeth was struck by how strong he was. She had always assumed gentlemen of society were not. Evidently frivolous activities such as dancing and socialising kept them more fit than she had assumed.

'Come along, Miss Mollie,' he urged in a gentle, coaxing voice while helping support her steps up to the road.

'I hand over her care to you now, miss, because I believe I see a pair of feet where they ought not to be.'

She laughed…honestly, how could she not? William Grant had gone pale and backed away as if he had witnessed something terrifying.

'On the contrary, the feet are exactly where they ought to be.'

Seconds later those tiny feet fully emerged followed by a perfect and beautiful lamb.

Perhaps there was some hope that William Grant would make a go of life here at Wilton Farm. He had not fainted at the sight of the birth and was now squatting down, watching and clearly fascinated by Mollie's dedication in licking her baby clean.

'This is truly amazing,' he muttered. 'A moment ago, there was but one sheep, Mollie...and now look, there is another one.'

'I never grow weary of this,' she admitted, unable to glance away from the fine lines creasing William Grant's forehead when he arched his dark brows. 'Usually, my ewes give birth in the lambing pen, but Mollie somehow wandered off. I cannot say how grateful I am that you happened by.'

Not that she believed it to be an accident that he had. He had ridden out to see the farm that would soon be his. At least the man was an early riser and that boded well.

It was time to tell him who she was, but she hesitated a moment longer because she wished to see the real William Grant. The one who was unguarded in her presence, believing her to be a simple country lass... which was exactly who she was.

She could hardly allow this unexpected opportunity to get a glimpse of the man she was about to commit her future to go to waste.

'I am always eager to assist a lady in need.'

'Even at the cost of your fine-looking clothing?'

'Worth the cost. I have never seen a lamb born. I admit to being in awe...of both you and Mollie. I stood by like a stump while you brought a life into the world as if you do it dozens of times a day.'

'Not that often, but often enough. And I admit it is a thrill each time.'

'I wonder if I will ever...' His thought seemed to go inward. He let the rest go unspoken.

'May I ask one more favour of you, sir?'

'I await your command.' Oh, again that smile! Without a butterfly in sight, she felt fluttery.

'Would you mind carrying Mollie home on your horse? She seems done in with her adventure.'

'It would be my pleasure.' Then he winked at her.

She could not imagine how he managed, but without straining, he picked Mollie up and mounted the horse. She was more than a little impressed.

Holding the lamb close to her heart, she walked along beside the horse.

'I confess to being lost,' he said, grinning down. 'Not that I mind in the least.'

She might not mind, either, although she was not going to admit it.

'If you are William Grant, you are not lost. Just over the rise is Wilton Farm.'

He blinked, long and slow, as if keeping time with his long, drawn-in breath. When he exhaled, the tips of his ears turned pink, his cheeks pale.

No doubt by now he had guessed who she was and regretted flirting with her. Hopefully he did not regret it terribly much because, much to her surprise and against her good judgement, she did not.

'Welcome home,' she declared.

Wilton Farm? Over the rise?

And she had pronounced him to be at home. Truly, he had never felt less at home, and yet something softened inside him at her words.

It was the oddest sensation.

But if Wilton Farm was just over the rise, who was the woman walking beside him, cradling a newborn lamb to her heart?

Surely not Elizabeth Morsely?

If so, he hoped his help with Mollie would offset his overtly appreciative attitude towards her. Truly, he had meant no offence, only to compliment.

But what must she think of him?

Exactly what she would have been told—that he was a flirtatious rascal sent here to learn responsibility. No doubt, while she looked at him with those lovely green eyes, her lips pressed in a tight line, she was reconsidering wedding him.

'May I ask your name, miss, since you know mine?'

Her mouth quirked and he nearly had the smile he'd been trying to win.

'Elizabeth Morsely. I believe we will be getting rather well acquainted in the next few days.'

Utterly flummoxed, he stared silently down at her.

'I do beg your pardon,' he finally managed to say. 'Had I known, I would not have—'

Dash it! He would have not let the fellow he had been in London be the one to greet her. Father's purpose for him being here was to change, not carry on as he always had. She had his measure now. This was not London and this woman was no game to be lightly played.

'Not behaved as you did?' she asked, her mouth still resisting that lurking smile.

'Again, I beg your pardon.'

'Think no more of it. I was in a desperate situation. Had you not gallantly come to my rescue, I cannot imagine what would have happened to this sweet baby.'

Gallant, was he? Well, that was something to aspire to.

She nuzzled her nose into the lamb's woolly coat. Unbidden, an image filled his mind. A wholly improper image wherein that pert and pretty nose was nuzzling his hair.

The woman was not yet his wife and, even when she was, he had no notion of what their marital relationship would be. But given the picture still happily jumbling about in his brain, he had an idea what he wished for it to be. The lady might not be the delicate Bo Peep he had imagined, but he liked her better as she was. A farm ought to have a mistress who was earthy rather than ethereal.

He tended to put women on pedestals which placed them out of his reach. It only now occurred to him to wonder about that tendency. Had he intentionally done so to place ladies and therefore marriage beyond his grasp?

He did not consider marriage to be objectionable. The example his parents had set made the commitment seem satisfying. Perhaps it was commitment he was wary of. Commitment was so permanent. Once vows were spoken, they could not be gone back on. In spite of it, here he found himself, with one foot at the altar.

Coming over the ridge of a hill, he saw Wilton Farm spread before him.

Whatever he had been expecting it was not this! Having never taken an interest in Father's investments, he had not known what to expect. What he had pictured in his mind was a small cottage, a barn…a few sheep being chased by dogs. He liked dogs, had even had one when he was a child.

From where he sat atop of Ace of Hearts, he saw land stretch away for ever, it seemed. Pastureland sloped upwards, meeting craggy-looking fells. Did all this land belong to Father...to William, if things went according to Father's wishes?

Nestled in the valley between the hills there were buildings constructed of whitish granite. Two of them were huge, set close together. Stables, he imagined. Between the stables was a smaller building. He could not guess what it was. Another structure was easy to identify as a carriage house. With the doors open he spotted a pair of utilitarian-looking wagons inside.

The building which most riveted his attention was the house. Although made of granite like the other structures, it might be the most charming home he had ever seen. But for all its homey look, it was quite large. There were several chimneys, two of which had smoke curling into the blue morning sky. The structure was somewhat V-shaped with the longest part forming the front of the house. The shorter wing faced north-west and would have a view of acres upon acres of pastureland.

It heartened him to know he would be able to host guests from London.

Surrounding the house was a low fence and within it a garden. Posies of every hue waved cheerily about in the morning breeze. Clearly, someone here took great enjoyment in its care.

The entrance to the yard was marked by an arbour. There was a path leading to a porch which spanned the length of the house. He spotted a man and a woman sitting in chairs, gazing out.

'Uncle James and Aunt Mary,' she told him. 'Aunt

Mary is the one responsible for the flowers. She adores growing and tending them. I wonder if…well, never mind. London will be different, but it is where they wish to live.'

Who would not wish it? he thought, trying to banish the edge of regret that he would not be living there.

'There are flowers in London,' he said.

Looking past the house and the buildings out to the pastureland, he saw too many sheep to count. Sheep which came with his soon-to-be farm. He knew nothing about the creatures other than that their wool made fine garments. And also that the one lying across his saddle was rather smelly.

Apparently, Elizabeth Morsely did not think sheep smelled. She continued to nuzzle the lamb in her arms as if it were the sweetest scented of creatures. Perhaps so new to the world, it was.

In the distance he heard a dog bark. He would not mind having a dog again. He was completely unqualified to run this farm, but he did know how to care for a dog. That was something, he supposed.

If Elizabeth Morsely accepted him as her husband, he would have a mountain of learning to do. About farming and about being a husband. He prayed he was enough of a man to live up to the responsibilities set before him.

'The lambing pen is inside the first stable we come to. Follow me.' She led the way down the hill, giving him a charming view of her skirt bouncing with her brisk gait. It would take a stronger fellow than him not to be captivated with the way the sunshine cast deep-brown shimmers in her hair where it swayed across her back in time with her skirt.

For the first time since he had been hauled to Father's office to answer for his sister's crime, he believed Father cared what became of his future.

He would always rather be in London, but Wilton Farm was more impressive than he had imagined it would be.

And as for the woman who was part and parcel of it? The very lady he had, until this morning, considered foisted upon him against his will? He might not have met her in a ballroom, might not have coaxed even a full smile from her...yet she intrigued him as if she were a lady of society gowned in satin and lace rather than wool, mud and lamb.

All the way down the hill he imagined how pretty she would look wearing the yellow hat he had purchased for her.

Chapter Four

Elizabeth sat in a chair across from William Grant feeling stiff, as ill at ease as she could ever recall being. Earlier today, during the hour they had spent in each other's presence, there had been an easy rapport between them which was now lacking. William must be as aware as she was that everyone was watching them, highly curious about how they were getting on.

Grants and Morselys might appear to be in lively conversation with one another but, every once in a while, Aunt Mary would slant Elizabeth a speculative glance. Minerva, William's younger sister, did the same thing, except that her glance was overtly curious. Thomas, the older brother and future Viscount, did not bother to hide a frown when he shifted his attention to William.

At least Uncle James and the Viscount paid them little mind. Heads bent towards each other, they were likely engaged in congratulating one another on a well-laid plan being nearly accomplished.

There was still the matter of her and William Grant giving formal consent to it all, but in all likelihood, it was going to happen.

While Aunt Mary and Minerva merrily chatted and arranged details for the wedding ceremony, Elizabeth and William alternated between staring at each other and then glancing awkwardly away.

They attempted a conversation which involved his admiration of dogs. It died quickly since the virtues of canines was not the subject on either of their minds.

Everyone had things to settle regarding the two of them. And yet it was the soon-to-be-betrothed who needed to lay down the rules which would govern their marriage. It could not be done with everyone having an eager ear for what they might say to one another.

She stood up. 'Would you like to visit the lamb we delivered this morning?'

Minerva spun on her seat cushion, staring with her jaw sagging. 'You delivered a lamb?'

'You have already met?' Thomas asked, nearly on top of Minerva's question. His expression indicated it was improper that they had. William must not have mentioned their encounter.

She supposed it was understandable given the censure in his older brother's frown. She had heard that in society, meetings between unmarried people were only conducted with a chaperon. In her opinion, what did it matter really, since they were likely to wed, anyway? As far as she could tell, William and Thomas were like day and night in character. She had always favoured bright sunshine to night shadows.

William stood up. 'We have met...it was early this morning. And, yes, Miss Morsely, I would enjoy paying a visit to the small creature and to Mollie. I believe the ewe and I formed a sort of bond.'

'You did?' Minerva's smile widened in apparent admiration. 'A bond with a sheep? May I come along?'

'No.' The Viscount frowned at his youngest child. 'Your brother has had quite enough of you tagging after him.'

Given Minerva's sudden frown and William's quick grin, there was more to the statement than was evident to her. Family matters were personal so she would not ask about it…which did not mean she was not highly curious.

Minerva did seem a lively girl. Perhaps she tended to pop up in places she should not. Judging by the humour in William's smile, she thought he had a close relationship with his sister…perhaps more than he did with his brother.

In spite of his scamp-like nature, Elizabeth's first impressions of William Grant were positive ones. Here was a man who faced life with good humour…at least it seemed so. Still, having known him for so little time, it was impossible to know for certain.

One thing was certain: the man was handsome and it was pleasant to look at him. Also, she liked the sound of his voice. It was slightly, but not altogether, deep… the rich timbre brought to mind dark honey stirred in warm milk. What she knew so far was very pleasant, but what she wished to do was get to know the heart of him.

What, exactly, did he expect of a wife?

Hopefully, while visiting Mollie and the lamb, she would discover what she needed to in order to decide once and for all if she would go through with the marriage. Theirs was not a love match. Indeed, it was a barely-know-you match. She must accept that right off.

But perhaps in time they might become…well, friends at the very least.

In a gentlemanly gesture, he extended his elbow to escort her from the room. She placed her fingers on his sleeve and felt a fascinating thrill skitter through them and up her arm. For all that she lifted her nose at London and its elegant manners, she had to admit that William's gesture made her feel feminine.

Having never been a lady of society, this was not something she was accustomed to. If the country mouse in her showed, he did not remark upon it by word or gesture. No matter what he was thinking, clearly, he had been raised to act a gentleman.

But what was he thinking? She would like to know what his genuine opinion of her was. Or perhaps not like to know as much as need to know. Socially, she was far beneath him. She did not want to dwell on the fact that he might feel embarrassed by her. There was no way to know such a thing until she asked…and then hope he would answer truthfully.

As soon as they were alone in the stable, she would do her best to discover the answers to her questions. No doubt he would have questions of his own.

'Well, here we are,' Miss Morsely said before sitting down in a pile of golden-hued straw.

William imagined it would appear rude if he sat anywhere else, so he settled down across from her. It was an odd sensation, having one's rump on the ground rather than a chair cushion.

Within a moment, they were being inspected by no less than six tiny black sheep. He could not identify which was the one from this morning…nor, for all that he thought he had bonded with her, could he identify which of the mothers was Mollie.

'Can you tell the difference?' he asked, not imagining how she could.

'Of course.'

Of course? He feared he would never have what it took to keep this place going successfully, which was what his father meant for him to do. Perhaps Father had the right of it…looking at the lady seated across from him while she cooed over baby sheep, he suspected there might be more to life than being an entertaining ball guest.

Obviously, Wilton Farm had been getting along well without him all these years. It was hard to imagine what he could do to improve anything…or even keep it running as it was. Unless the sheep needed to be taught the waltz, there was little he could do for the creatures other than haul them out of gullies or other tricky situations.

'It is interesting that the babies are dark and their mothers light.'

'Herdwick lambs are born black and turn lighter as they grow older.' There might be people in society who knew that, but he was not among them. The weight of all he did not know pressed upon him. How ever would he live up to Father's expectations? 'How many Herdwicks are there?'

'About five hundred, but…' she glanced at the tiny dark creatures exploring the hem of her skirt '…it is hard to know for certain since more are joining us every day.'

Who did she mean by 'us'? Certainly not him. Just when his self-esteem began to gasp and sink, she flashed him a smile. This was the sort of smile he had tried unsuccessfully to charm from her this morning.

Leaning forward, she set a lamb on his lap. 'Since he is alive and healthy because of you, you should name him.'

He lifted the tiny creature in his hands, turning it this way and that. 'Murray.' After his friend James Murray. Murray might find it amusing to have a lamb named in his honour. As soon as he put Murray down the woolly creature toddled off to his mother.

'I would imagine you have questions for me. It is a rather huge step we are about to take together,' he said.

'And you have them for me.'

'Shall we take turns, then?' He reached his hand into the pocket of his coat, felt the shape of the ring box hidden in it. His family had come to Ambleside in full expectation of a wedding…so had he. However, nothing was certain until Miss Morsely accepted his proposal. 'You go first.'

'Yes, all right then…' She gave him a tense-looking smile. 'I ask that you be honest with me, Mr Grant. There is no point to this conversation otherwise.'

He nodded, noting that Murray had curled into a fuzzy ball to nap at his mother's feet. 'Ask me anything, Elizabeth… I hope I may call you that.'

'It is fitting, I would think, given our unusual situation.' She shrugged, gave him a heart-warming smile. 'What I would like to know, is why you agreed to this arrangement. Life in Ambleside will not be at all what you are used to.'

'You wished for honesty and so you shall have it.' Even though the truth was going to make him appear shallow. 'Of the choices my father gave me, this seemed the least objectionable.'

To his relief, her smile did not falter. Her apparent acceptance of this much truth gave his heart a hard pump that he felt to his toes and back.

'Now I simply must know what the other choices were.' The tone of her voice made it sound as if they were the best of friends idling time away by telling tales.

'To become a member of the clergy. The other was to be cut off from funds…which actually did happen for a time.'

'Even though we have been acquainted less than a day, I can sense that neither sainthood nor poverty would suit you.'

'You do not feel I am terribly unworthy? You are not insulted by my reason for being here?'

'No and no.' She shrugged her slender, yet quite capable shoulders. He knew them to be capable after witnessing her bring Murray into the world. 'Neither of us is in this situation because we chose it.'

'That is honest. But tell me, Elizabeth, why have you agreed? Clearly you can have your pick of men.'

'There is my neighbour, Samuel, I might have chosen him, but…well, I decided not to.'

'Is he a beast? I promise to protect you from him if that is the case.'

'Oh, no. He is a steady, responsible fellow.' The slightest of frowns furrowed her forehead, her lips thinning a bit.

'Too old?' he suggested, seeking to make light of the moment. 'Perhaps he smells like sheep?'

'Not old…' She shrugged. 'There are many times

when I smell like sheep…but not every man a lady meets is… Well, never mind that. In the end, had I accepted one of his proposals I would have had to move away from Wilton Farm which would have broken my heart. But here I find myself with nothing really changed. With my aunt and uncle needing to move to London for the sake of Uncle James's health, I must make the same choice.'

'Ah…well, I am still young and last I checked I did not smell. And if you consent to marry me you will not have to leave Wilton Farm.'

She was silent for a long moment. He would give a lot to know what she was thinking.

'Would you truly not rather move to London with your aunt and uncle?' Who would not want to live in London? He did not understand her choice at all.

'No, that would not suit.'

'Is it that you love your life here so much or that you dislike London?'

'I do love it here, quite desperately. And as far as London goes… I could never live there.'

That was curious. London was the most marvellous place in the world. Naturally, her choice was her own to make so he did not defend London aloud. But in his heart, he was praising the city to high heaven.

'May I admit how grateful I am that you did not choose the neighbour? I would make a miserable pauper and a worse shepherd of souls.'

'Perhaps you will do better at shepherding sheep.'

'A sheep and a soul can hardly be equated but still, I freely confess that I know nothing about farming. It is only fair for you to know there is every chance I will be a miserable failure.'

She laughed and for some reason he felt grand.

'But tell me, why were you given those choices?'

She'd asked for honesty and, as frivolous as the truth made him appear, she would have it.

'I have been stubborn about taking on the mantle of maturity. While my friends married and settled down, I clung to bachelorhood. I earned a reputation of being something of a merrymaker with the ladies. Some of it deserved, but some of it not. Please believe I have never compromised a lady. My late mother raised me to be a gentleman.'

'It seems to me that sentencing you to life in the country seems severe. Aren't gentlemen of society known to be flirtatious?'

'It is expected of young men, who are new to society. I am thirty years old and it does make a difference in how one is judged.'

'I am twenty-five…also past the age to be wed. I imagine our marriage will put our families' minds at rest in that area.' She grew quiet again, seeming to mull something over in her mind. 'I do not mean to pry, so you need not answer this, but why did you not marry, William? Surely you had opportunities?'

'Not as many as you might imagine. It is my brother the ladies had their hearts set on.' How many times had he been speaking to a woman only to have her gaze shift towards Thomas? The conversation neatly steered towards an introduction. 'As a second son… I was second choice. I suppose I did not wish to take my brother's seconds. We have agreed to the truth and you shall have it.' Even though he had never admitted this to another soul, he would do it now. Later he would wonder why. 'I have only ever allowed myself to feel shallow emotions for ladies because of it. Better to enjoy a woman's company for a brief time and avoid having her use me to get to Thomas. It happened often enough that I decided to forgo the marriage market.'

'Thank you for being candid, William. But why agree to it now? I am no expert at what happens in society, but I do know that some gentlemen do marry later. You cannot be so unusual in that.'

'I might have been able to put it off a few more years if it were not for Minerva. Apparently, in Father's opinion, I am a risk to her future prospects. In my opinion she is more mischievous than I ever was… she was born that way. She is just like our mother was.' He grew silent, thinking about his mother and aching for her presence even after all this time. He was glad Minerva took after her.

At Elizabeth's nod, he pressed on. 'You may have noticed how lively she is…and too curious by far. Rumours of my…well, frankly, of my behaviour fascinated her. What led to Father giving me those choices is that she wanted to know about things a girl her age ought not to know. Rest assured, I refused to enlighten her. Then one night she disguised herself as a lad and followed me to my club to see what she could discover on her own. She got caught out. I kept her secret, but Father discovered it when gossip came to Thomas's ears. Father, and no doubt Thomas, too, feared that my influence on Minerva would damage her prospects. She is to come out next Season. So, here I find myself.'

'Surely you must feel some resentment for it.'

'I expected to, but…no, I do not believe I do feel that way.'

He had in the beginning. Why wasn't he any longer? He had every right to feel that way.

She laughed again and the reason hit him in the chest. Elizabeth Morsely was far better a bride than he had been expecting. Truly, he had assumed the glowing things Father was saying about her were to placate him.

How wrong he was. If he had been wrong about his bride, he might also be wrong about adjusting to life in the wilderness. And what was to say he could not bring society to the farm? There was no reason they had to keep separate places in his life.

In the moment, looking into Elizabeth's expressive green eyes…watching the slight tip of her smile…he thought he might make a go of it. No, not thought… he was determined to make a go of it. Which would not be easy. He had a strong sense that what he was taking on would be a great deal more difficult than what he was leaving behind. A great deal more satisfying, too.

And so—

'What do you say, Elizabeth? Shall we give this marriage a go? Announce the news to our families?' He felt the weight of the ring box dragging on his pocket. He stood up, then went down on one knee. Gently moving a curious lamb aside, he drew the box from his pocket and opened it. 'Will you marry me?'

Oh, my word…she had not expected this! To be proposed to on bended knee? He even pressed his hand to his heart while presenting a ring which had to be worth…she could not imagine how much, but it made her half-dizzy wondering.

She had never seen an actual diamond before and the way it winked and sparkled in the dim light of the stable stole the breath right out of her. So did the fact that, although they were strangers and the marriage not exactly of their choosing, William was making this moment special for her. It was not as if he had to, after all. Each of them knew this marriage was the least of their evils and so a simple affirmation of their intentions would have done.

His thoughtfulness touched her in a way he could not guess. For all the times Samuel had brought up the matter of marriage, he had done so in casual conversation. To him, asking her to be his wife was simply a matter of logic, something to be expected of lifelong neighbours having adjoining farms and common ambitions. There was nothing special about any of his proposals, the same as there had never been anything special between them.

There was nothing special between her and William, either, and yet seeing him on one knee, cupping the ring box in his hand, she could only wonder if perhaps there could be.

'It is a lovely proposal, William.' It thrilled her and yet…perhaps he was simply trying to charm her.

'You think I am putting on a show… I see in your eyes you think so.' He shook his head, smiling that wonderful smile which warmed her all over. 'The truth is, I have a good feeling about us. If we do manage to make a go of it, I want you to have been proposed to the right way. As years go by we will want to look back on this moment and smile, not wish we had done things differently.'

Oh, my goodness. William Grant did seem to have

a romantic soul. She believed he did mean what he said and so…

'It is a very pretty ring, William. Let's see if we can come to an agreement between us on how we will conduct our marriage. Rules will help us know what to expect from one another.'

Setting rules, establishing boundaries, did seem cold and unfeeling, but at the same time boundaries just might see them to the place where they did look back on this engagement and smile.

'This is your home. I am an interloper so whatever guidelines you deem helpful, I will abide by.'

'You may also determine guidelines. Once we wed, your name will be on the deed as well as mine. Although were it not for the fact that your father and my aunt and uncle are such great friends, I imagine my name would not be on the deed at all.'

'My feeling is that my father is fond of you, after all that happened. He was adamant that you not be turned out of your home.'

She was beyond grateful to Lord Rivenhall. How much did William know, or remember of that time? This was not the moment to ask.

'Shall we decide who is to be in charge of what?' she asked.

'I'll need your guidance since I have no idea what it is I ought to be in charge of.'

'Shall we begin with the house since we will both be living in it? We will not want to be intruding upon each other.'

'If you wish, but I feel wrong about it since I have only seen it once while you have lived your whole life here.'

'How about if I make suggestions which you can either agree with or dismiss and then make some of your own?'

'I agree!'

He truly did have a beguiling smile. No wonder the ladies of London were all taken with him. And, in her view, it was not simply to gain access to his brother.

'Lovely, we shall begin with the house, then,' she said.

The sleeping arrangement was uppermost on her mind, but she was shy of bringing up the subject. A man naturally assumed certain intimacy…marital rights if you will…from his wife. Marital rights were something she had given thought to when considering wedding Samuel. The idea had been mortifying. Not because Samuel was distasteful, but she did not feel a draw to him the way she did William. There had never been a time when her neighbour's smile made her desire that sort of intimacy with him.

Oh, but seeing her soon-to-be intended's smile… well and my goodness, thinking about such intimacy with him made her feel as if she ought to fan her face to cool the blush. Wondering about such behaviour with William was intriguing and not a bit mortifying.

Once again, she was getting ahead of herself. Such a relationship might grow between them one day, far in the future, but really, they had only begun to use their first names with one another. It was a lucky thing he could not see what went on inside her mind.

'Some rooms make sense to share in common. The drawing room, the dining room and the study…unless you wish to have a study of your own?' He might want that. 'We shall carve out a place for you if you do.'

'And what about the—?'

'The kitchen?' She cut him off because she still felt warm and prickly inside and she did not wish to discuss the bedroom in case that was what he was about to bring up. 'We might attempt to claim it as ours, but in truth it is Penny's domain. She does not mind if we visit, she will probably even feed us something, but to assume it is anything but hers would be a mistake.'

'I must also assume, then, it would be a mistake to bring a cook from London?'

'Yes, a rather large one. It would cause an upheaval for there to be two cooks in one kitchen. I do not recall a time when Penny was not here. But I promise, you will adore her cooking. She is the envy of Ambleside.'

'Agreed, then, no London chef.' He glanced about the stable, his gaze going from the rafters to the straw on the floor and the lambs sleeping in it. 'I assume there would be no need for my valet to come, either.'

'Honestly, no. He would be the only one of his kind in Ambleside.'

'As will I.'

Poor William must feel adrift. Ambleside was a world away from London...which she was grateful for but... 'I feel that you are giving up so much more than I am in this arrangement.'

'I wonder...' He grew silent for moment, simply looking at her. Then he shook his head as if clearing out the thoughts. 'What I am giving up is poverty. Also giving up a career as a clergyman for which I am unfit. I know less about shepherding souls than I do about sheep. But I am willing to learn about sheep.'

'I imagine it is easier than people. So, yes, I will teach you.'

'You will if we are wed.' Oh, that smile. She imagined it had persuaded more than one flutter-hearted lady to offer him a kiss. 'Will you have me, Elizabeth?'

'We shall make the best of our situation, I think. I already like you, William…so, yes, I accept.'

He stood up and reached down his hand to help her up. Setting aside the lamb on her lap, she took it and rose to her feet.

'One more thing, Elizabeth. You do not need to fear my past reputation. As your husband, I will never be unfaithful.'

She knew that, somehow. Sensed it in his touch. It might be silly to imagine she could know this by the way his fingers seemed so right cupping her hand… and yet she had the strongest sense that he meant what he said.

'Or that I will press my husbandly attentions on you.' He took a deep breath as if he were fortifying himself. 'I would like to have children, but the decision is entirely yours.'

'Oh…good, then,' she mumbled wondering how good it really was.

'Yes…all right, then, as far as the division of the house goes, is there a way for us to occupy different parts of it for sleeping?'

'All the bedrooms are on the second floor. Everything to the left of the landing shall be yours, to the right shall be mine.'

She might have seen a flicker of disappointment cross his smile. The question was, did he see the one that flashed in hers?

Still and all, she was relieved that he had not pressed the issue of his husbandly rights. Indeed, she could not be more relieved. Or was it disappointed? What she was…was confused.

'Let's go and share our happy news,' she said and started to turn, but he still had hold of her hand.

'Elizabeth?' His brows arched and he looked so…so very…well, whatever it was it made her sigh.

'Yes?'

'They are more likely to believe it if you are wearing the engagement ring.'

'Of course.' He slipped it on her finger, then let go of her hand. The warmth of his fingers lingered on her skin. How interesting, how utterly fascinating and delightful…and not like anything she had ever experienced. She was not at all certain that it was not her heart he touched along with her hand. 'It is very pretty.'

And by far the most expensive thing she had ever put on. She could not possibly wear the beautiful sparkler while tending sheep.

His expression held the oddest emotion. Before she could discern what it might be, he blinked…smiled.

'It looks just right on you.' He extended his elbow in that gentlemanly way he had. 'Our families might not be surprised, but they will be pleased.'

At the end of it, would she and William be equally as pleased? She kept the thought to herself because he appeared satisfied. His smile and his wink made her wonder if, just perhaps, she was, too.

Also, there was this one thing…she was captivated with the way his muscles shifted under her hand while they walked out of the stable. Other muscles would be shifting as well, muscles having to do with his manly stride. A stride that she assumed was normally much longer. Was he adjusting it to her shorter ones, or was he going slower to savour this moment of their engagement?

Whichever it was, she was having a delightful time imaging how strong his legs were, how muscular and…

This was a start, she supposed.

Chapter Five

If anyone would have asked William how he imagined his wedding to be, it would bear no resemblance to the one just accomplished.

Had he wed in London, the affair would have been grandly extravagant, with hundreds of people attending. The church would have been large enough to accommodate them with no less than a bishop to preside over the vows. The wedding of a viscount's son, no matter that he was a second son, would have been the talk of society for months ahead of time.

In London, there would have been a procession of carriages carrying the families to the church and people waving good wishes from street corners.

This morning, his family had walked to the church, leaving the Rivenhall carriage for Elizabeth, her aunt and her uncle to ride in.

Afterwards, it would be just he and his bride returning to the farm in the carriage.

In the moment, she walked beside him towards the carriage, flushed and pretty. He liked to imagine it was because of the wedding vows so recently on her lips.

Only moments ago, she had stood beside him, a ray of sunshine streaking through a stained-glass window cast her gown in a rainbow glow. His heart had nearly tripped over itself wondering if this was a sign of some sort.

It might or might not be true. But what was true was that he'd promised to be faithful to this woman for ever. Also true that he felt every word of the vow.

He had a bride…a wife…more beautiful than he could have ever dreamed of having…had he ever dreamed of having one.

Gazing sidelong at the woman he had just wed made him feel grand. On top of the world. It made him question why he had hidden from marriage for so long. And he had to admit that was what he had done, hidden behind a pretence of frivolity.

It was not as if he had not grown up with an example of a fine marriage because he had. He knew that marriage could be a great blessing.

In a sense he feared going through what his father had when his mother died, but grief was the price of loving. He knew and accepted that sad fact of life. His reticence had not been fear of loss.

But what, then? It seemed important to know this even though it had never been all that important before.

'You look beautiful, Mrs Grant,' he murmured, bending close to her ear. She smelled beautiful, too… like fresh air and green grass.

Somehow, Elizabeth's aunt and Minerva had managed in a short time to come up with a gown to rival any a London lady would wear. It had lace, frills and pearls in all the correct places, yet it was not those things that made it sparkle. It was the bride. Elizabeth was prettier than any ornament could ever be.

Stepping into the carriage behind his new bride, William took a moment to glance back at the intimate church where he had just become a married man. It was said that the land it was built on used to be an orchard and was chosen by no less a personage than William Wordsworth.

No…he could never have imagined this wedding. The one he would have imagined would have been so much more and yet, at the same time, so much less.

Birdsong had been the music his bride walked down the church aisle to, wildflowers her bouquet.

The guests had consisted of his bride, her aunt and uncle. On William's side it had been his father, his brother and his sister. No one had lined the sides of the road, tossing flower petals and shouting good wishes. Indeed, the only ones to cheer the procession had been a group of bleating sheep and their curious shepherds.

He would wonder if Elizabeth felt slighted by the lack of pomp and circumstance surrounding her hurried wedding, if she were not smiling.

But she was smiling, quite prettily, in fact, and that's what made this morning shine. It was also what made this sudden turn in his life seem promising rather than foreboding.

While he did not love her any more than she loved him, her expression did warm him more sweetly than the morning sunbeam warming his back. Until the last few days he hadn't realised he enjoyed morning sunshine. There was a slight chance that, in time, he might continue to.

Watching Elizabeth wriggle her shoulders into

the bench cushion, it struck him anew that she was his…his wedded wife…his to keep in sickness and in health, for better or for worse. He had vowed to do so a few moments ago and did feel the full responsibility of it.

Mrs Grant… Elizabeth Grant. Mr and Mrs Grant.

Surely he had been responsible for something important before…but in the moment he could not recall what it would have been. In the quite recent past his greatest responsibility had been to keep up interesting conversation in a ballroom. Suddenly that seemed shallow.

That was it, he realised. Perhaps the reason he had not considered marriage was that, at the core of his heart, he did not want what the ladies of London had to offer. A life of party after ball after tea…and all of it without great purpose other than having fun.

After his mother died, he'd believed a life of gaiety was his soul's desire. And that was how it had gone… until he had come to Wilton Farm and met an enchanting yet down-to-earth shepherdess who reminded him that there was more to life than acting the fun ball guest. He was now a husband, a landowner…a man who needed to learn responsibility.

Father would be relieved to know the direction William's thoughts were taking, that perhaps his scheme would—

Abruptly thoughts of Father, and the reason he had not wed before, now fled his mind.

In the process of settling back into the cushions Elizabeth sighed deeply, her bosom lifted, and his mouth dried as completely as his noble ideas.

There was more to being a husband than acting a

guardian. There was a particular intimacy which did not end with one exceptionally brief kiss which had been prompted by the minister as a symbol of sealed vows. Would there come a time when they would care for each other with a tender, amorous bond? He was willing…a bit more than willing, truth be told…

He had left that choice to Elizabeth. The decision to carry a relationship past friendly, to risk a love match, was hers to make.

'I have never ridden in anything so grand,' Elizabeth declared, running her fingers over the velvet seat cushion.

To him the luxurious interior of the carriage was commonplace. Truly, he was so accustomed to it he rarely gave it a second glance. The difference in their attitudes towards the cab pointed out that, despite the peaceful beauty of the moment and the sacred vows which now bound them, there was a great deal separating them. While he meant each and every promise, it remained that he and Elizabeth were from vastly different worlds.

What would happen when those worlds came together? Would they crash explosively, or would they meld as smoothly as milk stirred in tea? He could not be certain yet, but he had to wonder if he would dislike his banishment from society as much as he imagined he would.

His new home was large. Surely, he could invite guests from London as often as he liked? Perhaps a blend of the two, village and city, would see them to the happy future which unexpectedly blossomed in his mind.

* * *

Nothing about this morning felt real. Occasionally, Elizabeth would blink hard in an attempt to plunge back to reality. Perhaps she would sit up in her bed and there would be no William, no sale of the farm with her name on the deed...all would be as it always had been.

So far blinking had not worked, nor had the pinch she had inconspicuously given her wrist. Life was as real as could be and she was getting into an elegant carriage wearing a gown unlike anything she had ever worn. Or was she ever likely to wear again! One could not expect to feel enveloped in iridescence twice in one lifetime.

Wrapped up in silk and lace, it was easy to imagine she was walking on stars...a proper princess. But at the same time, being a princess was entirely foreign to her. What she must bear in mind was that she was a shepherdess, a rural farm lass to the bone. No matter what she put on it would not change who she was on the inside. Oh, but for a lovely few moments she chose not to bear it in mind.

Walking down the narrow church aisle towards William Grant, she did not feel the gap of their different stations. She was a bride and he was her groom.

In the moment everything went away except for the way he looked at her...at the turn of his lips, the warmth and approval shining in his eyes. For that brief time, she shut everything away except for him. He had suggested they have a proper proposal, one that they could look back on and be happy about.

So, when she vowed to keep him in sickness and in health, to cherish and...well to love, was what she said...and for this very instant she would pretend she really did. Some day she might, after all, so it might not be a fib in the end.

And then…oh, then…when the reverend said William could kiss her, she gave herself fully to his lips, brushing her mouth with the pressure of a whisper. For the sake of future memories, she took her vows to her heart where they would be kept for another time. Just for a little while she pretended that they were no different than any other bride and groom giving their lives to one another in this sweet, quaint church.

The truth was it could only be a matter of time before William realised she was not fit to be his wife. But for now, she rejoiced in the romance of the morning. Being wed in the lovely old chapel with flowers blooming in the garden beyond the windows, with birds singing joyously in time with the cheery bleating of sheep, truly…her wedding had been lovelier than she could have hoped for.

To her, it had been ideal, but now, walking away from the church, and the magic which had wrapped her up beginning to give way to reality, she could only wonder what had it been for her groom?

Lacking, perhaps?

Luckily he had agreed to being married here since it would have taken both families to drag her to London for the ceremony. A London wedding would be grand, full of pomp and circumstance. In London, William would watch his bride walk down the aisle of a huge and ornate church. Her gown would flutter about her shoes to the strains of an orchestra's romantic tunes. Lords and ladies would fill the sanctuary…all of them smiling and teary eyed.

There had been only one nobleman at her wedding.

Thankfully, Lord Rivenhall had been smiling. Her aunt had been teary-eyed while Uncle James sniffled aloud. Not that Elizabeth could understand why. It was not as if she was making a love match like her aunt and uncle had made.

Far from it!

But at least her new husband was smiling. She liked his smile quite well which was as good a start as any, she supposed. If she appreciated his smile, she might also appreciate what was behind the smile…or who was.

The carriage ride home was thankfully short. With the two of them glancing shyly back and forth at one another, it was an awkward ride. It was no wonder she was tongue-tied. What did one say to a stranger who had suddenly become her husband?

Coming to the front gate of the house, the carriage stopped and the driver opened the door. William stepped out before her, then offered his hand to help her down. His fingers felt so large and strong around hers. If she did not withdraw from his grip, would he continue to hold her hand? It would be forward of her to let the situation remain, even though they were wed. Slowly, she started to withdraw her fingers, only to have him hold on more firmly.

Her heart battered about as if she were smitten with her groom and he with her. As if the spell that had bound them during the ceremony remained. What a shame they were not smitten. The moment would be so lovely were it true and not something to be preserved in case it was a memory later to be cherished.

In the instant she was an odd blend of floating in

romance and wondering if this union between them would really work in the end. One foot in the clouds and one in the mud of Wilton Farm.

And hungry!

Coming inside, she realised how famished she was. Scents of their wedding breakfast, which had to consist of all her favourite foods, wafted from the kitchen. A wedding feast in London would be a more elegant affair, but not as tasty. Of that, she was certain.

'Ah,' William said, still holding her hand. 'I understand now why we will not need a cook from London.'

Something about the way he said 'we' made her heart skip about. Why would it do that? She had not expected to be 'we', especially with a man she had been appointed to wed…and he appointed to wed her.

Had this not been, for both of them, the least objectionable of the sorry choices they had been given?

The front door stood open and the voices of the rest of the family could be heard as they crossed the yard. They sounded happy and excited. It was an interesting thought…family was. One she had not had a moment to consider until now, but in the space of the morning her family had more than doubled in size. Now, in addition to a husband, she had both a brother and a sister…and a father!

She had no memories of her own father, only distressing images of a faceless man being pulled from the Thames or vanishing in various ways. And the one she had just acquired was the very man who'd rescued her from the terror fearing that what happened to her father would happen to her.

It nearly felt fateful that becoming his daughter should be so.

'Are you well, Elizabeth?' William asked, bending slightly at the knee to peer into her face. 'You look flushed. Come, let's sit down.'

He led her to the table which was set for the wedding party. Flower-filled vases ran the length of the table while colourful petals were strewn on the white tablecloth.

'Well enough, considering what we have just done,' she admitted while glancing towards the door where the others entered the house. 'It's just that all of us are family now and socially we cannot be more different from one another. Will this really work?'

'Do not fear, sweet bride…we are not as stuffy as our rank would indicate…well, perhaps Father and Thomas are, but Minerva balances them out. Besides, my father and your aunt and uncle have been friends for years and rank makes no difference to them.'

Watching them all chatting and laughing, she realised her fears in that regard were groundless. It was only her own insecurity prompting the thoughts.

'By the looks of it, they are happy to be related.' William inclined his head towards Aunt Mary and Minerva. 'I imagine your aunt has been offered residence at Rivenhall House by now and Minerva has been instructed on how to shear a sheep.'

William's sister and her aunt did seem to get along well. Perhaps the social status one was born to did not mean as much as she feared. Perhaps this did not need to be a barrier between her and her husband, either, if they did not wish it to be. With the issue somewhat settled in her mind, she relaxed and enjoyed her wedding breakfast.

It really was lovely getting to know William's family. She might have done it sooner had she not been so frightened of accompanying her aunt and uncle on their trips to London.

Minerva proved to be every bit the lively girl her brother said she was. Elizabeth enjoyed seeing how curious she was about everything to do with the farm. Lord Rivenhall was a cordial man who smiled often at his children…and at her.

She had the sense he bore as deep an affection for his troublesome son as he did his more serious heir. However, when Lord Rivenhall's gaze settled on Minerva, all he looked was worried.

All at once, William's sister gave Elizabeth a sunny smile. 'Mother's ring looks just right on you, Sister… and I am ecstatically pleased to be able to call you that and, please, do say you will call me sister, too?'

This was William's mother's ring? That would explain the tender look he'd had when he'd placed it on her finger in the stable. All at once the gold band seemed warmer, glowed brighter. It was quite touching to know it had belonged to his mother. For some reason, it validated the marriage…made it seem more of a real one.

'Mother's ring?' Thomas gave her an odd half smile which she suspected was an attempt to hide a frown. As the eldest son, the heir, Thomas must have assumed he had first rights to it.

The elegant band suddenly felt awkward on her finger. Surely it would have been more appropriate for a true lady to wear the delicate, sparkling ring.

'It looks lovely on you, my dear,' Lord Rivenhall assured her. 'My late wife would want you to have it.'

Perhaps that might be true had her son made a love

match, or at least married a lady who was his social equal. Lady Rivenhall certainly would not have wanted her first born to feel slighted over it being given away when it ought to have been his.

Warm, bread-scented breath brushed her ear, sent a chill along the side of her neck and distracted her attention from Thomas's insincere smile. 'It's true,' William whispered. 'She meant for the ring to go to me one day. Thomas got Grandmother's ring which is twice the size.'

'I do not wish for him to have hard feelings over it. Is there a lady he had in mind to give it to?'

'Not yet. Thomas is too busy learning to be a viscount to think of marriage. Just give him time, Elizabeth. This whole thing, our marriage, happened too quickly for him. Thomas likes life to be orderly and predictable. He is most comfortable with events planned far in advance. If I had given you Mother's ring a proper year in advance of the wedding, he would be happy about it.'

'Don't look dour, Thomas,' Minerva announced. 'You know Mother and William are peas in a pod. It is right that his wife wears her ring.'

Thomas blushed, apparently embarrassed that his inner thoughts had been exposed. He pressed his lips together and then gave Elizabeth a curt nod.

'Forgive me, Elizabeth. My sister is correct. Our mother would be delighted to see you wearing it. And it does look exquisite on you.'

'The matter is settled and put behind us,' William declared.

But was it really? She suspected the dissension between William and his brother went rather deep.

'The ring is no longer Mother's, but Elizabeth's. From somewhere up above, Mother is smiling her approval... I feel it.' William clapped his hand over his heart, also smiling. When his gaze shifted to Thomas, the smile sagged somewhat.

'You do?' Minerva gave her brother a great wide blink. 'I feel it, too. Right here in my heart.'

With a ring so clearly treasured by one and all, she only hoped no would be offended when she took it off. Truly it was far too great a treasure to wear while tending sheep, which she would be doing first thing tomorrow morning.

Given their circumstances, a honeymoon trip would be inappropriate...uncomfortable in the extreme. As she saw it, her job as William's wife meant teaching him how to become a responsible farmer whom his father would be proud of. This was a feat which could not be accomplished on a romantic tour of France or Italy. Besides, she would feel backward visiting the fine places he would be used to.

The meal and the afternoon passed in pleasant conversation. It was agreed that her aunt and uncle would leave with the Grant family after dinner, spend the night in Windermere and then travel on to London with them. They would live at Rivenhall House until they found an apartment of their own.

It was all so lovely, except that she was going to miss them dreadfully. Except that, aside from the staff, the only person she would have was her husband...a near stranger. Except, except, except—this was now her life and she must deal with it in the best way she knew how. And she did have her home which was a huge comfort.

* * *

After the meal, they all took a walk around the farm and after that returned to the house for tea.

Apparently, Minerva thought everything was grandly romantic. All through the afternoon she had been casting both her and William odd, curious glances. Unless she was wrong, Minerva was intensely interested in what would happen between her and William when everyone went home, and they were alone behind closed doors.

Having been raised on a farm, Elizabeth knew what was what between male and female. Still, knowing that her sister-in-law was wondering about it in regard to the new bride and groom made Elizabeth uncomfortable in an odd, itchy-under-the-skin way. Surely everyone must be wondering what kept her in a constant state of blushing.

What her young sister-in-law did not realise was that this bride and groom would not be alone together behind closed doors. William would retire to his half of the first storey and she would retire to hers.

Perhaps they might spend time in the study, chatting and becoming more acquainted over a late-night dessert, but that would not be anything akin to what Minerva was envisaging.

Which, while gazing at her groom's profile while he sat beside her speaking with Uncle James, made her envisage it, too. To redirect her mind, she asked. 'Where in London will you look for your apartment, Aunt Mary?'

Before her aunt could answer, Minerva spoke. 'In Mayfair, of course! I so wish for you and Uncle James to live close by. I can introduce you to everyone and it will be so very grand.'

My word. Aunt Mary and Uncle James were to see their dream of living in London fulfilled in a grand way.

And she was going to live here with her exceptionally handsome husband which had not been her dream at all but…well, dreams had a way of changing, did they not? This time last year she would have sworn this to be impossible…believed that a star would fall out of the sky, and she would hold it in her palm before such a thing would happen.

'The sun is getting low,' Thomas pointed out. 'We ought to be on our way so we can reach Windermere before dark.'

'We can only hope the railway will approve the spur people are talking about,' Lord Rivenhall commented. 'It will make our visits more convenient.'

And cut precious pastureland with rails! Endanger grazing sheep and corrupt the air with smoke!

Just when she was heated and ready for a discussion about it, Minerva spoke up.

'We cannot leave yet, Father. I have a surprise for the newlyweds.'

The inflection in Minerva's voice when she said 'newlyweds' caused a ripple of heat to race under the surface of Elizabeth's skin. Aunt Mary smiled brightly as if she knew what the surprise was.

William arched his brows, casting his sister a glance which was something halfway between a grin and a frown. Honestly, she had never seen anyone make that expression before. She could not determine what it meant.

Apparently, Minerva understood it. She gave her

brother a bright smile and said, 'Do not worry, it is a grand surprise which you will both thank me for.'

'What do you mean?' William's expression turned sceptical.

'I cannot say, or it will ruin the thrill.' She stood up, clapping her hands. 'You must come and see for yourselves.'

Evidently Minerva was not so grown up or so sophisticated that she could not skip…for it was what she did, skipping happily from the drawing room and up the stairway.

William shrugged, indicated with a nod that they should follow. Coming to the head of the stairs, they followed her to the left, then to the third door down on William's side of the first floor.

The master's chambers. What possible surprise could there be in those quarters? Coming to the doorway, she froze on the threshold, her chin sagging.

An explosion of multi-hued rose petals was strewn on the floor…in a direct path to the large master bed which had the covers turned down and even more petals scattered on the sheets.

She gasped in horror.

Luckily, William was laughing so hard his sister was not likely to notice Elizabeth's thoughtless response. Minerva had clearly gone to some trouble to decorate the room and she did deserve thanks for her effort.

'What a sweet gesture, Sister,' she said while standing resolutely in the doorway and not a toe over. 'Thank you for thinking of it.'

William had no hesitation entering his new chamber. Walking inside, he turned in a circle while nodding his head, then with a great smile sat down on the bed.

'Thank you, Minnie. I appreciate your effort on my behalf.'

'It isn't for you as much as it is for Elizabeth. Ladies do enjoy a spot of wedding-night romance, you know.'

'My question is, what do you know about wedding-night romance?'

'Not nearly enough since no one will enlighten me. But I do listen and I read things, so I know that if I wish to have a niece or a nephew, flowers, especially roses, help in some way.'

From the foot of the stairs, she heard her father-in-law's voice calling up, 'Minerva! We must be on our way.'

'All the way home I shall be wondering what you will name the child.' Spinning on her heel with a happy squeak, Minerva rushed out of the room, leaving Elizabeth and her groom staring at each other across a sweetly scented chamber.

He grinned at her, but she had no idea what her answering expression was. It could be anything from horror to fascination.

She felt those and everything in between so she said the only thing to make any sense. 'We should go bid them goodbye.'

There it was again…'we'…and used so casually. She absolutely was not going to look at that turned-down bed. She spun about, hurried down the corridor.

Laughter followed and then she felt the warmth of his hand at her elbow. 'She meant well,' William said. 'I promise. She always does.'

Chapter Six

How was a person supposed to sleep in such silence?

Giving up hope of it, William tossed the blankets off his legs, then got out of bed. He walked to the window, then shoved it open, listening for any odd noise which might sound familiar. But wait…what was that? He squinted his eyes to be sure that what he was seeing was true before he raised an alarm.

There was a fire in the pasture! In the moment it was too far out to be a threat to the house or the stables, but no matter, flames were always a concern. Even in this wet environment he did not feel inclined to dismiss it. Flames could eat up a city street in a moment.

As children, he and Thomas had been forced to run from a fire once and it had been frightening in the extreme. Thomas had had the brilliant idea that the two of them should sneak away from their governess and go exploring. It had all been great fun until they'd smelled smoke while passing a print shop. The front door crashed open and a screeching man in an apron rushed out. Smoke billowed out after him, then the windows exploded, sending people running for cover. Three other business had burned by the end of it.

No fire could be assumed harmless.

Rushing away from the window, he hurriedly put on his coat and shoes, then dashed out of the house where he could keep a closer watch on the flames. In London one might send for the fire brigade, but not here.

Dashing out of the house, he wondered if Ambleside even had a fire brigade. Even if they did, he could not summon help fast enough to prevent the meadow from burning.

Once outside, he was relieved to see the fire had not spread since he did not know what he would do about it if it had. He ran towards the field. The pasture stretched away from the house on a slight downward slope. It seemed to glisten in the moonlight.

Between where he was and the fire were the two stables and the carriage house. Since he could do nothing to stop the fire, he would alert Mr Adams and together they would get the animals out of harm's way.

Again, to his relief, the fire remained small, but it could not hurt to take the precaution. Since he was now a citizen of Ambleside, he was going to make it his goal to see that the village had a fire brigade, in the event they did not already.

Light leaked out from around the stable door. Good, Adams must have seen the flames and was already taking steps to protect the animals.

He rushed inside, a shout ready on his lips, but he ran headlong into a woman. She started to topple. He grabbed her forearms to steady her.

'Elizabeth?' he gasped.

'William! Hello.' She cradled a lamb in her arms which he took quickly from her. 'What are you doing out here in the middle of the night?'

'The same thing as you are, getting the livestock to safety.'

'To safety?' She blinked, cast him a speculative gaze as if he had become suddenly unbalanced. 'What do you mean?'

'Yes, to safety! Surely you have noticed the blaze in the meadow. It is quite far off, but I have seen fires move quickly before.'

Gently, and without undue rush, she prised the lamb from his grip.

'That is so…so brave of you, William. But that is a fire we need not fear. It is only a campfire for the shepherds. It is safely contained within the sheepfold.'

'Sheepfold?' He was greatly embarrassed to admit he did not know what it was. What sort of farmer was he going to be?

'It is where the shepherds bring the sheep for the night. It is an enclosure, a low wall made of stone.'

'And the shepherds sleep outside with them?'

'Some do. But there is a shepherd's hut for those who wish to sleep indoors.'

She'd called him brave, but he could only wonder what she really thought. Halfwit was no doubt what she'd meant.

'Well, then…since there is no emergency at hand, I shall return to the house.' And lick his wounds of humiliation. He pivoted about to do just that, but then— 'Elizabeth, what are you doing in the stable at this hour?'

'Mr Adams sent word that this sweet baby was having trouble coming into the world. But here she is, safe and hale, and so is her twin, over there with Mama.'

His bride was quite unique among the women he knew. He could not imagine which of those gently bred ladies would know how to help with a birth, difficult or otherwise...let alone rise from the comfort of her bed in the wee hours of the dark to do it.

She must think him an incredible dunce. There was more to living in the country than he could have guessed. He had never felt more inadequate...more like a fish flopping about on the riverbank.

'Now that I know all is well, I shall walk you back to the house...as long as your work here is finished, that is.'

'Give me a moment to settle her back with her mother.'

'I'll wait for you outside.' Where he could take a breath and gather what he could of his pride.

Moments later, he heard the stable door slide closed, then Elizabeth's quiet footsteps in the grass as she joined him near the path to the house.

'William, it means a great deal to me that you came rushing out to save the lambs. I think you were heroic.'

Did she? What a shame there was nothing to have been heroic about. He thought he would enjoy seeming a hero in her eyes. With a nod to acknowledge her remark, they began the walk back to the house.

Off in the distance the campfire continued to merrily snap and blaze. Ah, and now that he knew about it, he could see the faint outline of the stone sheepfold.

If he meant to be successful at farming, and he thought he ought to be, there was much he needed to learn. And he suspected he would be required to rise at dawn to learn it.

Thinking about the life he'd left behind and the one he was about to learn, he realised there was something which would make life at the farm familiar... more comfortable. Having visitors from London! A bit of society would go a long way towards making life satisfactory in Ambleside. Also, the purchase of a proper carriage would not be out of line. When he took Elizabeth on visits to Windermere, or other quaint and picturesque villages nearby, it was only proper that they ride stylishly.

A whisper of feathers swooped overhead, followed by the hoot of an owl.

He felt a million miles from London. No creaky wagon wheels broke the silence. No shouts of drivers to one another as they brought their passengers home from a late night at their clubs. No call of lamplighters going about their business.

The night was far quieter than he was used to. He wondered if he would ever become used to it. Even the shrill call of a constable's whistle would have been a welcome distraction from the silence closing him in on all sides.

Suddenly a breeze came up, rattling the grass. Something, he had no idea what it was, made a rustling noise in a bush to his left. The sound seemed unnerving to him, but he would bet his wife did not think it was. Growing up here she probably found the sounds comforting.

Indeed, just now she closed her eyes, lifting her face to the moonlight. Her chest lifted with the deep breath she took. 'It is a bit of paradise even at this hour, don't you think?' she asked.

It might well be, but it did not have to do with the crisp, clean air. It was because with her face turned towards the moon, he could see how incredibly beautiful her smile was...that part of the night was heavenly. And the way the breeze captured wisps of her dark hair, blowing it about her cheeks...catching it in the corner of her mouth. In a moment he might hear a choir of angels singing.

Which was the poetic thought of a London gentleman, not a sensible, down-to-earth farmer. He wanted to make a go of it in Ambleside, but wondered if it was possible.

Nothing was what he was used to. No valet...no footman or butler. This was all... He took a glance at the pasture with moonlight shining down, heard the bleat of a wakeful sheep...so foreign to anything he knew.

There was not much choice in the matter now, not that there had ever really been one. He was a married man, half owner of a farm. In the wink of an eye, he had gone from being responsible for nothing to being responsible for all this...and her.

Once morning came, his mind might not be so unsettled. In the morning birds would sing, the same as they did in London. The same sun would be shining down on both places. By the light of day his situation would look more hopeful.

He would invite his chums from London to visit. The coming rail spur would make it convenient. The railway would also bring tourists beyond the confines of Windermere. Soon the area would have more inns, restaurants and other establishments which spoke of civilisation.

Even if those things did not happen and he remained without society, he would do his best to make a go of his life here. He wished to prove to his father that he was fit for more than the ballroom. Perhaps if he was successful here, Father would look at him with approval the same as he did Thomas.

He needed to prove he was a success at this business to himself as much he did to Father, to be honest. And to his wife. Now that he had one—a dark-haired beauty who was far more appealing than the Bo-Peep he had conjured—he did want to be a man worthy of her respect.

There was so much he needed to learn about how to care for this property. At present he could not even discern the difference between a docile campfire and a raging blaze.

'No one expects to you know it all at once,' she said.

He had not realised he'd uttered that thought aloud. 'I hope you are a patient woman, Elizabeth.'

'More than that—I am determined.'

His mind wandered, watching that errant lock of hair still clinging to the corner of her full, pretty mouth. What he wanted was to kiss it away. To turn her towards him on the path and do what he had never done: be the one to offer a kiss. He was nearly itching with the desire to brush that strand of hair away from the corner of her mouth…nip it with his teeth and discover if it was as silky as it appeared.

In his mind being the one to give the kiss somehow indicated commitment. Not that exchanging wedding vows had not been a commitment, a very great one, but while they had given their lives to one another, they had not given their hearts.

Even without that, he did like her quite well. Liked her and wanted to kiss her. If he made it back to the house without giving in to the temptation, it would be a wonder of self-restraint.

If he got a wink of sleep, it would be a coup. No pair of pretty, shapely lips had ever haunted his thoughts before...ever nudged at his heart seeking entry.

Only Elizabeth's.

Only his wife's.

Coming back into the house with William, Elizabeth had one thing on her mind.

Rose petals.

Were they still on William's chamber floor...on the bed? Had he slept among them? An image filled her mind unbidden...which did not mean she was going to cast it out swiftly. Because there was her groom, his large body splayed across the mattress with the sheet barely protecting his modesty. Red and pink petals drifted in a swathe across the sheet and under it. She imagined petals under her bare feet as she crossed the room to touch him and see if he would awake.

She had to blink hard to return her attention to the here and now.

Climbing the stairs nearly elbow to elbow, they reached the top and then stood where the corridor divided her space from his.

For an instant which seemed to stretch longer, they stared silently at one another.

She could not help but wonder where his thoughts

were. Probably nowhere close to the imaginative place her mind was visiting.

'Did you clean up your sister's gift or sleep in it?' she blurted, because she was wondering about it rather intensely. She doubted that she would be able to rest without having an answer to the mystery.

'I did not sleep.'

That answer did nothing to appease her curiosity, but she could hardly press him further on it.

He cleared his throat in a manner which sounded uneasy.

'There is something I must make clear. I mentioned it before, but…well…' He smiled, but his mouth looked tight at the corners which made it not a smile at all, but a grimace. 'It is to do with our marriage bed. Rest assured I will not pressure you on the matter, Elizabeth. I realise you did not choose me. So, what happens in there—' he nodded his head down the corridor in the direction of his closed chamber door '—you do get to choose that. You may trust that I will never force my attentions upon you.'

Very well…fine. Naturally the last thing she wished to have was forced attentions, which did not necessarily mean she did not wish to have 'attentions'.

The idea took her by surprise. Perhaps knowing a man for a long time was not a requirement for having delicious thoughts, but rather knowing that said man was one's husband made possibilities flourish. And perhaps seeing how handsome said husband was…well, standing so close and smelling so manly and wonderful…

My word! Show her the bride who would not welcome this man's voluntary attentions. This one would, which only went to point out how unsatisfactory forced attentions would be.

'Thank you, William. I appreciate your...well, your...'

His what? Restraint...respect...or was it his uninterest? And if he was uninterested in her, how did she feel about it?

Confused was how. 'Just...thank you for understanding.' Because she did not understand. Just because William Grant was her legal husband did not mean she was suddenly smitten with him and, recent thoughts aside, wished to share his bed.

Indeed not! Although...given that they were wed, it was customary for such a thing to happen. Customary for a bride and groom who actually knew each other before the vows were spoken, that was.

Simply because she felt drawn to him, to his scent and to the fine, masculine build of his body...also to the sound of his voice which she found herself hearing even when she was not with him...none of that meant she knew him. She had never been so unsure of what was in her mind, much less in her heart.

'It is late,' he murmured, then took a step deeper along his side of the corridor. 'We should get some sleep.'

Should, yes. But what would happen when she closed her chamber door?

Would she lay upon her lovely soft bed and fall into the arms of slumber, or would she summon an image of her sheet-draped husband...indulge in a fantasy of herself falling into his arms instead?

'Goodnight, William.' She retreated a few steps along her side of the corridor, which placed them several feet apart.

'Goodnight, Elizabeth.'

Once more they stared silently at each other. How she wished she could see behind his eyes and read his thoughts.

Her thoughts continued to wander, taking a sweet path to his bathing chamber where rose petals floated about him while he reclined in the tub.

'I hope you sleep well,' she added.

Why was she hesitating to be parted from his company? It was late and morning chores would be upon them soon.

Oh, but the corridor was dim, romantic, with moonlight streaming in the tall windows. He looked so handsome...so appealing that she simply did not want to let go of the moment.

'I hope you sleep well, too, Elizabeth.' His voice was nearly a whisper...a breathless whisper.

The sound hit her square in the heart as if cupid had shot an arrow at her. She had to give herself a good mental shake to regain her reasonable, practical mind. 'Would you like to begin learning how to run your farm tomorrow?'

'I imagine I need to begin some time.'

'Very well. Until tomorrow then.'

She would not sleep. She could not possibly get a wink until...not until she—

With a quick dash, she crossed the line separating her side of the first storey from his. Rising on her toes, she kissed his cheek. 'Once again, thank you for coming to the aid of the sheep.'

'There was nothing that needed to be aided.' He touched his cheek where her lips had quickly planted the kiss.

What could that mean? It could mean he liked it, or it could mean he was wiping it away.

'But it was your intention to help and that is what matters.'

With that, she spun about to run to her chamber where she would now be able to sleep, as long as she could forget the scent of his skin and how the stubble of his beard scraped her lips in the most intriguing way.

Opening her door, she glanced back down the dim corridor. He stood where he was, gazing steadily at her, but she could not read his expression. Thinking back to the beginning, when she had first learned of the turn her life was about to take, she had not anticipated William Grant. Not imagined him as any more than a way to keep her home.

She had not anticipated that marriage would change her greatly. Her husband would go about his business on his side of the house and she would go about hers on hers. In the common areas they would be polite in each other's presence and then go about their separate lives. Now, getting to know William Grant, liking him quite well—nothing was as she had expected. Moment by moment it was all changing. Her expectations of a marriage shifting.

How naïve she had been. Wed only a day and she feared she would fail at her own rules. Feared, too, that she would not mind failing at them!

She had not slept, in part because there had been no time to do so, having settled in her bed so late and rising so early. Now, with dawn nearly ready to tint the sky, she stood in the corridor at the dividing line, listening for William's door to open. Surely, he must be up and anxious to be about the day.

Nothing…no footsteps, no rustle of fabric.

'William,' she called softly.

Again, nothing so she called again, this time a bit louder. The animals needed care, would be wondering where she was. If nothing else, he would want to feed his horse. After several more moments of waiting, she felt rather annoyed.

'William Grant! Are you ready to work?' She shouted this loud enough that Penny, already busy in the kitchen, must have heard.

This would not do at all. If the man wished to live up to the responsibly of owning half a farm, he would need to get out of bed. Even if he did not wish to live up to it, she wished for him to.

As boldly as a woman wed for many years, she crossed the line in the carpet, marched towards his chamber door and pounded upon it.

What was that? Snoring!

Clearly, there was nothing for it but to open the door and march inside. It was either that or…well, there was no *either that*. Gathering her sense of righteous ire, she stormed into his chamber, nearly stumbling over the hem of her workday gown.

While the rose petals were absent, her groom was lying on the bed exactly as she had imagined him. But there were some things that her virginal imagination had not supplied. There was a dusting of dark hair on his arms. It grew on his chest, too. His manly-looking ribcage rose and fell in the peace of deep slumber.

William Grant did sleep as bare as her daydream had suggested. What the daydream had not accurately conjured was how all-over muscular a man he was. Naturally, there was no way she could have imagined it, especially since she had always assumed London gentlemen were too refined to have such a solid form.

It was a breach of their agreement for her to be standing in his bedroom...worse of one for her to be gawking at him in his vulnerable state. Yet, wed was wed and there was nothing untoward in what she was doing. But the fact remained that while he dozed and she stared at him doing so, eggs were waiting to be collected, the lambs' nursery ready to be swept and new straw laid down.

'William!'

This roused him somewhat, but not enough for him to crack open his eyes. No, indeed, he turned over on his side, snuggling his wide bare shoulders into the mattress.

'Deliver my breakfast in an hour or two, if you will.'

She flushed hot and cold at once. Something was about to be delivered and it was not breakfast. She stomped towards the water pitcher and heard him resume snoring. Having been standing all night, the water would be good and cold. Plucking the pitcher up, she dumped the contents on his back, neck and head.

He sat up with a yelp. He grabbed the sheet when he leapt up, but it did not do a great deal to cover him.

'At Wilton Farm, the place you now reside, breakfast is not delivered.'

She looked steadfastly into his eyes because if she looked any place else, he would see that it was not completely anger in her eyes, but something altogether different. And she was angry and wanted him to see that and nothing else.

'Additionally, you will eat after the livestock eats and the morning chores are completed.'

'Elizabeth?' He blinked at her, his gaze fuzzy and unfocused. 'I did not mean that you… I woke thinking I was in London.'

'Clearly you are not. Which means you are no longer a gentleman of leisure. Life at our farm begins before daylight. I will expect you in the hen house within fifteen minutes.'

Wed little more than a day and William had already offended his wife.

He had not meant to. He had been so deeply asleep that he'd thought he was at home in London and that breakfast was being served far too early. Not that he took breakfast in his room at home, but it was what his brain registered coming out of a deep sleep.

He would need to be especially diligent in learning what to do in the hen house in order to appease his bride.

Coming downstairs, he realised he did not know the first thing about hen houses. He could not recall ever having occasion to visit one. In this new life of his, he imagined he would have occasion to do many things he never had before. And he did want to learn them. He had a new life now and he wanted to do well at it.

Hearing noises coming from the kitchen, he went that way, poked his head around the door frame.

'Excuse me, miss,' he said. 'May I ask where I might find the hen house?'

'Good morning, Mr Grant. How delightful to see you this fine day.'

Perhaps it was a fine day. For him it was far too early to know.

The woman plucked a muffin from a tray she had just removed from the oven and placed it in his hand. 'Here you are, then, to start the day right. You will find the hen house in the farthest stable from the house.'

'Thank you.' The muffin felt warm in his palm and smelled delicious. He lifted it as if in salute.

'I would suggest you eat it before you get there. Your wife did not look a bit happy when she left the house. Elizabeth nearly always looks happy.'

Which meant he was making a muddle of being a husband. He had better be a quick learner if he did not wish to have cold water dumped upon him again. Or worse, to be sent packing back to London. He did not wish to go back and not only because he would be ashamed to the bone.

There was Elizabeth, his wife…while he had seen anger in her eyes this morning, and rightly so, he had seen something else as well. In her beautiful green gaze, he had seen a flicker of a promise. It suggested that perhaps this might become more than a 'lesser of two evils' marriage.

Rushing out of the kitchen, he ran in the direction the cook had pointed, gulping down the muffin as he went.

Coming into the stable, he noted how large it was, and how well kept. He paused to listen, heard hens cackling, then followed the sound past several stalls which he thought might be used for wool shearing. The door to the hen house was open so he went in.

Without looking at him or acknowledging his presence, Elizabeth shoved a basket at him. 'Take the eggs out of the nest and place them in here. When you've gathered them all, take them to Penny so we may have eggs for breakfast.'

The first hen he reached his hand under pecked him aggressively. 'Ouch!' he exclaimed, staring at a dot of blood welling on his hand. For some reason, his painful exclamation made the corners of Elizabeth's mouth quirk. He imagined she was fighting a smile at his expense.

Then she dumped the scoop full of feed she had been holding on to the hen house floor. Chickens hopped out of their nests clucking, scratching and pecking about the floor.

'You might have done that before I tried to get the eggs,' he grumbled.

But then she laughed and he did not feel like grumbling any more. He stared at her lips, remembering how they'd felt on his cheek last night. It was probably the least intense kiss he had ever been offered, yet it had affected him the most deeply.

No wonder he'd overslept this morning, given that it had taken him a long time for his cheek to cool off. Longer even for his mind to stop picturing what those lips might feel like kissing his mouth. That was a thought he would like to dwell on longer, but Elizabeth pointed to the empty nests and advised him to collect the eggs while the hens were distracted.

Acting quickly, he plucked them from the straw, then placed them in the basket. Already he had learned some valuable lessons. First, do not oversleep. Second, the cook made the best muffins he had ever tasted and she seemed quite kindly. Then third, feed the chickens before raiding their nests. And fourth? Ah, yes, number four was the best. He had learned that he would do almost anything to see his bride smiling at him.

'Very good,' she said with that very lovely grin encouraging him on. 'Now, wipe that muffin crumb from your chin and then carefully take the eggs to Penny in the kitchen. After that, meet me in the lambing pen.'

Doing as she commanded, he hurried away, hoping as he went to be given another treat.

Penny thanked him for bringing the eggs, but did not offer him anything else to eat.

Judging by the smells in the kitchen, he wondered if rising this early might be worth it if only to have breakfast.

Dashing to the stable where the lambing pen was, he went inside. Forget breakfast being a reason to rise early. When he came inside Elizabeth was humming to the lamb she cradled against her heart. She bent her lips to kiss the top of its head.

It might be wrong to wonder if she would ever hold him that way, or kiss him with such tender affection. Such a thing was not in the agreement they had made and he had promised to give her the lead in this area of their marriage.

'Is this what I do next?' he asked because he dared not allow his thoughts to travel too far down a forbidden path.

'It isn't required, but...'

Bending, he reached to scoop up a small sheep that had just toddled up to inspect the leg of his trousers. He hummed to it even though his humming voice was as off key as his singing one was. Then he kissed the top of its head. He glanced at Elizabeth, seeking her approval.

'Did I do it correctly?'

'That depends upon why you did it.' There was that particular expression of hers which twitched the corners of her mouth, withholding a smile which clearly longed to be released. 'Did you do it because you genuinely like Murray? Or were you trying to get back into my good graces for oversleeping?'

'If this is Murray, I do like him…and his mother, whichever of them she is.' His wife was certainly pretty early in the morning. 'And I am trying to get back in your good graces. For demanding breakfast as much as oversleeping.'

She laughed. The lovely tinkle shot straight to his heart. If he never had any more of their marriage than her laughter, it would be more than he would have hoped for. Hearing Elizabeth laugh was far better than the other choice he'd had.

He cringed at the thought of trying to preach a sermon to a chapel full of parishioners who would be either falling asleep or frowning at him.

So far being wed to this beautiful stranger, who was becoming less and less of one by the moment, was intriguing, cold water notwithstanding.

'Well,' he said while setting Murray down in the straw. 'Do I correctly assume that I am to change out the dirty bedding for clean?'

'Yes, William. You will need to learn everything from bottom to top.'

What, he had to wonder, did the foreman do? Back in London no one in the family went into the stable except to visit a favourite animal or to order a carriage to be readied. Since he did not think she would appreciate him asking, he kept the thought to himself. But they were paying the fellow to do something.

'Mr Adams is now caring for your horse; you will learn this.'

Had he voiced his thought aloud again, or was she simply adept at reading his mind?

He understood some wives were skilled at it, but only after a long acquaintance with their husbands. Perhaps there was something special between him and his bride, an uncommon connection. He dearly hoped so. The two of them were bound together for the rest of their lives. It would be good if they got along well. Better than well, truth be told.

To that end he bent his back to the chore she was explaining as well as demonstrating. He felt uncomfortable watching her move straw around with a pitchfork. At home in London, a gentleman would never allow his wife to perform such a task. Not that said wife would be willing to do it.

Watching her going about it while looking so cheerful, he set his mind diligently to learning everything she had to teach him. And just maybe he would be able to teach her a few things about society so that when they visited London she would feel comfortable.

While they were from two different worlds, he did not see the difference as a great barrier between them. He would teach her of his life and she would teach him of hers. How to begin? Ah, the bonnet. The gift would be an excellent place to start.

Every woman he knew adored a frilly bonnet. He could hardly wait to see her smile when he placed it on her head and tied the ribbons under her pert and pretty chin.

Chapter Seven

Elizabeth could only admit to feeling a bit of pride in how hard William had worked today. For a London gentleman, he had done well. At least she thought so. More than once she had noticed Mr Adams casting him quizzical glances.

What she hoped the stableman understood was that this being William's first day, he had everything to learn. Her husband was bound to become more knowledgeable as time went on.

Her husband…thinking of him as such gave her middle a tickle…was clearly doing his best to please her. All throughout dinner he had looked exhausted, as if he might drift to sleep mid-sip of Windsor soup.

Walking along the corridor to the library, Elizabeth was happy to be inside and the long day finished. Wind and rain beat against the windows she went past. She supposed it was quite cold outside.

It was nice in here, though. It would be cosy in the study where William had asked her to meet him.

Coming into the book-filled room, she saw him sitting on the couch, his legs straight out before him and his arms stretched out on the back cushions. Since he faced the fire, his back was to her, giving her a second to admire the back of his head…the deep brown-black shimmer of his hair where it swept the nape of his muscular neck.

Hearing her, he stood, turned and indicated with a crook of his fingers that she should join him.

'Bless you.' He grinned widely when he spotted the tray she carried. 'Is that cake?'

She nodded. 'Chocolate.'

'How did you know it is my favourite?'

'I didn't, of course, but it is mine.'

'Well, then, perhaps we shall grow to be soul mates. Come, let's enjoy the fire and listen to the rain while we discover what else we have in common.'

'Listening to blustery weather when one is warm and toasty inside is a delight.'

'It is, especially when there is cake to go with it.'

Conversation lagged while they ate dessert and listened to the tap of rain, the crackling of the fire. Oddly enough, the silence was not uncomfortable.

'Tell me something about yourself that I do not already know, Elizabeth.'

'That would be everything since we do not know each other at all.'

'That isn't quite right. I do know a few things about you.' The way he raised his brows at her made her forget to swallow the cake. 'For instance… I know that you are dedicated to lambs. That you value hard work and adore this farm, so much so that you were willing to wed a stranger in order to keep it. I know you dislike London and society. I learned this morning that you are an early riser and a patient teacher.'

'I poured water on you, William… I was beyond impatient at the time.'

He laughed, the rumble deep and…well, she really did need to eat the bite of cake poised on her fork before it plopped off on to her bosom.

'I had just ordered you to deliver my breakfast at a later hour. Who could blame you for it?'

'Even so, my reaction was rash and I apologise. I promise not to do it again.'

'Think no more of it.'

'You did work awfully hard today. You must be exhausted.'

'Today I discovered muscles I never knew this London gentleman possessed.' His quiet laugh caught her heart, making it go soft. It was a relief to know she had wed a man with an easy nature. 'But here we are, just the two of us, in front of this pleasant fire while we indulge in cake and good company. Now, tell me something I do not know about you. Tell me something that you are fond of.'

Such as, in this very moment she was imagining him leaning towards her and kissing her…and how she was wondering what it would be like to have him touch her hair and… Never mind. They were only just getting to know each other. Perhaps one day it would be more appropriate to allow her mind to wander, in case it had not already been doing so quite happily.

'My favourite colour is yellow,' she said in order to point her thoughts to a more mundane subject.

'Splendid!' His smile stretched so wide one might think she had revealed a delicious secret. 'I have a small gift for you.' He stood, walked over to the bookcase and picked up a hatbox which she had not noticed being there when she came in.

Why would she have noticed, being caught in her husband's smile as she had been…and also the knowledge that this man was, indeed, hers for all time? It was going to take some time to get used to the notion. Even now she found it unbelievable. She was Mrs William Grant. Elizabeth Grace Grant. It was a good-sounding name. If only that was all there was to being a wife, a change of name. For all that her original intention had been to go about their separate lives, she was no longer sure it was possible.

She touched the elegant-looking bow on the box. The hatbox would be a fine gift even if nothing were inside.

'When did you have time to make such a purchase?'

'Before I left London. I wanted to give you something and…well, here it is. I hope you like it.'

It was thoughtful of him, truly. It made her glow inside thinking he had wanted to please her before they had even met. She opened the box, moved aside the tissue which was exquisite looking all on its own. Seeing a flash of yellow within the folds, she withdrew a stunningly pretty and exceptionally fashionable hat.

Her breath hitched for a heartbeat. How much money had William spent on it? While exquisite, it was impractical. She dearly hoped the matter of how they spent the farm's income would not become an issue between them.

He was clearly used to finery and she was used to utilitarian. Why, the first time the hat blew off her head in a breeze, it would be gobbled by a sheep or carried off by an envious bird. She would simply have to store the hat safely away, along with her wedding ring.

Although, having had the ring on her finger for a while now, she was coming to enjoy the happy wink of the diamond. It would be a shame when she took it off. She ought to have done so first thing this morning, but felt it could not hurt this once to leave it on. But it was William's mother's ring and she would need to be more careful of it in the future.

'Now you must tell me something that you like,' she said.

He nodded, looking thoughtfully at her. Taking the bonnet from her hands, he placed it on her head. Smiling, he tied the ribbons under her chin, tugging the bow into place under her ear.

'I like the way you look in the hat.'

'That is not something about you, it's about me.'

'No, it is my feeling about how you look in the hat.'

'I fear you will not see it often since it shall be stored safely in my wardrobe.'

'You will look fetching no matter where you choose to wear it, but it will look splendid on you when we visit London.'

London! That was one place she would not visit! The very thought of it made her stomach twist. She wondered if he would be disappointed when she told him that when he visited London he would do it alone. No matter what, she would not set one foot in that city.

'I would like to know something that you like which does not have to do with this hat. Perhaps some happy thing from your childhood?'

'That would be puppies. I have not had one since I was a boy, but still, I like them.' That was particularly good news since there was a litter of pups in the stable and she would like to give him a gift in return for the hat. Tomorrow he would get a grand surprise.

'Tell me something you dislike,' he said.

London, of course, but she decided it best to keep that to herself for the moment. Even if he did remember the time when his father found her, he would not realise how deeply scarred she had been by the event.

'I greatly dislike the spur the railway is proposing.' She shook her head, felt the satin ribbon slide along her throat as if it were his…never mind that. 'It will ruin Ambleside. Our rural lives will be threatened by tourists. Let them remain in Windermere where there are already inns, restaurants and shops. That is what I dislike.'

'Quite passionately.' He lifted a brow at her.

'Quite.' She settled back into the cushions, then took a moment to let the tap of the rain and the whoosh of the wind outside the window soothe her.

'Tell me something you dislike.' Since she had exposed her heart on the matter of the detested spur, it was only fair to know what got under his skin.

He gazed at her for a moment, shrugged, then smiled.

'Seeing how pretty you look in the hat, I can't think of a single thing that bothers me.'

'I suspect you are every bit of the flirt your reputation claims you to be.'

His handsome smile grew wider. No wonder women lathered him with attention and offered kisses.

'I was, but no longer. I am now a married man and it makes a difference. Any compliment I give you, my wife, will be from my heart.'

Had she not been sitting, that revelation would have blown her over. It seemed very sincere.

She understood that it really had nothing to do with her or any great undying passion he felt for her which would keep him faithful. No, it was better than that. No matter that society saw William Grant as rogue in need of reform, she knew differently.

From all she could tell, her groom was a man of integrity, one of high standards. In her opinion, a gentleman of high standards could be trusted more than one guided by a grand passion. Passion could die. Good character lasted a lifetime.

'It is true, I think.'

He pressed his back into the couch cushions, then yawned. 'What is true?'

'You are the gentleman your mother raised you to be. She would be proud of you.'

'She always was, no matter what mischief I got into…' He yawned and then, with a smile still lingering on his attractive mouth, he fell asleep.

Eventually, she would wake him and tell him to go to bed. For now, she was going to take a moment to simply look at him, this stranger who was hers. However, he was not as much the stranger he had been moments ago. Sitting here in his presence, feeling so peaceful, she felt optimistic. They might well have what was needed to overcome the social distance that lay between a gentleman and a shepherdess.

Feeling suddenly sleepy herself, she slid closer to him and did what felt the most natural thing in the world. She rested her head on his shoulder and closed her eyes. His arm came up and curled about her shoulder, tugging her in. This, too, seemed the most natural thing in the world.

Drifting into a doze, she felt grateful that her life, in the moment, was a great deal better than it might have been.

The next morning, William hurt everywhere. He hobbled to the stable with mud from last night's rain caking his shoes. He thought the sun was coming up, but heavy clouds lingered, blocking the light, for as early as the hour was, he was running later than he ought to be.

With his muscles screaming at him in protest of the abuse he had subjected them to yesterday, it had taken longer to dress. Longer to hitch along to the kitchen in the hopes of getting something warm and tasty to energise him until breakfast. Bless Penny, she had rewarded him with a muffin still warm from the oven.

By the time he had fed the hens, collected the eggs and taken them to the kitchen, his muscles had loosened sufficiently to be merely sore.

Hurrying back to the lambs' pen, he was relieved that it had not begun to rain again, but he thought it might soon. He would need to work quickly to make up for the time he'd lost. He would rather that Elizabeth did not know he had lagged. It was more important to him than ever not to disappoint his bride.

Although she had not said so, he thought the hat he had presented to her was a disappointment. At the time he'd purchased it, he had not known how different she was than any other woman of his acquaintance. Any of them would have adored the hat. In his defence, having never met her, how could he have known that she valued hard work more than she did pretty frills?

Even yellow frills.

While the gift might have been a disappointment to Elizabeth, for him it had been a great treat. She had looked pretty in an elegant way. Wearing it when they visited London, she would rival any born-and-bred lady.

This morning, his desire to work hard and prove his worth might have a little to do with making up for the failed gift. Might...but he suspected his motives went deeper than that. For the first time since he had lost his mother, he actually wanted someone's approval.

No, that was not right. He had wanted Father's approval quite desperately. Sadly, his way of going about it, of hoping Father would see Mother in him, was all wrong.

He would not make the same mistake again. It mattered to him what his bride thought of him. Perhaps because she expected something of him. In the past all anyone had expected of him was to bring fun...or mischief...to a social gathering and to do it without bringing undue shame on the family. To not misbehave too badly was hardly a worthy goal to aspire to.

His wife expected him to behave as an equal partner of Wilton Farm. He would work his fingers raw—more than they already were—in order to see her smiling in approval of him. Approval, hers in particular, was a far better motivator than disapproval was.

In the past all he'd wished for from a lady was for her to think he was a fun companion for an evening... an evening which would be forgotten when the next social gathering came along.

Something had changed rather quickly within him, he decided while snatching the pitchfork and energetically removing dirty straw from the pen. The obvious change was that he was a married man. Still, it struck him as odd that he would suddenly feel a need to live up to responsibility. He had not felt such devotion to duty since he was a child and had the care of his dog. A wife could certainly not be equated to a dog, but she did inspire the more noble part of his character.

Months ago, the thought of rising before dawn would have been laughable. Often dawn would see him going to bed after attending a ball or socialising at his club. Something had changed him. Or someone. No woman he had ever met inspired him to change his ways. But Elizabeth? She was not like any of them. She was better. She was his.

Last night he had just started to doze away on the couch when he felt her head nestle against his shoulder. It had seemed the most natural thing in the world to gather her to him, to drift off to sleep together as if it had been their desire to become man and wife and not had the marriage foisted upon them.

Funny he did not feel the resentment which might come from being foisted upon a woman. He did not feel it within himself, but, more importantly, he did not feel it from her, which must be the reason he'd pushed himself out of bed this morning, groaning but not complaining, even if it did feel like the dead of night.

It was not as if he were the first one to rise at Wilton Farm. He would not have had the pleasure of a muffin if that were the case. Bless Penny for her pre-dawn work and the smile with which she went about her chores. Perhaps it was because the cook wished to please Elizabeth, the same as he did.

He also thought of how he wished to please Father.

It would be an amazing thing to see Father's gaze settle upon him with pride, as it did upon Thomas. He wanted that quite a bit.

But that was not the true reason he had pushed his aching body out of bed in the dark so that he could learn farming. It was to please his wife, as the pitchfork in his sore hands attested to.

With the dirty straw removed, he began to spread the clean in its place.

'Which one of you is Murray?' he asked.

He snatched up the first lamb to come and inspect, then nibble his trousers. Nuzzling its head, he hummed a quick tune, then set it down.

His wife was far better at this than he was. No doubt it was because she had been doing this all her life and was devoted to the tiny creatures, while he was devoted to—

To her? The thought slammed upon him so quickly he hadn't had time to consider it. One could hardly equate wanting to please someone with being devoted to them. Surely it was far too soon to be devoted to Elizabeth. He admired her and thought she was lovely in body and spirit…but devoted?

Confused more like it.

The stable door slid open. He turned to see his bride standing in the opening, a basket draped over her arm. It must have started raining again without him noticing. He watched heavy drops blowing every which way behind her as she drew the door closed.

'I've brought breakfast,' she announced with a nod at the basket. 'No need to go out in the storm just to eat it in the dining room.'

'Except that you came out in the storm to bring it here.'

'I enjoy stormy weather.'

Show him the man who would not work hard to gain this woman's respect. More, her affection. From all he could tell, she worked harder than any lady he knew. It occurred to him that he did not know any ladies who actually worked. How could he ever have imagined how attractive such a thing would be...how quickly he would become—

Devoted? He really did not know what else to call what he was feeling for her. Not that he could demonstrate his burgeoning feelings. He had given her the lead in that area of the marriage.

He would resolutely refrain from coaxing her to give him a kiss. However, he was having no success at refraining from imagining it. As much as he would like to feel that curvy, full mouth nipping his, he needed to be the one to give the first kiss. Only not until the time was right.

When, or if, it happened, he wanted the kiss to be different than any other. This would not be one that a lady offered and he accepted. No, this would be a kiss that he gave, expressed by both his lips and his heart.

She had not done up her hair this morning, but left it loose to tumble about her shoulders. Delicate-looking tendrils curled along the column of her throat.

Since he had made no promises about not imagining seducing her, he mentally caressed those dark, silky strands between his thumb and finger. Watched himself lift them to his cheek and...

'You look flushed, William. Perhaps you are working too hard.'

'I could do this all day long,' he admitted truthfully.

He could do it all night long, too, since he was not referring to cleaning the pen.

'While I appreciate your effort, we will take some time to eat.'

He glanced about, wondering where an appropriate place would be.

'There is a nice spot in the other stable.'

'How do you do that?'

'Do what?'

'Know what I am thinking?'

She shrugged, causing the hair lying across her bosom to shift and shimmer.

'Your face gives quite a bit away.'

'No one has ever said so before.'

No one had ever been his wife before, either. Could holy vows make such a difference? He had no way of knowing…perhaps it was just something between the two of them and they would have made the same connection in a crowded ballroom.

But, no. Had they met in a ballroom he would not be who he was now, nor would she be who she was. To him, she might have been simply another lady to enjoy a spot of fun with, kissed and forgotten.

One thing Elizabeth would never be was forgotten. If he failed at farming and she sent him home to London tomorrow, he would not forget her.

Taking off his coat, he held it over their heads while they dashed from this stable to the carriage house, then to the far stable.

Thunder crackled and boomed across the roof, sounding like a pair of giant's boots. Elizabeth rushed into the stable mere steps ahead of William. He was so close she felt his warm breath on her hair and smelled raindrops on his clothes.

'We might be here for a while,' she pointed out while sluicing water from her hair and shaking it from her skirt.

'It is lucky we are already wed.' He winked at her, giving her a deliciously mischievous smile. 'In London being alone with a lady regardless of the necessity would result in a hasty wedding.'

'No need to fear that again.'

As always, she was grateful to have grown up in Ambleside where the rules of behaviour were not so stringent. Not that immorality ran amok among her neighbours, it was only that standards of conduct were more reasonable.

Simply because a man and a woman spent time alone together did not mean that anything untoward would happen. Country people were far more sensible than city dwellers, in her opinion.

Most were, that was. Some people wanted the rail spur to cut up beautiful pastureland and they were not half-sensible.

'What a relief you and I are not bound by such nonsense.' She indicated an area near the midpoint of the stable where there were a few tables with chairs near a warm, glowing stove.

'What are the tables for?'

'Uncle James thought it only right for the employees to have a place to gather and relax away from the sheep.'

'I can see the need. Five hundred sheep and six shepherds?'

'It is not always only our shepherds. At times, shepherds from other farms work together—for instance, when it is time to bring the sheep down from the fells.

Also, it won't be long before the shearers arrive to trim winter wool off the animals and ready them for summer. It is only right for the men to have a place to rest from the work.'

'I admit, I never gave a thought to how much work goes into clothing me. From this day on, whenever I put on my trousers, I will be more appreciative.'

'It is encouraging to see that you are coming to understand the value of our flocks. Shall we eat?' Funny, having been wed such a short time, she found she greatly enjoyed sharing mealtimes with her husband. They never lacked for things to say and, when there was silence, it was comfortable.

She could honestly say she had never taken to anyone as quickly as she had William. Which, under the circumstances, was a fortunate thing.

It was a pleasant meal with each of them speaking of this and that thing of no great importance.

She ate more quickly than she normally did because she did not want her gift to give itself away before she'd had a chance to present him with his surprise.

'I'll be right back, William. I am going to get your gift.'

'My gift?'

Giving him a nod and a smile, she hurried towards the far end of the stable, opening the door to the tool room.

Making kissing noises caused four puppies to come dashing towards her, followed by their mother who wagged her tail happily.

She plucked a basket from the wall, put the puppies inside and then covered it with a square of tattered red wool.

'I'll bring them back soon, Mama. I promise.'

She petted the dog on the head to reassure her, then left the room to go back to William.

He stood at a window looking out, his hands shoved in the pockets of his trousers while he watched the storm.

She put the basket behind her to heighten the surprise. Suddenly she felt nervous about the gift. Hopefully, he wanted a dog. Just because he had enjoyed having one as a child did not mean he would enjoy one now.

While there were several dogs at the farm, they were working animals, not house pets.

'What have you there?' William asked, coming forward to stand in front of her and her hidden-but-wobbling basket.

'Pick a hand,' she said in order to draw out the fun.

'Left.'

She shook her head.

'Right.'

When, out of mischief, she shook her head again, he leaned in close. With only inches between them, he reached behind her back to claim the basket. His shirt touched her bodice, a rush of hot breath skimming her cheek. She caught the scent of hard work on his skin.

Exactly how many ladies had offered up their kisses to him? Dozens or hundreds, no doubt. Likely, every single lady in London had either done it or dreamed of doing it.

Perhaps…well maybe…since they were wed, and married couples did it all the time…all she need do was turn her head to the right and—

'Puppies?'

His delighted gasp snapped her back to reason. She

would probably kiss him one day...after they'd known each other for a proper amount of time.

'For me? All four of them?'

'Only one is the gift, although I suppose they are all yours since they will become working dogs. But pick the one to be your companion. It may live in the house if you like.'

'I cannot choose. They are all—'

A black pup with white paws scrambled over the edge of the basket. William caught it and set the basket down at the same time.

'This one,' he said. Holding the pup in one hand, he turned it from side to side, inspecting the wriggling creature. 'It reminds me of the one I had as a child. Oscar was his name.'

'What will you call this one?'

'Oscar Two. But I will call him Oscar for convenience.'

'Is this one as much like the one you had, then?'

'Not as much, but it is a good, solid name for a dog.' He smiled at Oscar Two with such warmth she knew she had chosen the gift well. 'You won't mind him being in the house?'

'I will enjoy it. I had a pet dog once and she was quite special to me.'

Her name had been Happy. Her aunt and uncle had given her the puppy in hopes of bringing her out of her melancholy after having been lost in London.

It had worked. Happy had made her happy again. Although the scars she had of that time were still with her.

'This Oscar is one of her descendants.'

'Is he? I thank you for him. I suspect he is a far more appropriate gift than the hat was.'

'Oh…well. The hat is the most beautiful one I have ever seen.'

'Not at all to your taste, though.'

It had been a thoughtful gift. One he had taken his time to purchase for her, a perfect stranger. She did not have the heart to admit he was correct.

'But it is! I adore it.'

Had anyone else given her such an utterly impractical thing, she would not adore it… But William? Injuring his feelings was not something she wished to do. She would wear it and smile…only not while tending sheep.

Soon, there was to be another meeting to protest the rail spur. Between now and then she would find the courage to put it on and wear it in front of her modestly dressed neighbours. They might think that by dressing that way, she was encouraging the influx of fancy tourists to Ambleside and therefore changing her stance on the spur. If they did, she would proudly straighten her pretty yellow bonnet and set them straight.

By now all the pups had escaped the basket and were merrily sniffing for fallen crumbs from breakfast.

'I need to give the rest of these back to their mother,' she said.

He helped her gather them and stuff them back inside the basket, where they did not want to go.

Pressing the red wool on top to hold them in, she turned to go back to the tool shed.

William caught her elbow. Slowly, he slid his hand down her arm. Even under her coat the pressure felt good…delicious. Better than chocolate. What she had to wonder…she really did have to because there was no way not to…what his hand would feel like on her bare skin.

'Thank you again. Oscar is a perfect gift.'

His fingers were at her wrist now, curling around her rapidly ticking pulse.

'You may regret saying so later on tonight.' Oh, please let her voice sound casual, unaffected by the way his touch made her feel melty. She was barely ready to acknowledge the twist of her heart to herself, let alone for him to know it.

'May I call upon your help when he cries in the night?'

No! It was difficult enough to keep her emotions a secret in the middle of the morning. Within the dark intimacy of his chamber, she would have no chance whatsoever. Keeping her growing attraction to herself would be difficult, especially when there was no legal reason to do it. No moral reason, either.

The one and only reason for it was that she feared giving her heart to him too quickly. Everyone knew that relationships needed to be cultivated slowly. Needed time to grow and blossom, did they not? Nature was an excellent example. Plants that grew too quickly tended to have roots which did not stand the test of time. Some of them did not, anyway. Some quick growers did quite nicely. Until she knew which they were cultivating, she would follow good reason.

Although his gaze on her in the moment was particularly warm and his smile softened to something intriguing, and just because he had still not let go of her wrist, did not mean he felt the same way she did.

Good reason, she reminded herself. 'If you find him

too difficult this one night, you may leave him in my chamber.'

Because she did not dare to put one foot inside his. If she did, she might abandon good reason and see rose petals, whether they were there or not.

It was not a surprise that the puppy slept through the night given that William had sat up in a chair all night long, holding him in the crook of his arm.

While Elizabeth was all the way on the other side of the corridor, she might have heard the pup's cries had William put him down. She had said she would not come to help, but she had a tender heart when it came to baby animals. The last thing he wanted—or to be honest the first—was for his bride to come to his chambers.

It had been far too close a call in the stable this morning. He had come within a heartbeat of breaking his resolution to allow Elizabeth to decide the direction the carnal aspect of their marriage would take. He had been so close to kissing her.

There was a reason he had never taken a kiss from a woman…only the ones freely offered. He had held to that gentlemanly code of behaviour to keep from becoming too deeply involved with a lady. Admittedly it was his own code of behaviour that some would scoff at, but none the less it worked for him.

This morning had been different. He'd wanted so desperately to draw his wife, complete with her basket of puppies, in and kiss her. He did not want to take a kiss he knew she wanted to offer. No, he needed to be the one to give it to her. But had he done so, he would have offered his heart along with his lips. At this point in their marriage, he did not know if she wanted more than to be partners on the farm. Perhaps at most bosom friends.

Oh, wait…perhaps not that. What he meant to think was that friendship was easy between them.

The storm had passed in the night. Gazing out the window, he saw the sky beginning to lighten. Although he had not slept and the sun not yet risen, it was time to go to work.

'Wake up, Oscar, it is time to go back to your mother while I gather eggs and clean stalls.' He stood up, placed his pup in the large coat pocket, then went out of the room and down the stairs. 'If we are lucky, we will start our day with a treat from Miss Penny.'

As it turned out, Oscar not only got treats, but prolonged snuggles and kisses which nearly made William late for gathering eggs.

In a hurry he carried Oscar back to his mother and siblings, then went on to the hen house. On the way there he realised that his muscles no longer ached. For some reason that made him feel rather proud. Going inside, he scattered chicken food on the floor, then began to gather eggs.

'Good morning, William,' Elizabeth said, stepping into the small space.

'Good morning, Elizabeth.'

'I did not hear Oscar crying. The two of you must be getting along well.'

'You could say so. But the reason he wasn't crying was because I held him all night.'

She started to laugh and all he was able to do was stare at her lips. How long was he going to resist them?

Even with the mood as far from romantic as could be, he wanted to kiss her.

'Where is he now?' she asked.

'I left him with his mother for the day.'

'Good idea. Today you are getting a promotion.'

As husband or farmer? He held his breath, waiting for her to reveal what it was.

'Just when I've become so bonded with the chickens.'

'Well, life does go on. As soon as we deliver the eggs to Penny, we will go to the fields and meet the shepherds. It is important for you to learn everything they already know.'

'Lead the way, Mrs Grant. I live to learn what you have to teach.' Which he did mean, but not only in the way he had stated. He wanted to learn how to be a responsible husband. But what was it she needed of him? To learn to be a farmer only?

After spending only days with her, he knew what he wanted. And yet the last thing he was going to do was try to convince her to give it to him. It was what he had done with women all his life.

Elizabeth was different. Even if she were not Mrs William Grant, it would be true. She was an amazing woman. All he wished was to be worthy of her respect…and, in time, perhaps to be worthy of her love.

There, he had declared it in his mind. Now he needed to wait patiently to discover what was in her mind. Between now and then he would put his mind to becoming an outstanding shepherd.

Something struck him as funny, so he laughed aloud.

Elizabeth lifted a brow at him in question.

'I just thought of my sister. If Minerva got wind of my new duties, she would come in an instant. She has the finest sense of adventure of anyone I know and such a curious mind.'

'We shall see if you think shepherding is so adventurous by tomorrow morning.'

Tomorrow morning? Now it was his turn to lift a brow at her.

'Do you mean I will be spending the night out of doors? In the pasture?'

'Yes, unless you choose to sleep in the shepherd's hut. Either is acceptable and if you do choose to sleep outdoors—' her hesitant smile flashed into a grin '—as you know, there is a campfire to keep you warm.'

Chapter Eight

Mid-morning sunshine chased away last night's storm and with the land warming nicely, Elizabeth decided it was time to take Mollie and Murray to the pasture to join the flock.

With a bit of luck, she would encounter her husband returning from his night with the shepherds. She was anxious to learn how it had gone and if he had managed to enjoy it at all. Last night would have been far from anything he was used to.

She hoped he'd got on well with the shepherds since they were now in his employ. This farm could simply not operate without them. Even though the adult sheep were in no great danger from predators, the lambs were vulnerable.

As owner of the farm, William would not be required to perform shepherds' work any more than he needed to gather eggs or clean stalls, but he did need to understand the things which kept the farm running smoothly.

Entering the lambing pen, she thought about how she'd missed his company last night. Indeed she had! More than she could have guessed. The hours seemed to stretch on and on. All during her morning chores, she had wondered why that should be. Until recently she had got along splendidly without William Grant in her life.

But now? What would her life be like without him to laugh with? Thinking of never knowing what it felt like to feel her heart warm at his smile made her feel... adrift, although she could scarcely imagine why she would feel that way. Being wed so short a time, it was not possible to become so deeply attached to him that she felt half there without him.

Even breakfast had been lonely in a way it never had been before. Going about her early morning chores had been dull with no one to instruct. Without William to instruct, that was.

This morning, after so much rain, chores had been a muddy business. The hem of her gown was soiled nearly to her knees. Her fingernails would require a dedicated cleaning once she returned from delivering Mollie and Murray to the pasture.

She reminded herself that it was a good sign that William had not returned. It must mean he was fitting into his new role. It could not be an easy thing for him, given that he was a gentleman born and reared.

While her groom might be from an aristocratic upbringing, she detected no condescending attitude from him towards her or anyone else. If he felt above the place he now was, it did not show by word or deed.

'Come along, Mollie,' she said, then scooped Murray up in her arms. 'I imagine you will be glad to get back to the pasture and show this sweet baby off to the other ewes.' And, if she were lucky, she would meet

William along the way and they could return to the house together.

Coming out of the stable, she turned for the path leading to the pasture.

'Hello!'

She spun sharply, spotting a man in the yard sitting atop a smartly saddled horse. Without a doubt he was a gentleman. She could not imagine what he was doing at Wilton Farm this muddy morning. From the looks of it, he had ridden his animal through a great deal of muck. All she could think of was that he was here to visit William.

'Good morning,' she answered, offering a bright smile. If this was William's friend, of course he was welcome.

'Good day, miss.' He dismounted, then handed off his horse's reins to her.

'If you will be so kind as to see my horse is tended to.'

That would be a challenge given she had a lamb in her arms and was being closely trailed by its mother. Surely he could not have failed to notice. She attempted to point him towards the stable, but he continued instructing her on what he needed and doing it in an annoying way. While his words were phrased as a question, they were clearly a demand. A proper guest would never demand hospitality from his hostess. William's friend was—

'And if you will be so kind as to inform your mistress that I have arrived and desperately require a bath and a meal.'

Her mistress!

'And whose acquaintance do I have the pleasure of

making, sir?' Please do not let her sound as offended as she was. If this man really were an acquaintance of her husband's, he would be welcome, whether he actually was or not.

Before he could answer, footsteps rounded the corner of the stable.

'Murray!'

The namesake of the sweet creature in her arms?

William's smile declared he was pleased to have this visitor standing in the yard. 'What the blazes are you doing here?'

'I heard that you had wed and moved to…whatever wilderness this is. Mile after mile—it all looks the same. I could scarcely believe it was true, so I came to see the truth of it for myself.'

'It is good to see you, man! It is true. I am a married man.' William smiled when he said so, which made her feel a little less like the mud smeared on the visitor's boots.

'May I point out that you look somewhat worse for the wear?' Murray slapped William on his back.

'I spent the night in the pasture watching over sheep. What is your excuse?'

'It was a miserable journey from Windermere on a muddy road which took far longer than it ought to have.' Her 'guest' cast a quick glance her way as if to ask why she continued to stand by listening to their conversation when she ought to be tending to his demands, but then quickly gave his attention back to William.

She had never felt so invisible in her life, nor so dismissed.

'Even though I see you with my own eyes, I cannot

believe it. I can imagine no one less likely to live in the wilderness than you. Or to be wed, for that matter.'

What he said was unsettling because this man had clearly known her husband for a long time while she had known him briefly.

It was easy for Elizabeth to imagine him as married since he was married to her. So far, he seemed to be adapting well to the situation. The arrival of this high-born gentleman pointed out the fact that she did not really know her own husband beyond the boundaries of the farm.

Seeing these old friends together, laughing, joking and clearly bonded by the past, illustrated what a great gulf lay between William's class and hers. Could a noble gentleman actually find common ground with a simple shepherdess?

Moments ago, until the arrival of William's peer, she had been hopeful of it, but now doubt made her stomach tighten.

'I would introduce you to my wife, but apparently you have met already.'

'No, I only just arrived and have not been to the house.' Murray grinned broadly. 'She must be quite exceptional in order for her have snatched you away from London. The word about town is that Lady Penelope has not ceased weeping since the rumour began to spread.'

'If Penelope is weeping, it has nothing to do with me.'

Who was Penelope? If she was important to William, he might have let her know before she started to— Oh, never mind that. If the woman was weeping over William, there must be good reason for it.

Suddenly the visitor's gaze shifted towards her, his

frown bordering on contempt. 'Girl! Why do you continue to stand there gaping at us? My horse needs attention.'

William gave a brief bark of laughter. Coming to her, he plucked the reins from her hand.

'You have met my wife, James.' He led the horse to Murray, deposited the reins in his fist and then walked back to stand beside her. Not just stand, but place his hand on her shoulder and give it a squeeze.

'Elizabeth, may I present Lord Carlton, James Murray as far as we are concerned.' William took the lamb from her arms. 'Murray, may I present my wife, Elizabeth—Mrs Grant as far as you are concerned.'

James Murray turned pale, his mouth opened and closed like a landed fish.

'You must believe me to be a great boor, Mrs Grant. I apologise with all my heart.' He placed his hand over his chest to demonstrate his sincerity. 'Please forgive me. I have never been known for my tact…and truthfully, Lady Penelope has not been weeping all that much. I exaggerated for the simple jest of it.'

'Elizabeth, Murray might be a boor, but he is also sincere. You may accept his apology as such if you wish… or we can send him packing back to Windermere.'

William was smiling when he said so which indicated he would like nothing better than for his friend to remain.

'We would be delighted to have you stay with us, my lord.' At least she would be delighted for William, if not for the man's company.

'I shall do my best to behave, I vow on my honour as a gentleman.'

How could she not wonder what the visitor was really feeling? Perhaps he wondered why his friend had chosen a country mouse over a refined lady. The confidence which had been building within her, the hope that perhaps she and William's stations in society did not matter so greatly, took a sudden dive. She all but saw it rolling in the mud, sputtering and choking.

How could she ever have thought she could live up to the ladies William was used to? Doubtless, she would fall far short of Lady Penelope when it came to manner and refinement. The woman probably looked like poetry in motion, every move and word perfection. Elizabeth would wager she had never got grime embedded in her nails or the hem of her skirt muddied. Had never been mistaken for a servant.

Not that the mistake was not understandable. She did look like a servant...in fact, was rather glad to look that way as opposed to fluffy and useless. It was James Murray's attitude of dismissiveness that made her feel unworthy. Every human deserved to feel worthy, as far as she was concerned.

'Here is someone else you need to meet,' William said.

She loved his grin, well and truly did. Watching it restored her smile and her spirits to a degree.

He placed the lamb in his friend's arms.

'Meet Murray. I watched while Mrs Grant helped bring him into the world.'

'You named the beast after me?' James Murray held the lamb stiffly. 'What do I do with it?'

'Nuzzle its head with your nose and sing to it.'

'Surely not!' He handed Murray back to William.

With a wink at her, William nuzzled the lamb's head, although he did not sing.

'I'll show you to the stable where you can leave your horse. If Mr Adams, our foreman, is busy you will need to tend him yourself.'

He placed Murray back in her arms. 'I think you will get a glowing report about my night in the pasture. Be sure and ask how I remained awake and vigilant the whole time.'

She watched for a moment while the two of them walked slowly towards the stable.

'I do not believe you spent the night outside alone,' she heard James Murray say.

'I was not alone. I was with the shepherds.'

Her husband seemed completely at ease with his friend, a man of his own station. Until this moment she thought he'd felt completely at ease with her, too. Could a man really stand with one foot in each world? Just when she thought she might know who William Grant was, she feared she did not.

An unworthy thought crept into her mind. She felt horrid for thinking it, but she could not very well unthink it. She wished her husband had not had a life before the one he now shared with her. It was unfair, she knew it…and yet, once considered, it lodged in her in her heart like a burr.

A burr that hurt dreadfully.

But she had also lived a life he knew nothing of. How was she to know, really, in the short time they had been wed, who he was at heart? How was he to know who she was at heart?

What they needed was time. She had tried to remind herself of it before, but in the end she'd rushed headlong into feeling a great deal for her husband.

Once again she told herself they must take their

marriage one step at a time, one revelation about each other at a time. In the end she hoped the steps they took together would lead them to a satisfying life together. More than satisfying. What she wanted was a marriage that would bring them joy for all their lives.

Of course that would be more easily accomplished if she thought she was worthy of him socially, that she would not be an embarrassment to him if they visited London.

London...the very thought of going there left her anxious. She did not belong there. Which only made her wonder if he felt the same way about Wilton Farm...that he did not belong? Until now she had not thought so. He'd seemed so eager to learn.

Now that James Murray was here, the distance between their worlds was made startlingly clear. What would happen once his friend went home? Would William wish to go with him...to the place where he belonged and to a lady who wept for his return?

She also wondered if she could go back to her life as it had been if he decided to leave. Life before William Grant had been incredibly good. Had she not wed him in order to keep it?

She had not married William because she wanted a husband, but because she wanted to keep Wilton Farm. Surely she could carry on with the life she'd had if he went back to London. Surely she would not spend her days weeping over the loss.

With dinner ended, Elizabeth retired to her chamber. William invited Murray to sit with him on the front porch. For all that was different than when they spent time together at the club, what was important remained the same. Enjoying one another's company.

Instead of an expensive copper ceiling overhead, there were stars. The chairs were utilitarian instead of plush. The whisky was fine even if the crystal they sipped it from was not of high quality. Much was the same and much was different. It was interesting that the things which remained the same were the important ones and the ones that had changed did not matter a great deal.

Back in London, he and James would be laughing about the latest scandal being gossiped about at the club. One which might have involved him in some way.

Taking a sip from the glass while looking up at the heavens, he did have to admit how good it was to have his friend here. Despite the fact that he was putting his heart into becoming a successful farmer, he still missed London. Missed the noise, the street vendors and society. It was beyond unlikely he would attend an event in Ambleside that was half as elegant as a ball.

He could travel back to London with Murray for a visit. A visit would not make him a failure. As long as he returned, all would be well. But that would mean leaving Elizabeth so soon after their marriage.

Everything had happened so quickly for them and yet, already, he enjoyed knowing she was as close as upstairs. Imagining her up there, snuggled in her bed, her dark hair splayed across the pillow…perhaps with her pretty hard-working hand tucked under her cheek in slumber…it did something to his heart.

No, he had no wish to return to London without her. What would be the point when half of his heart would remain here? He could not help but wonder if the charms of the city would hold the same appeal as they had even a short time ago.

As he glanced over at Murray sipping his whisky, a sudden playful spirit took hold of William. Mischievous more than playful, truth be told. He stood up, pointing at the pasture. 'Do you see that?'

'There is nothing really to see, William. I'm not certain how you fill your days out here.'

Oh, this was going to be grand! Playing a prank on Murray would be great fun…and also prove that William was not the only one foolish enough to consider a campfire within a sheepfold to be a raging threat.

'Look! The pasture is on fire!'

'Yes, I do see it, but it is quite far off. I'm sure no harm will come of it.'

'I imagine someone said the same thing back in 1666 when the Great Fire of London first began to smoulder.'

'I do not know what we are to do about it in any case.'

'We could put it out. It is still small enough to be handled.'

He yanked on Murray's sleeve. 'If you are not willing to put out the fire, we should at least get the animals out of the stables.'

'My horse!' Murray leapt to his feet, at last looking alarmed. He dashed down the front steps, running across the yard.

He could not recall ever seeing his friend run before. His awkward loping gait made William let loose the laugh he had been holding in.

'What? Do you wish the horses to perish, man?' Murray exclaimed. He opened the gate, glancing behind to see if William was following.

Which he was not, since he was doubled over in laughter.

'I cannot imagine what is wrong with you, Grant.'

'It's but a campfire!' William wheezed. It was all the funnier in the face of Murray's stunned expression. 'Have you never seen one before?'

'You have become addled out here with nothing to do.' Murray stomped back into the yard.

'No, I see things more clearly than I ever have, if you want to know the truth.'

Things such as coming upon his bride in odd moments hugging a lamb to her heart, looking so lovely, so full of tenderness. Seeing how beautiful and happy she was in those moments, he would feel his heart swell with the pleasure of simply standing and watching her.

He did not share this with James, but he kept it to himself. A treasure for his own mind only.

'Addled...too much fresh air. Next time I see you I will not know who you are.'

That might be true. He felt the change within himself. Whether it was a good thing or not, he was not yet sure. He did not wish to lose who he had been. Nor did he wish to give up who he was striving to become. Perhaps he could be both men at once.

By inviting society to Ambleside, such a thing might be possible. Surely his rural neighbours would be glad of it. Nights would not be so quiet. His guests from London would bring some needed entertainment to Ambleside. Farmers and aristocrats, alike, would be invited to the parties he would host at Wilton Farm. City life and country life would blend.

More than that, his way of life and Elizabeth's would meld into one. This was the very thing their marriage needed in order to flourish. A happy outcome could only be assured by blending what he wanted of his future with what she wanted of hers. City and country would meet in the middle. He and his wife would do the same.

'You must return for the house party I will be hosting,' William announced.

This time Murray laughed. 'You? Hosting a house party?'

'My wife and I.' He dearly hoped she would approve of his sudden decision.

'You have never hosted anything. And I imagine Mrs Grant has not had reason to entertain society. Are you certain this is something you ought to attempt, my friend?'

If he had not been certain before, he was now. Murray had challenged him with the question. There was nothing to be done but answer the challenge. Besides, he was the one to have said he would do it. All Murray had done was to question his ability to see it done.

'I have attended so many affairs, how can I fail at hosting one of my own?'

It was important to do it and so he would...somehow.

'But Elizabeth...you must consider her feelings in the matter. I do not mean to disparage her in any way. I feel awful about our first meeting. But you know as well as I do that many of the women we associate with might be unkind. Even if they do not intend to slight her, they have clear opinions about who belongs to which class.'

It was true. Some ladies would feel that associating with Elisabeth Grant would be akin to socialising with their own staff. No matter that, his wife outshone every one of them. Frills and fancy manners had nothing on Elizabeth's practical gowns and capable hands.

'I intend to make a go of my marriage, James. At the same time, I cannot forsake who I have been all my life...nor can my wife forget who she is. This is the only way I can see ahead for us.'

For all the difficulty in accomplishing said country visit, it could be the very thing to draw him and Elizabeth closer.

Or it might rip them apart.

Chapter Nine

It had been two days since James Murray had gone back to London and Elizabeth still could not wrap her emotions around the man…or rather his attitude towards her.

Walking beside William towards the village to attend the meeting against the rail spur, she watched their long afternoon shadows stretching away. If this was all there was to them, shadows on the ground, they would be equal. Shadow was shadow, one not grander than the other…although William's was much larger than hers was. But shadows were an illusion and did not change the fact that William was superior to her socially.

Her first meeting with James Murray had made it pointedly clear. Murray had dismissed her as beneath him, a woman of no consequence, until he'd discovered she was wed to William. As soon as he knew she was married to the second son of a viscount, his manner towards her had changed.

He had been as sorry as he could be over the mistake, but the fact remained she was the same person after the revelation as before. Nothing about her had changed except that her last name was now Grant.

There was no reason to believe that anyone of her husband's acquaintance would see her as anything but a servant. Which she was not, but to them she would never be more than that. Not that there was anything wrong with being in service. No one was more treasured than Penny was, or anyone else in her, and now William's, employ.

Her mind whirled in confusion, and she had no idea what to do about it. It could only have been confusion which had led her to wear her fancy yellow hat to the meeting. She had put it on, admired it even, in front of the mirror, knowing full well it would cause a stir among her acquaintances.

Still, it was William who would cause the biggest stir, being dressed head to toe in London finery.

'Where are you, Elizabeth?' William asked while they walked. 'Are you worried about what that Samuel fellow might have to say about me snatching you away?'

'What? Samuel?' She had not given him much thought, really. 'He will know by now and I suspect he might be surprised. Not heartbroken, though.'

'I will not have to fight for you, then?'

The arch of his brows, the playful smile on his face chased away the shadows within her, leaving only those bobbing on the path. How could she not laugh? Her husband had a way about him which made her want to be with him all the time.

'Are you the fighting kind, William? Samuel is not.'

'I might not have had occasion to use fisticuffs in the past, but I believe I would fight if the need arose.'

'In regard to Samuel, I do not believe it will arise. But fighting for what is right… I would do that, too.' As the coming meeting would attest to.

'May I hold your hand, sweet wife?' he asked. His smile, as always, turned her warm from the inside out. 'Would it be too forward?'

She extended her fingers towards him, felt them tingling in anticipation of his touch. Marriage did allow for certain liberties. This one would not be out of line with what they had agreed to. Ahead, their shadows joined. Something about seeing it gave her hope.

He stopped, looked at their entwined hands, then smiled. 'Thank you for wearing the ring. It looks exactly right on you.'

To her great surprise, he lifted her hand to his lips, kissing her fingers where the gold band sparkled in the late afternoon sunshine. My word, but she could not recall anything that ever felt so grand. Perhaps there really was no reason their stations in life should come between them. It could be her mind creating a problem where there was not one.

But then she saw Samuel staring at them, his expression quizzical while they approached the meeting place. He was not the only one doing so. Her husband was being gawked at from all quarters. He was not one of their own, their glances announced. They probably knew by now that he was the son of Viscount Rivenhall and that he was the new owner of Wilton Farm.

William could only be feeling what she had felt upon meeting James Murray. While he might not be one of their own, he was her own. For as much as he had offered to defend her, if only in jest, she would do no less for him. And not in jest. When had her allegiance to him become so strong? She was not certain, but she had vowed to cherish him and so she would.

She squeezed his hand tighter. If he felt uncomfortable under the neighbours' consideration, he did not show it. She supposed it was years of proper breeding which allowed him to appear congenial no matter the circumstance.

Once inside, they took their places on the benches. She was incredibly pleased to have this man on her side. For all that everyone cast him dubious glances, she knew they could not fail to be impressed.

Once he came out against the rail spur, people would listen. Never before had a gentleman of society spoken up for her side of the debate. Second son of a viscount he might be, but he was still influential.

There was really no need to introduce him. Gossip spread as quickly here as anywhere else, so they already knew who he was and that she had married him. It was unlikely they knew why she had wed him since it was assumed that one day she would marry Samuel. Some things she would not enlighten them on.

However, a proper introduction was in order. It was best to get it over and done before discussion of the spur began so she stood up.

'Good afternoon neighbours…friends. I assume that all of you have learned that I recently married. I am pleased to introduce you to my husband, William Grant.' There was a great silence while people looked him over in his elegant garb and then over at Samuel in his worn work clothes.

'Mr Grant is recently from London, but is now an Ambelsidian.' Was there such a word? Perhaps not, but she hoped they understood that he was now one of them.

Their faces gave nothing away. It was possible that they felt offended for Samuel and so they were reluctant to welcome William. But then one man stood—Samuel, whom she had not really jilted since she had never accepted one of his proposals.

'Welcome to Ambleside, Mr Grant. I offer my congratulations on your marriage. I'm sure we will be the best of neighbours, the same as Elizabeth and I have always been.'

William stood, nodding at Samuel. 'Thank you, sir. I appreciate your kind welcome.'

Both men sat down.

With Samuel bearing no grudge, she hoped the rest of her neighbours would look kindly upon the stranger in their midst.

'It cannot hurt to have a noble voice to support our cause,' declared Mrs Peabody who hated the spur nearly as strongly as Elizabeth did.

Then Bart Miller stood up, looking ready to spew his strong opinions in favour of the spur.

'Fine, intelligent gent like him might support the spur since it will make it more convenient for his London friends to visit Ambleside. Why have them spend all their money in Windermere when they can spend it here?'

Of all the selfish attitudes! It went to show that Bart cared for money more than he did the lovely pristine place they all called home. His attitude was enough to make a person boil over. Nothing could make her steam hotter under her new yellow hat than hearing his nonsense spoken aloud for everyone to listen to and perhaps, quite foolishly, agree with. Had she not been standing, indignation would have shot her off the bench.

'You, Mr Miller, know nothing at all.' Her voice was as steady as she could make it while defending the quiet beauty of their countryside. 'Just because the rail would bring inns and restaurants, it does not mean people will forsake Windermere to come here and frequent them. The only thing that will change is that our pastures will be cut up with iron rails. Foul smoke will darken our skies and choke us.'

Some of her neighbours nodded energetically, but others shook their heads just as energetically.

If only everyone was as sensible as she was. 'And the trains' whistles will frighten our sheep half to death. Our ewes will miscarry and the quality of our wool will suffer.'

She was not really sure about quality of the wool, but the thought alone should give everyone pause. Surely no one would put the value of a more convenient journey from Windermere ahead of their livelihood. It was an easy enough journey as it was. Four miles only.

She glanced down at William who, strangely, was staring at the tips of his expensive boots, his fingers linked together, tight and tense looking. He must be as passionate about the issue at hand as she was. Once he stood to speak, her adversaries would pay attention.

'Mr Grant,' she said. 'Please stand and share your feelings about this ridiculous spur the railway is planning to foist upon us.'

He glanced up at her with the oddest expression in his eyes. Giving a quick and nearly imperceptible shake of his head, he stood. Perhaps she ought to have talked to him first about presenting an opinion, but she'd spoken before fully thinking. Still, she was certain he would not mind and that what he had to say was bound to influence others.

Her heart fluttered madly because he was the most handsome man in the room. And he was hers, they shared a name and a home. What else might they share if things continued to go as well for them as they had been? Another part of her fluttered which was somewhere south of her heart and north of her knees. What a curious and delightful feeling.

She sat down so that the company's full attention could rest upon her husband.

He cleared his throat, then when he spoke his voice carried all over the room. 'In my opinion, the rail spur is an excellent idea.'

Had William tossed a bucket of icy water in his wife's face or ripped the bonnet off her head and stomped it to shreds, he thought she would not look at him in such horror. She bit down on those full, beautiful lips, silently letting him know she had plenty to say and would do so once they were away from the neighbours' curious ears.

Judging by the way her cheeks flashed between red hot and pale, she was doing her best not to leap up and rail at what she had to consider his betrayal. She had asked for his opinion on the matter and so he had given it. He did not wish to betray her cause, but neither did he wish to betray himself and his own ideas.

He had better explain before she walked out of the meeting and went home, where he would return to find his horse tethered at the gate and his belongings scattered among the hedges.

'Shall we discuss this at home?' he suggested.

'Now that you have begun,' Mr Miller said, 'I would like to hear more.'

'Elizabeth?'

'Oh, please do enlighten us, Mr Grant.' Still sitting, Elizabeth shot him an offended-looking glare.

As much as he would rather speak in private, he now had no choice but to continue.

'Ambleside is lovely as it is and I will not say otherwise…but it is set apart from a world that is quickly changing. Since we can do nothing to prevent it, I believe we ought to embrace it.'

Elizabeth shot up, her glare at him as sharp as a honed arrow. She did not seem concerned that the attention of her friends and neighbours was intently settled upon them…a pair of newlyweds having their first spat. He dearly hoped that, in the end, this was all it would amount to. A simple spat that all married couples had upon occasion…only, more privately.

'One of the things we cherish about Ambleside is that it is a refuge from all that change,' she announced. It was hard to miss the way her fingers curled into her fists as if she were striving to keep them from trembling. 'Here, Mr Grant, we live much the same way our grandparents did. Our grandchildren will live with the same simple values that we hold dear. Our quaint little village does not need all the noise and chaos to be found in your London!'

'It is not my London, Elizabeth. Many people enjoy living there.'

'Ladies, how many of you wish to have your children's safety endangered while they are at play? There are all sorts of miscreants in that populous city who might easily travel here and be a threat to them.'

'It is unreasonable to think they will, not with so

many children in London they might accost,' Mr Miller pointed out.

Elizabeth gasped at his callous remark, pressing her hand to her middle.

Needing to move quickly from the foolish remark, William said, 'Gentlemen, which of you cannot say that a bit of socialising at the end of the day would not be welcome?'

As it was, all the end of the day brought to Amble-side was dinner, a sit by the fireplace and then bed, which was all well and good for the happily married among them. For those who were not, a place to gather and discuss the trials and victories of the day would be welcome.

'I propose that we open a pub. On our own we will not have enough customers to make a go of it, but those coming from Windermere and beyond will make the establishment profitable,' he said.

Elizabeth's clear nemesis, Mr Miller, charged to his feet, a great grin on his face.

'It is precisely the sort of establishment I have been wanting to open. Why should it be only city gentlemen who have the comfort of society? We farmers need it as much as anyone else.'

Elizabeth spun away from him to glare across the room at Miller.

'We have a pub! We do not need another. Two will be the ruin of Ambleside…of home and hearth.'

Ah, he did not know they already had such a retreat. Clearly he had a bit to learn about his new village.

Elizabeth spun away from Miller to glare at him again. She shook her head, which caused the hat to sag over one eye. As fetching as it looked, there was still one eye visible which accused him of all sorts of villainy.

'And it will be all your fault, William Grant!' With that, she ripped the hat fully off her head and flung it at him, then, with a narrowed glare, sailed out of the meeting.

He would say he had made a mess of things, but all he had done was speak what was in his heart. The points he'd made were valid. A bit of society would do Ambleside a great deal of good and would not result in children being accosted while at play.

'If you will excuse me,' he said to the stunned on-lookers.

Going out after Elizabeth, he heard one person applauding. It could only have been Miller, who was probably mentally building a pub to rival the one already in business.

Where was said pub? What would he not give to be escaping to his club in London right now? Dash it! Not all that much, he realised. The last thing he wished was to saddle Ace of Spades and ride back home.

Somehow, remaining at Wilton Farm and making amends with his wife seemed a happier choice than sipping whisky with James Murray in London. If he could not manage to make amends, he would at least do what he could to convince her that he had no desire to ruin Ambleside. Only that he hoped to make it a livelier place to live.

Watching her stride quickly ahead of him, he did not know if this was possible. She had to know he was behind her, but she made no attempt to acknowledge his presence. He did not like feeling invisible to her.

'Elizabeth! Wait!' he called, but apparently he was mute as well as invisible.

Well, that would last only for the time it took to get home. He was not going to let a wedge of silence keep them apart. Something good had been building between them and he was not willing to let it go easily. She might try to force him to leave Wilton Farm, but he would not. This was now his home.

What he would do was stay and work hard for the farm…and do it while enjoying the company of friends from London. As far as he was concerned, farming and society were not exclusive of each other.

Father would be vastly disappointed if he ran home to Rivenhall. But he had disappointed his father on many occasions so that was not his reason for refusing to leave if she asked…or even demanded he go.

For all that Elizabeth was furious with him in the moment, he hoped she would not always be. The true reason he would not give up here was that he did not wish for her to see him as a failure. Her opinion of him meant a great deal.

Which made this moment, striding home in the wake of her anger, feel uncomfortable…prickly. No… more, it made him feel determined. He had told her he would fight for her and so he would.

He was not sure what his battle tactic would be. It would not be capitulation to her will, he did know that. What he also knew was that, somehow, he would earn his way back into her good graces. The rail spur would come, or it would not. Either way it was not up to him.

Getting her to smile at him again, though? He would give it his best go.

Chapter Ten

It was getting harder to ignore the voice in her head which suggested she was behaving like a pouting child.

Two days had passed and she still had not spoken to William even though he had tried on several occasions to engage her. Had she seen anyone else acting as she was, she would have judged them to be shrewish. Oh, but the man had betrayed her and she could never recall having been betrayed before.

Her conscience gave her a bit of a nip. A disagreement was not necessarily a betrayal. Nowhere in the wedding vows did it say they must be in agreement on every subject. But really, he might have told her of his feelings on the rail spur before she'd presented him as her supporter.

Again her conscience nipped. She had not asked his opinion, which she ought to have, she supposed. It was only that she considered him a reasonable person. Reasonable people did not support the spur. Which in turn meant it was reasonable to assume he did. She could not recall ever being so embarrassed in her life.

What she needed to do was go to the lambing pen.

It had always been a place where she'd found the solace to face the problems dogging her.

It was a drippy afternoon, not quite raining but not dry, either. She shrugged into her coat. In buttoning it up she noticed her bare finger. She missed seeing the ring glimmering there. In her anger she had taken it off because it seemed wrong to feel as she did and wear William's mother's ring. If the woman was looking down, naturally she would be on her son's side.

More than missing wearing the ring, she missed sharing smiles with her husband, laughing with him and feeling a lovely glow thrumming under her skin. She simply missed William Grant, a man she had not even known this time last month. It was stunning how attached she had become so quickly. It was a wonder her heart was not dizzy.

Oh, but that was not true. Her heart was dizzy. Dizzy for the sight, scent and touch of the man.

Waking across the yard, she pulled her coat tighter against the drip. Pulled her heart tighter against the yearning to absolve William of his wrongdoing. *Nip, nip, nip...* All he had done was speak his mind the same as she had.

It might be easier to understand all this if she believed she knew who he was. Until the meeting she had assumed he was her ally in everything. Believed that as husband and wife, although new to the roles, they had each other's interests at heart. Vying ideas did not mean they did not.

For now, she held on to her anger because it was the easier emotion to indulge in and she still felt hot with embarrassment over the way she had been forced to charge out of the meeting... Oh, my, but her conscience had a nasty nip.

All right, she had chosen to, but still, she was angry. To suddenly discover he favoured pubs had been a shock. What other establishments might he promote in Ambleside? A place that was perfect as it was.

It had been a mistake to allow William into her heart before she thoroughly knew him. It was unlike her to act so unwarily. She had been blinded, she supposed, by his handsome face and a smile which suggested an easy-going nature. She had been completely misled by her fluttering heart. How could she have guessed he would become so adamantly opposed to what was good and sensible for her safe little village?

In the future she would be diligent when it came to unguarded feelings for William Grant. If he stepped close to her and her heart flip-flopped, she would simply back away. If her belly softened in desire when she looked too deeply into his eyes, she would turn her gaze to something unpleasant, such as the fact that he might prefer to spend his evenings at the tavern than with her.

No doubt that was where he was this very minute.

Stepping inside the stable, she sighed in relief. All she needed was time with her lambs to settle her soul. Just before she stepped into the large lambing stall, she heard singing. Although the voice could not carry a tune, it did sound pleasant...happy in the attempt.

She stopped outside because she did not want to share her special space with William...did not want to share any space with him until she'd regained her sense of reason. Because it was not at all reasonable to be drawn to a man who thought so little of her as to humiliate her in front of her neighbours. Leaning against the wall, she knew she should go back to the house, but he'd stopped singing and began to speak.

'Let go of my trouser leg, Oscar.' Then he laughed and she had to force herself to look harder for her sense of reason. She had never known it to be so elusive. 'And you, too, little sheep! Have you a name? If not, you shall be known as Scamp for ever. At least to me. The pretty lady who delivered you into this world would not approve. She thinks you are sweet as a blossom. But the hole in the knee of my trousers says otherwise.'

Oscar started to bark in the high, shrill way puppies had. 'You two go over there and play or I'll never get the straw swept.'

This would not do. William Grant sounded far too congenial while she was…well, it was no wonder she had been fooled by him.

'Do you know,' she heard him say, 'I miss London quite a lot. But where I live, there are no lambs to eat my trousers, no puppy to chew everything else. I'll admit this to you and no one else. I do not mind raking straw. There is something soothing to it. And I'm getting used to the nights being so quiet. If I went home, I would miss it here.'

He sounded sincere, but she had been fooled by him before…but then not by him, but by her perception of him. She did not wish to be fooled again. Apparently, she was to be denied a moment of solace to sit in her private spot and work things out. At the same time, she was not going to cower outside the door.

She turned to go, but then heard him sigh. A shuffling sound indicated he had settled down in the straw.

'All right you two…oh, all right, three then. Come here and help me think.'

Oh, the man had his nerve! To sit and think in her spot! Especially when she was waiting to make use of it. There was nothing for it but to demand he go somewhere else and do it. Spinning away from the wall, she stood in the doorway, hands anchored on her hips.

'William?' How could she have whispered when she meant to sound indignant? Because he was half-reclined in the straw with twin lambs on his lap and Oscar nestled on his shoulder and licking his ear.

'Elizabeth! Come and sit with us.'

Oh, but the man was a charmer…her charmer. And yet this sweet and tender scene would not sway her.

'We cannot go on as we have been. Come and sit, we will discuss what happened.'

'I do not think an apology will help,' she declared, all bristly with righteousness…*nip, nip, nip.* When had her conscience become so demanding?

'No? An apology would help me.' He reached one of his big, manly hands towards her. 'Come.'

She backed up because looking at it made her feel things she did not wish to. 'What do you mean?'

'I mean, I would accept your apology.'

'If I did sit down to talk, it would not be to apologise! Why on earth would I when you are the one—'

'Who was not allowed to express an opinion you disagreed with?'

Only because it was a wrong opinion.

Gently, he set the lambs aside, put Oscar down in the straw and rose to his feet.

He stood in front of her, one arm braced high on the

door frame. It was as if he engulfed her, wrapped her up in his scent and heat.

This would not do at all. Neither would backing up, perhaps allowing him to sense how he made her feel mushy inside even if it was against her will, mostly. What was wrong with her?

'Have you even given a thought to the fact that what I said at the meeting had merit?'

'Naturally not.'

'You, my dear, are a stubborn woman.'

'I am a reasonable woman and I am not "your dear".'

'Are you not?' With the hand not bracing his weight on the door, he touched her hair, twined the strands around and between his fingers.

For some reason she did not yank it away, but simply stood, mesmerised by the dark strands sliding and looping against his skin.

'My opinion on matters might not be the same as yours. But, Elizabeth, I do have a right to them. And my opinion is that you are "my dear". Do you wish to debate my own feelings with me?'

She blinked, breaking the spell he was clearly weaving about her. Ducking out from under his arm, she rushed out of the stable. Hurrying through the drizzle, she realised even if she was not being childish or acting a shrew, she was a coward. At least William was not that. He had no trouble speaking his mind. And what was on his mind was going to leave her restless all night long…again.

'My dear?' she mumbled.

After everything…he felt that way? In her heart, and quite against her will, she imagined the corridor between her quarters and his shrinking.

* * *

William lay upon his bed, staring at the ceiling. If he could call back his words about Elizabeth being 'his dear', he would. Not because they were not true, but because 'his dear's' reaction to them had been to withdraw even further from him.

At first, he'd had in mind to flirt with her, coax and cajole her out of her anger. He was accomplished at such manoeuvres with women, after all. When he came down to it, he found he could not. As his wife, she did not deserve to be manoeuvred. Besides, she was a woman not easily manoeuvred.

Not being reared in polite society she was more immune to vain compliments than a socialite would be. Ladies of his acquaintance would accept compliments as their due; fluff and preen over them. Elizabeth, being grounded in what was practical, was more suspicious of vain flattery. Truthfully, calling her 'my dear' had not been vain flattery, but had sprung from his heart.

Winning back her affection was not going to be an easy thing because what he'd said about her being stubborn was true. Unless he claimed to come around to her way of thinking on the rail spur, she might not get past the rift between them. Since he would not do so, he faced a great challenge.

Nothing in his past had prepared him for such a serious matter in regard to a woman. And yet, here he was, an emotional mess without ever having kissed his bride. It would be an easy thing to fall in love with her.

Tossing off the bed covers, he went to the window to gaze out at the night and think about the direction his mind was taking. He was not sure he had the pluck to give his heart to a woman who seemed not to want it. Lost in thought, he took bare notice of the rain having moved on.

Then suddenly his vision focused and his chest cramped on a sucked-in breath. One of the stables was on fire! Windows pulsed with a red glow. The ground beyond the open door was tinted orange. There was no mistaking this blaze for a campfire.

On the run he grabbed his shoes off the chair and shoved his feet in. Dressed only in trousers and shoes he was indecent for going out, but no matter that.

Dashing down the corridor, he crossed the invisible line that separated his half from his wife's. He banged on her door and shouted, 'Fire!' Without waiting to discover if she had heard the alarm, he fairly flew down the stairs, then out of the house.

Oscar was in that stable! He had left the pup there this one night to keep company with the lambs. He went cold inside, fearing that harm might have come to his small friend.

Closer to the stable he spotted moving figures. A few of the animals were already in the yard, dashing about in fright. Mr Adams appeared in the doorway, framed in an awful red glow. Adams dumped a lamb into the night and then rushed back in.

William could not imagine what might have happened to start such an inferno. From out in the pasture, he heard shepherds shouting. Appearing shadowy in the moonlight, they dashed towards the stables. It would take them a long time to get here on foot.

Too long, dash it!

Rushing inside after the Adams, he noted that the worst of the flames came from the lambing pen. Fire sparked and snapped so loudly that he could not hear the man shouting at him even though he stood only steps away. Wicked, fearful flames flared to life in the back of a stall, instantly eating a pile of straw and lashing at the ceiling.

Those flames needed to be put out before they caught the roof on fire. If it was not, the fire might spread to the rest of the stable. He pointed to the area, but Adams shook his head, indicating that there were still animals in the lambing pen needing rescue.

He wanted to argue that the fire needed to be put out or the animals in the rest of the stable would be at risk, but before he could, Elizabeth rushed inside.

She, too, had not bothered to dress, but wore only a nightgown. In the same instant that she ran for the remaining lambs, a ball of black fur dashed from whatever place he had been hiding and began leaping about William's leg.

On a run he took the pup outside, scooping up a cat on the way out. Leaving them both several yards out in the paddock, he raced back inside.

The flames engulfing the straw pile were beginning to blacken the roof beams. A pile of blankets lay stacked against a wall. He snatched two of them, then ran to the back of the stable.

The flaming stack was too high to be able to try to smother the flames on top. Instead, he slapped blankets, one in each hand, in a windmill fashion at the bottom of the pile in the hope that the burned straw would fall in on itself, drawing the flames away from the ceiling.

His skin was hot, his eyes dry, he coughed from the smoke filling the stable. Hitting the fire with the blankets was not working. He could not imagine anything that would.

But then a shepherd appeared beside him with blankets in hand. He slapped the flames in time with the rhythm William set. Then the Mr Adams rushed up to do the same and then—

Dash it!

'Elizabeth, get away!'

It looked as though she shouted 'No!', but he could not hear anything but the fire's roar. Elizabeth's white nightgown billowed about her, looking a pure invitation for sparks to ignite. Her long hair lashed about and he swore fingers of fire actually reached for the strands.

When two more shepherds ran to their aid, he picked his wife up and carried her outside. Judging by the way she kicked, squirmed and wriggled, she did not approve of being hauled away from the danger. But hauled she would be since she hadn't the sense to seek safety on her own.

What did it matter if she thought him a brute? As it was, she already saw him as a betrayer of all that was right and reasonable. She opened her mouth with what was bound to be a severe come-uppance.

'Don't bother, Elizabeth. You can tell me what you think of me later. Right now, you need to help the animals. They have to be reassured that they are safe so they do not rush back inside.'

There was Oscar again, cringing and whining about his ankles with this small tail tucked under him. He picked the pup up, shoving his small trembling body at Elizabeth.

'Begin with this one.'

It looked as though she wished to say something,

but the words went no further than her lips. She stared at him quite oddly, her gaze slipping from his face to his chest.

Ah… He only now recalled that he was but half-dressed. No doubt she was offended at his lack of clothing. If time had warranted and the situation was not what it was, he would point out that she was not properly garbed, either. He dared not look too hard at her because one blaze for the night was enough. The last thing he needed was to be battling a blaze within as well as without.

Although he shot her look back at her, he could not claim to be offended. No, indeed. Trying his best not to glace at the curves her nightgown clung to, he gathered his resolve to fight the fire without. With matters so urgent, the fire within was something he would face at a later time.

'Stay here.' Hopefully, his voice relayed the urgency of her doing so.

He rushed back inside, quite honestly surprised that she did as he asked—no, demanded—of her.

It took nearly an hour of hard, hot work for them to get the flames out. There was a great deal of damage, but luckily not to the structure of the stable. Since the roof remained intact, what damage there was could be repaired over time. Scrubbing and rebuilding interior walls would be the main thing.

Tomorrow, by the light of day, they could better assess what needed doing. Praise Good God above that the flames were out and no animals had been harmed.

The more difficult repair, he decided, would be his relationship with his wife. Painting over a wall was bound to be an easier task than convincing her that he was not truly a heavy-handed heathen who carried women about willy-nilly against their will.

With the lambs and ewes reunited, they had calmed enough so that Elizabeth could return her attention to what was going on inside the stable. Having Oscar snuggled in the crook of her arm asleep, she found his small, warm weight and rhythmic breathing to be a solace, for as much as she wished to go back inside and help the men, she understood her time was better spent here with the animals.

Besides, as far as she could determine, the blaze was nearly out. The smoke had gone from wicked grey to white because of bucket after bucket of water being dumped on the flames. Even the noise which had been a roar a short time ago was now a whisper. She heard the men speaking in normal tones rather than shouting as they had been.

At last, they came out, each one of them looking dirty and exhausted. Mr Adams emerged first, nodding at her. He looked sober but victorious. The shepherds came out next, slapping each other on the back while they trudged back to the sheepfold. Last of all, her husband came out. His grin robbed her of breath.

It was not as if she had never seen a man without a shirt on. But she had never seen one who looked this... not one with his muscles all sweating and glistening, and all in the cause of saving their stable and livestock.

He was utterly heroic which made him irresistible in her eyes. A hero who leapt from the pages of a novel could not be more valorous. She was quite undone seeing him so...so very...everything wonderful was what.

Yes, he had picked her up and carted her off when she did not wish to be carted off…and yet, where was the outrage? It ought to be ready to spew from her lips, but strangely, the only outrage she felt was at herself for wanting to press her, not outraged, lips on the attractive spot where his shoulder joined his arm and—

Wait! What was that? She hurried close to him to get a better look. Concerned about the red blister on his shoulder, she nearly missed how the scent of ash and sweat pulsed from his skin…nearly, but not quite.

'You have been hurt!'

'Have I? I hadn't noticed.' He lifted Oscar from her arms.

'Come along with me.' She placed her fingers lightly on his elbow, looking first to make sure he had not been burned there, too.

Going inside the kitchen, she indicated that he should sit at the table. At once, Penny bustled over with a bowl of steaming water. She set it on the table and then went to bring a stack of towels, her braid bouncing with her quick steps.

'Is everything well in the stable?' she asked. 'It looked a proper fright from the kitchen window.'

'None of the animals was lost,' Elizabeth said. 'Things inside are burned and will need rebuilding, but the structure is not damaged. We will know more in the morning.'

Apparently reassured, she looked at her employer, blinked hard as if she had only just noticed he was sitting on a stool half-dressed. She slid a sly glance at Elizabeth, bit her lips together and then declared, 'I'm for my bed since it seems we are none the worse for the mischief.'

'Goodnight,' William said.

'There will be extra for you at breakfast, sir,' Penny said, hurrying out of the room without glancing back.

'Does it hurt?' she asked.

'Some, but I have dealt with worse. And I have been promised extra breakfast.'

She tried to ignore his cockeyed grin, but she was a woman, not a stone. The burn did not look horrid, only blistered. 'Cleaning and salve ought to see it right within a few days.' Going to the pantry where medicinal items were kept, she selected a jar of ointment and hurried back with it.

'Let me take him.' She lifted Oscar from the crook of his elbow, then settled the pup on a blanket in the corner of the room. 'I imagine the poor baby will sleep half of the day tomorrow.'

Returning to her ash-streaked husband, she dipped the towel in water. Warm rivulets trickled down her wrist and arm, reminding her that she was no more decently dressed than he was. Not that it mattered. For husbands and wives this lack of attire was commonplace. Not so commonplace for this husband and wife, but still, being alone together and neither of them properly garbed, did not feel sordid.

She swiped the dripping towel across the back of his neck, then along his shoulder, careful not to get too close to the burn. 'You were wonderful tonight, William.'

Oh, but wait…she was angry with him. She only now remembered. Well, given all they had been through tonight, the ire she had harboured seemed trivial. Perhaps she would bring it up tomorrow, or perhaps she would not. She dipped the cloth again, this time cleaning the back of his shoulders.

He sighed; his posture sagged in what had to be vast

relief at having the night's ordeal over with. 'You were brave as well, my dear.'

Hearing the endearment did not make her feel bristly like it had the first time. One reason for it could be that she believed he meant it…another could be that she was simply too weary to become annoyed.

'I apologise for carrying you out as I did. It's only that I feared your gown catching fire…and your hair… I swear it nearly did.'

'I will admit you were right about one thing, William.' She let water dribble from the towel down the centre of his back. 'I was more helpful outside with the animals.'

My word, he was finely built. And he was hers. Not only that, she was also his. What was wrong with her, allowing her mind to wander and not focus on her task? If one could call it a task at all.

'Let me see the front of you.' He pivoted on the stool. She forced her words to seem businesslike. 'Perhaps you have another burn which you did not notice.'

As soon as she drew the cloth across his neck, water mixed with ash dripped down his throat, rolling over the muscles of his chest. It was then that she realised what a fool she was. Business? Honestly, she had never attended to business remotely like this.

'But as for the other,' he said, catching her hand and along with it, her heart. She dropped the towel. It fell on his lap. 'I hope you understand that I cannot apologise for feeling as I do…about the railway's plans for the spur.'

She did not want to admit that he was right, but, with angry Elizabeth being shoved aside by dreamy Elizabeth who wanted nothing more than to feel the swell of his ribs under her fingertips, she had to admit he was correct.

How would she feel had he been the one to be angry at her for what she believed? Clearly, his actions of to-night proved like nothing else could have that he was devoted to Wilton Farm. He had risked his life for it. Nothing spoke louder of his intentions than that did.

Letting go of her hand, he picked up the cloth and gave it back to her. 'But I do beg your pardon for not making my opinion on it clear before we went to the meeting.'

'And I should have asked, not assumed. The spur will come, or it will not. What either of us thinks about it will make no difference on how the railway decides. It is not up to us. I also apologise for acting so horribly towards you. I promise I am not normally like that.'

'I imagine we have some learning to do when it comes to marriage and each other,' he said, his voice soft…a caress as much as a sound.

It was true, they did. She found she was looking for-ward to it when before she had wanted to keep their marriage in the margins of her life. This, the under-standing blossoming between them right now, would be a beginning to that learning.

The honesty, the openness of heart they were shar-ing, was ever so much better than the anger she had harboured. She vowed to herself she would never be that shrewish person again. She would listen to his ideas and either agree with them or level headedly dis-agree. What she would not do was act as if he were her enemy. The opposite was true. He was her ally…her knight and her hero.

In the spirit of honesty…and learning…she could

only admit that she wanted nothing more in this moment than to kiss him. If she did, how would he react? Kissing was nothing new or special to him as it would be for her, but still...

What if?

Chapter Eleven

The intimacy of Elizabeth's touch was nearly his undoing. Although it was not her fingers touching him, but the wet cloth.

Lucky thing it was the cloth or there would be no 'nearly' about it. He would be utterly and completely undone. He was within an inch of giving in to the temptation to answer what he saw in her eyes. The look was familiar enough to read with ease. His wife wanted to offer a kiss.

She was too shy to carry through with the request, he saw that, too. He knew what to do to get her to overcome it…present a smile that teased, or a wink that invited her to claim what she wanted. How easy it would be to encourage her. And how unthinkable.

Elizabeth was different…better than any woman he had known. He could not possibly treat her as if she were not. If he allowed her to kiss him, she might feel she was the same as the others, kissed and forgotten. She would never be that.

All of a sudden, her hand stilled halfway between his throat and his heart. Looking him in the eye, she tapped one finger on her lips. Funny, but he guessed she had no idea she was giving away secret thoughts. Her eyes softened. Her mouth tensed. He wobbled on the stool.

'Shall we put some salve on that burn?' she asked, her brisk tone doing nothing to hide her tender expression. Dipping her fingers into the ointment, she came up with a creamy scoop.

Her touch was remarkably light. He barely felt it when she smoothed the salve over the burn. Not on his skin, he didn't, but in his heart...he did feel it there. He looked for something to talk about to keep himself from coaxing her to offer that kiss. If she did ask for one, he would only turn her down. He would have to because he meant to be the one to kiss her first.

She was special to him. When the time came to kiss her, it would be meaningful. It would be binding. He would surrender his heart along with his lips. It would be a kiss to ignite the marriage of a lifetime—when the moment was right.

'I would like to invite guests from London, Elizabeth. Would you mind terribly?'

That ought to make her forget offering a kiss.

Her fingers jerked slightly, then went still. When they resumed the gentle circling motion on his shoulder she said, 'I would enjoy that.'

What? He knew very well she would not. He also knew he was going to have a difficult time forgetting the kiss that had been in her eyes. Had been because it was gone now, replaced with some expression halfway between fearful and determined.

'Are you certain?' he asked.

'I am certain I will be uncomfortable with it. I will not know the first thing about what will be required.

But you deserve to have your friends visit your own home… So, yes, let us host a country visit. Isn't that what it is called in society?'

'Truly, you do not need to say yes.'

'But I do if we are to make a go of our marriage. We must support one another, even when what we want might be at odds with what the other wants.' Finished with the salve, she set it aside.

'You truly do wish to make a go of our marriage?' His heart leapt to his throat, beat hard and nearly choked the breath out of him.

'William…' her voice sounded soft, whispery, with the barest hint of uncertainty '…there is no one I would rather learn about marriage with than you. We shall make a go of it, I think.' She wiped the salve from her fingers on the towel. 'I suppose we are finished here,' she said.

He stood up and held her gaze while she held his heart. 'No, Elizabeth… I believe we have only just begun.'

He cupped the back of her head in his hand, tilted her face up and looked hard into her eyes, trying to see what was behind them. To make certain for one last time that he was not making a mistake. The prettiest green eyes he had ever seen gazed back at him in utter trust. Her eyelids dipped closed at the same time that her lips opened just enough to sigh.

He slipped his hand from her neck to her chin. He drew her close then waited, half a breath only, to savour the moment of what was truly his first kiss.

'Wife,' he whispered, inhaling the scent of her breath.

'Husband.'

He lowered his mouth upon hers. Having waited a lifetime for this, he found it to be a more tender, compelling and poignant moment than he would have dreamed. Not only that, sparking through the tender was simmering heat which, once released, would be impossible for him to come back from.

One day he would take a kiss past tender and let it explode in a blaze which would truly bind them in the way husbands and wives were bound...body and soul. He wanted that with her, but he also wanted it to be right in every way for both of them. He needed to know she wanted all of him.

When they came together that way, he wanted it to be in the name of love. In the beginning love had not been what mattered, it would grow perhaps...but now it mattered greatly. What they had now was understanding, friendship and affection. It was a good start, but far from where he hoped to be before—

Well, one day, perhaps.

He set her back at arm's length, but could not find it in him to let go of her, so he kept his hands on her shoulders, tracing small circles on her skin with his thumbs.

'I am done in, my dear,' he said and it was not a lie. 'I imagine you are, too.'

'Oh, my, yes! Entirely exhausted,' she exclaimed a bit too brightly.

She walked to the corner of the kitchen and picked up Oscar. William had to admit to forgetting his dog was even there.

'That was a wonderful kiss, William,' she told him while they walked out of the kitchen, her shoulder brushing his arm. 'You are very skilled.'

'What would you say if I told you this was my first kiss?'

'I know it is not. You told me so, yourself.'

'There are kisses and there are kisses…not all of them equal. Those kisses I told you about, Elizabeth, they were only games of amusement. This time with you was not. I want you know—you are the first woman I have ever offered a kiss to.'

She blinked at him and placed Oscar in his arms. Going up the steps towards the bedrooms, moonlight flooded in the windows. He noticed a glint of moisture at the corners of her eyes.

Stopping at the invisible line between their corridors, he kissed her again. 'And know this, too, Elizabeth…you shall have my last kiss as well. No matter what people say about me, I am faithful to the bone.' He traced the curve of her smile with the tip of his finger. 'Goodnight.'

He spun on his heel and hurried down the corridor to his chambers. If he did not move now, he might not. Having cast his lot, he felt equal parts relieved and worried. But glad, too…and amazed.

Going back to the time he had been summoned to Father's study and given an ultimatum, he could scarcely believe that not only had his circumstances changed, but how he felt about those circumstances as well.

Looking back on his life before, he likened it to a pond dried out by long drought. Looking forward, he imagined his future as full and saw the dry pond become an overflowing spring.

Elizabeth was fairly certain she was floating rather than walking beside William while they walked to the stable to get a better look at the damage done by the fire last night. Her marriage had taken a turn in the wee hours of the morning, shifted in a way which held a great deal of promise for its future. It was rather unbelievable that something which had begun as the lesser of two evils now filled her with such a sense of hope.

Oh, my word, she had gone to sleep feeling his kiss and woken still feeling it. She had never been kissed before and so had nothing to gauge it by, but she thought this kiss was special…more than special actually, more like momentous.

She glanced over at her husband while they walked in the early morning sunshine. Oscar wagged his tail madly in the crook of William's arm. The playful quirk at the corners of William's mouth made her feel like dancing.

Perhaps he was reliving last night's intimacy, the same as she was. To her way of thinking, the stable had not been the only thing burning. How long, she had to wonder, could the echo of a kiss linger on one's mouth? She was certainly going to delight in finding out. But for now, she must give serious attention to the stable. Please let the damage not be greater than her budget.

Oscar's litter mates gambolled about the paddock. Mr Adams must have let the litter of pups out to play. When William set Oscar down to join them, they wrestled and tumbled as happily as if last night had not happened.

Going inside, she gasped, brought back to the here and now. Last night had happened and with a vengeance. Everything was black. Not all of it burned, but all of it layered in soot. And the smell was awful enough to make a person hold her breath.

'What a blessing that all the lambs have already been born and are just old enough to join the flock,' she said. 'They could not possibly remain here.'

'It is going to take a great deal to fix this.' William turned in a circle, looking at the ceiling, then the walls. He bent to peer at a pile of ash that had once been the gate and sides of a stall.

'More money than I have set aside, I fear.'

'It is oppressive in here. Let's go outside and discuss what needs to be done.'

Back outside, sunshine seemed more precious than ever.

'If it is money you are concerned about, you need not be.'

'When it comes to Wilton Farm, money is always a concern,' she pointed out.

'When it comes to the funds I receive from Riven-hall, money is not a concern at all.'

'What do you mean?' Finances were always a concern. She had grown up learning to make income come out on top of expenses.

'I mean that with the money I get from the estate, you are a wealthy woman.'

He grinned while he said so, but she felt rather stunned by the revelation.

Perhaps she ought not to have been. As the son of a viscount, of course he would be wealthy. It was only that with everything else she had buzzing about her mind regarding the change in her life, she had failed to consider this one.

'I suppose I ought to have mentioned it right away.

It is only that there was already so much to deal with, I did not think of it. Honestly, having money is just something I don't think about since I've always had it.'

'Since I never have, I shall not know how to act as a wealthy woman, William.'

'I will teach you.' He smiled that smile which melted her inside. There was a great deal she wanted to learn from him which had nothing to do with money. 'You have quite a head start where teaching is concerned so I am relieved to have a chance at my turn.'

'I will do my best to learn, but I do not want to change who I am. What if, with all that wealth, I become a wasteful spendthrift?'

He laughed, which made her feel better, but she really did fear such a thing. She would need to be diligent to remain thrifty when, apparently, there was suddenly no need to be. Because thriftiness was a virtue which she had always valued.

But compromise was what they had vowed last night. She did need to learn how to live in her husband's world. The tricky part would be not losing her own in the process.

'I cannot imagine you will. For a start, simply accept that you need not worry about how we will pay for repairing the stable.'

'Simply?' For him it might be simple. Growing up without monetary issues to be considered would give a person a different outlook on life.

'What you need is practice. Look at me. Practice has made me an excellent egg gatherer. You must admit how skilled I have become at it.'

'Oh, you have! The best I have ever seen. How do you suggest I practise being wealthy?'

'We will need to go to Windermere to order what we need to repair the stable. I propose we spend the night at an inn. We will purchase some gowns for you.'

'I have gowns.'

'And they look fetching on you…perfect for caring for lambs. But you will need something more appropriate for entertaining guests.'

Gowns in which she would feel perfectly awkward. But he was correct. She could hardly greet his London friends in anything she currently had in her wardrobe.

'And we shall purchase good, sturdy work clothes for you.'

'Agreed.'

There was something in his smile that shot straight to her heart. Honestly, it had from the first time he had come upon her in the gully.

'I wonder,' she said, feeling shy and bold all at once. 'If we ought to kiss to seal the agreement.'

'I like kissing you.'

And he proved it, right there in the morning sunshine with chirruping birds and a litter of gambolling puppies to witness.

For a woman on her way to purchase new gowns, his wife seemed glum. He had never met a lady who did not enjoy the pursuit. Perhaps she disliked riding into Windermere in the work cart. He was not overly fond of the conveyance himself, but they did need to bring back supplies to begin the repairs to the stable. Besides, it was the only transportation available at Wilton Farm.

One would think the beauty and cheerfulness of the town would brighten her spirts, but the closer they got to the livery where they would leave the wagon for the night, the quieter and more withdrawn she became.

'What troubles you, my dear? Don't you find Windermere to your liking?'

She shook her shoulders, as if to free herself of whatever dark mood had settled upon her spirit. 'I like Windermere... It's only the inn. I dislike inns.'

'All of them?' he asked, stopping the wagon at the livery door. 'Or only the seedy ones? Some are excellent.'

'Especially the excellent ones.'

He helped her down from the wagon, suddenly regretting his plan to stay the night at the finest inn in Windermere.

'But why?'

'It has to do with when I was lost in London as a child. I was staying at an exceedingly fine inn then, too. I confess that I have never recovered from it. Would you mind terribly if we went home tonight instead?'

'It will be late, but if you would rather, of course we will go home.' He hesitated, then asked, 'Would you like to talk about what happened to you in London?'

He knew, of course, since Father had been the one to find her. William had even seen her from a distance. He and Thomas had peeked around a doorway to get a look at her. Mother had shooed them off, saying the child was sick and distraught and did not need them peering at her.

Perhaps he ought to have brought up the subject sooner, but the last thing he wanted was to bring up a stressful subject.

'I still bear scars, William. London still holds great fear for me. It might seem silly to fear an inn that is not even in London…but I just do. I will feel much better at home.'

And then, upon walking into the livery, he knew exactly how they would travel there. At the back of the large livery there was a fine-looking carriage for sale. Did it come with a team? he wondered.

Instinct told him that this was not the time to bring the purchase up with his wife. Better to wait and let it come up in easy conversation when her mood was restored. Later when she saw it, already knowing it belonged to them, she would probably approve. He hoped so, at least.

He could not imagine who would not approve of a more comfortable way to travel. In the event she did not, he began to gather his arguments in favour of it.

'Would it be difficult for you to have lunch at the inn? I have it from Minerva that the food is delicious.'

They went out of the livery. He gave the carriage one last, longing glance. It was exactly what Wilton Farm needed.

'We can eat somewhere else, if you wish,' he said because the inn was across the road and Elizabeth stood silently frowning at it.

She took a breath, squaring her shoulders as if she were preparing for a battle. 'I suppose I might manage lunch.'

'I would rather have you enjoy it somewhere else than manage it here.'

'No…honestly, I feel foolish letting something that happened so long ago haunt me. No harm actually came to me from being lost. You father, bless him, found me before it did. So…let's have lunch at the inn.'

He put his hand on her shoulder, pulled her in for a

hug. 'There is a big difference between then and now, Elizabeth. You were a child when you were lost before. Now that you are grown you are resilient enough to deal with it if it were to happen again.'

'I will not need to deal with it since I do not intend to go to London.'

'If I can convince you to go, there will be another difference between then and now. You will have me. I promise that nothing will harm you. You are mine and I will keep you safe.'

She smiled, then, and it touched his soul. She was his, Mrs Grant, his wife…and he would protect her from any threat, imagined or real.

'That reassurance should keep me through lunch.'

'Good, we will need our strength to face our respective battles.'

'Are we going to war, William?' she asked when he took her arm, leading her across the street to do battle with the inn.

'Indeed we are…you to lunch and the dressmaker and me to wherever one purchases proper farming attire.'

'We shall be sure to eat heartily then.' She laughed when she said so which was a relief.

He hated to see memories of what had happened to her as a child shadow her eyes. They were gone now that she was laughing, but it wrenched his gut to think of what she had endured.

Elizabeth felt pleased with herself, in all. Not only had she survived lunch, but she had enjoyed it.

How could she not, spending the meal with William? All through it he had made her laugh and forget she disliked inns. Although this was not the inn proper, but only the dining room attached to it. Until today she'd made a habit of crossing the street rather than walking in front of the fearful establishment. Which had been an absurd and cowardly thing to do. Windermere was not London.

More than that, this time was not that time.

William was correct in pointing out that she was no longer a helpless child. And yet it was the other thing he had said to her that gave her the backbone to have lunch at a place which reminded her of the time she was lost and forsaken.

He would protect her. For as self-reliant a woman as she always believed herself to be, knowing he was there for her touched her deeply. Somehow, his promise made her feel empowered rather than weak. She did not feel at all like a dainty damsel in need of protection.

William said he would protect her and he would, she knew it. In giving her that security, he also gave her what she needed to draw on her own courage.

Taking that empowered spirit with her, she walked to the dress shop while William went to purchase proper farmer's clothing. For him it must be as daunting a prospect as her purchasing gowns. And not only one gown! She would need several of them for the purpose of looking pretty while entertaining guests. Elizabeth could not imagine what the dressmaker would think. She had never purchased anything that was not useful and durable.

A silent giggle ticked her throat because she imagined her husband had never purchased a garment for any other reason than that. Entering the shop to face the unknown, she decided that she quite adored William Grant…thanked him even for making her stretch what she was comfortable with.

Two hours later she left the dress shop with four gowns ordered. She had felt positively sinful spending that much money on fluff.

She had put on the first dress and stood on a dais in front of a long mirror, feeling guilty in the extreme, but then…well, little by little she'd become accustomed to seeing herself in lace and frills. To her surprise, she'd enjoyed the unique experience, halfway at least. Trying on the second and then third gown, she'd felt better about things.

Ah, but then came the fourth gown, which was a ball gown and quite low cut in the bodice. The dressmaker insisted she needed such a thing. Elizabeth had put up a stiff argument over it…until she put it on and then…my word! Just—oh, my word! All she could envisage was William's glance of approval when he saw her wearing it.

Stepping out of the shop, the late-afternoon sun shone in her eyes which was why she did not quite understand what she was looking at.

William stood outside the shop, grinning and pointing to a fancy carriage…but the thing that puzzled her was seeing their good, trusty farm wagon tied by thick a rope to the rear of the carriage.

'Do you like it?' His grin could not possibly grow any wider.

She had the sinking feeling that the fancy conveyance was going to take up residence at Wilton Farm.

Before she could come up with an answer which

would fall politely somewhere between the truth and a lie, he said, 'I've purchased it for us…as a gift.'

'A gift for us, William? Or for you?' He could not be serious. What were they to do with such a conveyance in Ambleside? 'I promise you this is the last gift that I would choose to give "us".'

'It is exactly what we need and for a few reasons.' His smile did not falter, not by the slightest dip.

'Our neighbours will laugh at us,' she accurately pointed out. No one in Ambleside travelled in luxury.

'Only to hide their envy.'

'I do not want them to be envious. I have always got along well with my neighbours. I do not wish for that to change by putting on airs.'

'Perhaps to you it would be putting on airs. For me, this is a normal mode of travel. Nothing at all pretentious about it.' He opened the door, indicating that she should look inside.

If he meant for her to be swayed by the plush-looking interior, she simply would not be. It was one thing to be suddenly wealthy and quite another to flaunt it to the neighbours. Standing firm on the steps of the shop, she shook her head.

'It is time to practise compromise, as we discussed,' he said brightly, closing the cab door.

Standing two steps up as she was, they looked at each other eye to eye…or faced each other off for the challenge, to be more precise.

'Am I to assume you have also purchased that team of horses to go with the carriage?' They were elegant-looking creatures and a good complement to the carriage.

'A carriage cannot draw itself. Meet Blueberry and Otis.'

'Those horses will need to be fed. How much do you imagine that will cost?'

'We can easily afford their care.'

Oh, yes. They were wealthy. This was not a concept she could easily become accustomed to. The idea of never wanting for funds was as foreign to her as taking a walk on the moon would be.

'The compromise I present,' she said, frowning in the face of his grin, 'is that you ride home in the carriage. I will ride in the farm cart.'

'That is nearly a compromise, but not quite. A more proper one would be we ride in the cart for the first half of the journey and then we ride in the carriage for the second half.'

The sunshine which had been beaming down a moment ago disappeared behind a scuttling cloud. Whichever way they got home they would need to do it in a hurry, since it looked like rain was on the way.

'Come,' he said, taking her hand and leading her to the cart which was loaded in the back with supplies. He helped her to climb up and then got in after her. 'We ought to be on our way home before the weather turns.'

All at once the carriage lurched, drawing the wagon jerkily after it.

'I assume we also have a driver?'

He nodded, grinning. Her heart fell all over itself seeing the pride he took in the new purchase.

'We can afford him. Also, before you ask what we will do with him when he is not required to drive, he has agreed to work in the stable. With the new animals, Mr Adams will be glad of the help.'

She could only imagine what a sight they made...a fancy carriage towing a humble cart and she and her husband riding in the cart. It would look beyond absurd to witness the fancy horses in front with sturdy wagon horses tied to the rear of the procession.

'People are staring at us,' she pointed out.

Being stared at was something she supposed she would need to get used to. Even if William did not stand head and shoulder above anyone in Ambleside socially, he would still be stared at. By the ladies, she meant, since he was also head and shoulders above any other man when it came to handsome looks.

His reaction to the stares was to shrug. 'It will happen upon occasion. I do not think anyone means ill by it. Besides, I have prepared a couple of arguments to support my side of this purchase.'

'Truly?' She could not wait to discover his reasoning.

'We have agreed to have guests from London, and we cannot ask them to walk from Windermere. Our new carriage will transport them in comfort.'

'All right, I suppose that makes sense.' The comfort of their future guests was important.

'And the other reason is that it will transport us in a proper manner. If one day, we have children, we will not wish for them to travel unprotected from the elements.

Children? They had not gone quite that far in their marriage, but…well, one day it could happen and she would want them protected.

'You do know how to support an argument, I must say.' She had promised to live in a spirit of compromise and so she would.

It was a lucky thing the second part of the compromise was to ride in the carriage. Rain, it appeared, would be arriving soon. All at once, riding inside a dry and comfortable carriage did not seem at all unpleasant.

For all that she'd fought having a fancy carriage, she could not help but admit it would be a boon for travelling on inclement days. And if they were required to travel at night…perhaps they really did need the fancy conveyance…and the driver and horses to go with it. As long as they really could afford this, as her husband assured her they could, she would not be greatly opposed to the comfort.

William had closed the door on both the weather and the dim light of early evening a quarter of an hour ago. What a timely purchase the carriage had been. He was grateful that it had been for sale. The carriage and team had been a settlement of a large debt, the liveryman had told him.

Rain tapping on the roof of the cab sounded comforting. Especially so since, had he not got lucky in this purchase, that same rain would be beating down on their heads.

'I must admit, William, you do win this compromise. It is better to be inside.' She snuggled up to him when she said so.

With her head leaning against his shoulder, he did feel a winner. 'One does not win a compromise,' he pointed out. 'That is not the point of it. We both win.'

'Humm,' she murmured sleepily. 'Or both lose.'

'What is it? Have we won or lost?'

'Won.' She covered a yawn with the back of her hand. 'But I hope we are as wealthy as you claim because my gowns cost an extravagant amount of money.

I imagine the gowns alone argue for keeping the carriage. I could not possibly allow them to be ruined by foul weather...and I would look silly...' Her voice trailed off, her eyes closing.

'We will keep it, then?'

When she spoke it was while she was drifting halfway between sleep and wakefulness. He nearly missed hearing what she whispered. 'I think we must, for the sake of the babes.' Her head nodded, then jerked up.

He eased her down so that her cheek rested in his lap. 'Our babes, you mean?'

She answered with the most delicate snore he had ever heard. Well, she had said what she said. He would hold those words close to his heart until the time came when they were ready for that next step in their marriage.

In the meantime, he would wonder what compromises they would make as steps towards that goal. Knowing she could not hear him, he whispered, 'I could so easy fall in love with you.'

A lock of hair crossed her cheek. He reached for it, but she sighed and wiped it away from her face with a languid flick of her fingers. If only the ride home were not so short. He felt he could sit right here, just watching her all night long.

It was hard to imagine that only a month ago he had not known her. How could she ever have been no more than a means to avoid becoming a clergyman or a pauper? He could never have imagined that the woman with the ewe stuck in the gully would become so dear to him. Nor that he would be sitting here studying the line of her jaw and the slope of her pretty nose, wondering what children between them would look like.

He thought about his mother, too. In his eyes, she had been the soul of irrepressible joy, always ready for a spot of fun. All his life he had striven to copy her... to honour her memory in that way.

The only noise inside the cab was his wife's soft, slow breathing, and outside, wind huffing against the windows. With time to simply think, he brought up more memories of his mother. She had loved him no matter how he had behaved. Nothing he did was ever unforgivable. Her touch was always tender, her words ever gentle.

She was the best mother a boy could have. And, he recalled, there was a great deal more to her than laughter and gaiety. He had heard her desperately weeping once when he was quite small. At the time he did not understand why, but there was supposed to be a baby brother or sister coming to the family and then suddenly there was not. Mostly, Mother was jovial, sometimes she was sad...but she was always strong.

'What do you think of this, Mother?' he whispered into the dim light of the cab. 'In trying to live up to being as irrepressible as you were—or are still, I would wager—I ended up married. You heard us speaking of children? What do you think about that? Am I too irresponsible for such an important duty?'

Something tickled the back of his neck, making him shiver. He did not think there was a draught in the carriage, or a spider.

'If that was you, I wonder what you meant by it. Perhaps that I should strive to copy all of who you were and not only the part of you who adored parties?'

He watched his bride breathing, the lift and fall of her chest while she nestled against his thighs.

'You would approve of all this, wouldn't you, even in spite of how it came to be?'

And then the oddest thing happened. Even with no light in the cab, the ring on Elizabeth's finger glimmered, gave a quick, happy wink. It must have caught some source of illumination. He was going to choose to believe the illumination to be his mother's spirit, laughingly and lovingly giving her blessing.

Too soon, the carriage stopped in front of the door of the house.

He bent low, kissing Elizabeth's cheek to wake her.

She blinked, sat up and smiled. 'I was having the loveliest dream.'

'What was it about?'

She blushed—even in the dim light he could see it staining her cheeks. 'I will keep it to myself for a while,' she answered.

And he would keep what happened while she was sleeping to himself.

For a while.

Chapter Twelve

The need for another compromise presented itself the morning after bringing the new carriage home.

Elizabeth was not surprised by it, naturally.

When William had insisted the carriage be parked in the carriage house, it evicted the farm cart from its long-accustomed spot. Not only the wagon, but several other large farm tools.

Mr Adams was not at all happy to have the good, practical tools sitting in the elements and a rather useless carriage protected. He had accepted the new employee who would be helping in the stable with better grace than he did the carriage.

In the end Adams was appeased because what she and William agreed to was that a new building would be constructed which would be even larger than the current carriage house was. And as part of the agreement, Adams would have new, larger quarters built within it for himself.

In the end everyone was happy. As far as compromises went, she and William were doing splendidly.

* * *

It had been three days since the carriage came home and while they had not had occasion to use it, she had visited it a time or three. For reasons she could not explain, she found great comfort sitting in the snug cab. It was as if something good had happened here, but for all her thinking she could not recall what.

Within those three days tradesmen had begun to build the new carriage house. She had never seen anything come together so quickly. Also, her gowns had been delivered. In the past her gowns had taken a few weeks to be completed. This unusual efficiency must be what came of doing business with the son of a viscount. For all that the special treatment was foreign to her, it was not so horrible.

Standing in her chamber this evening with the gowns spread across her bed, she wondered what to do with them. There was clearly not enough room in her wardrobe.

The ball gown alone would take up all the space.

Oh, but it was the prettiest thing she had ever seen, so fluffy and pink. She picked it up, clutched it to her chest and twirled about. She had never owned anything so unsuitable as pink.

Lost in delight, she nearly missed hearing the quick rap on her chamber door. Gown still pressed to her heart, she opened the door.

'William?'

'I realise I have crossed the line, but shouting for you seemed disruptive. But it is the line I have come to discuss…that gown is fetching, by the way.'

'It cost you a great deal of money.'

He shrugged, 'I wish to make a proposal about the imaginary barrier.'

'What do you propose?' she asked, noticing that his gaze went soft watching her hold the gown under her chin.

'I propose we move it. I believe our friendship has got to the point where we might break the line in half—one section in front of your door and one in front of mine. It will avoid raising the household when we wish to speak with one another after we have retired.'

'It is the practical thing to do. Yes, I agree to it.'

'Good, then…that was easy.' He stood for the longest time without speaking and then, 'Put on the gown and come down to the drawing room. It is time I taught you how to dance.'

'But I—' He hurried away before he heard her protest. She was fairly certain it was on purpose.

She did know how to dance already; however, she imagined that the exuberant country steps she was used to would look silly in this beautiful gown.

It had been a long day of working with the sheep and she was bone weary, but still, she did long to put on the gown again. Ever since she'd first tried it on, she'd wondered what William would think seeing her wearing it. If the way he had looked at her holding it was anything to go by—

All right, then.

It was not until she had peeled off her workday gown, quickly washed and then stepped into this one that she discovered the problem. There was no way she could fasten the back of the dress on her own. It needed two women to accomplish the task.

How disappointing, but she would need to learn to dance in her old brown gown. Unless…well… But, no, asking William to fasten it was unthinkable. Except that it was not. Husbands and wives did…

He was her husband, she was his wife… Before she could think more deeply about it, she rushed downstairs, the back of the gown open and the front hugged to her chemise.

Standing at the fireplace and gazing at agreeably tame flames, William wondered if Elizabeth would come down. The invitation had been impulsive and she was not an impulsive person. For certain she would not put on the gown. For all that he wished to see her in it, he knew he had asked too much.

Then he heard fabric rustling. Without turning, he knew she wore silk and not wool. One did not have to look to know the difference. Wool sounded down to earth, straightforward and no nonsense. But silk? The soft whirr and swish while a lady walked was an invitation to seek enjoyment in her company.

Knowing that Elizabeth was coming towards him made his heart leap as it never had before. Even without seeing her he was dancing. Then he turned. He felt his jaw fall open, but nothing could have made him snap it closed. She was wearing the gown, but not all of the gown. It sagged away from her, held in precarious place by her small work-worn hands.

'Since Penny has already retired, you will need to help me with fastening the back.'

With her free hand, she neatly touched his chin and closed his mouth, which made him jump and brought him back to the delightful situation he found himself in.

She turned about, apparently waiting for him to do up the back of the gown. Which he would do, as soon as he stopped staring in fascination at her back, at the rise and fall of her quick breathing. Her chemise was plain, but sheer enough that he could see pink skin blushing under it, along with the curve of her spine and the shape of her waistline where it began to flare to her hips.

His heart welled so large in his chest he feared he might stop breathing. Or thinking…he must have stopped since it took her casting a questioning glance over her shoulder to make him blink back.

'I assume you know how?' she muttered.

'I can understand why you might think so given my reputation. I assure you—I am not nearly as skilled with buttons and ties as you must think.'

'Well, then…' her voice was soft in that way she spoke sometimes, nearly but not quite a whisper '…we shall simply fumble our way through.'

He did fumble, but it was his heart doing so more than his fingers.

'Do you know any dances?' he asked in order for his brain to have a place to land which would not tempt him to break his vow of allowing her to lead the way in this area of their marriage.

'I know a few leaps and stomps but those would be rather disrespectful to the gown, don't you think?'

What he thought was that having anything covering her was being disrespectful to her womanly— Dash it, he needed to retreat from thoughts of that nature and concentrate on the reason he had asked her to come downstairs. Dancing was a skill she would need in London. Many ladies had dance instructors to teach them. But he was not going to give another man the pleasure of Elizabeth's company when he wanted it himself.

More and more often, he craved being with her. Discussing the line in the corridor had been an excuse to see her. The invitation to dance had been but one more excuse to remain in her company. It seemed he could not get enough of spending time with her. There was no one, he realised, that he liked better than his wife. In a truly short time, he had gone from not knowing her to wishing to never live in a world without her company.

With the last button done up she turned to face him. 'Won't we need music of some sort?'

Music? Somehow, he had failed to think of that.

'Come.' He caught up her hand, felt her roughened fingers curl around his…roughened and yet gentle. He had seen those very fingers touch lambs and pups with unbelievable tenderness…touch him that way, too, when she'd tended his burn. He had held many delicate, feminine hands in his life, but swore he had never held a more womanly hand than the one he now held.

There was a set of glass doors in the drawing room which led to a patio. He opened them and led her outside. 'We shall dance to the music of the night,' he said.

'Frogs…owls…' She cocked her head, listening. 'There is a melody to it. One can nearly hear the moon and the stars chatting with each other.'

'What would you like to learn? Shall I teach you to waltz?'

'If you are feeling very patient.'

He did not need patience in the way she thought, but he did need it in another way. With a mental shake, he reminded himself that he was teaching her to dance.

She needed to learn this social skill the same as he needed to learn how to care for sheep.

One, two, three…he led her in the steps. Then he twirled her so that her skirt flared out in a pink froth which caught a glimmer of moonlight.

She tipped her head back, laughing. He watched the muscles of her neck ripple. He felt a tingle race over his own neck, then down. A vow was a vow. He repeated it, making a mantra of the words.

'You have a natural sense of rhythm, I think.'

'I suppose a glide is not so different than a leap, only more refined.'

'It occurs to me…' one, two, three '…that I ought to learn leaps and hops. Surely the people of Ambleside dance.'

'They do, but not often.'

'Surely not! We must change that. What do you say to a party here at Wilton Farm? We shall invite the neighbours.' A brilliant idea came to him. 'What if we invite the neighbours and my London friends at the same time?'

'We could do that, if we wished to have the most awful party in the history of parties. With the differences of our guests' places in society, no one would feel comfortable.'

'You and I are of different classes and I do not get the sense that you are uncomfortable with me.' Not with the way she giggled when he twirled her under his arm. 'They might come to feel the same way with time and familiarity.'

'Farmers are stubborn.' She shook her head.

He nodded, shrugging. 'Aristocrats are haughty.'

One, two, three, her hair shimmered in the starlight.

'We shall simply have to lead by example. Let our marriage be a lesson,' he said.

'I am not misreading you, am I, William?' It was a bit hard keeping an intelligent conversation going while concentrating on the sensuous shift of her back under his fingertips. 'For I feel you are becoming content living here?'

'No, my dear, you do not misread.' He twirled her out and then pulled her closer than the dance warranted. He dipped his mouth towards the sweet curve of her ear. 'And I hope I do not misread that you do not mind that I am?'

He slowed the dance so that there were no steps to it, merely a gentle swaying of their bodies which were not quite touching, but at the same time not quite *not* touching, either.

'Have we come to another compromise, then? An understanding that we do not mind being with each other?' she asked.

'I propose something else…an understanding…that it isn't that I don't mind being with you, but that I like it…very much.' His words grazed the curve of her cheek. He felt it lift with her smile. 'And you like being with me.'

'I accept that.' She hesitated half a heartbeat before saying, 'I also propose, no…admit, that I like kissing you.'

His lips were already brushing her cheek so when she touched his chin and turned his face there was nothing for it but to answer the call to a kiss. Night music went even better with kissing than it did with dancing. The unique strain was made for such a moment. The melody circled his shins, swirled up his thighs, beat a tempo in his ribcage.

'Elizabeth Grant, you have a wonderful mind for compromise and admissions.' He set her away because it was either do it or break his vow, then led her towards the parlour doors. 'Did I forget to mention how beautiful you make that gown look?'

'In a sense, you did.'

'Only in a sense? I am remiss. I would have been had I not been struck silent by your beauty.'

'Silent, William?' She laughed and his knees went soft. 'But I did see it…in your eyes. I know because I am not used to being looked at in that way.'

Her lips formed one of those smiles that she had, pressed thin, tight and twitching at the corners in a playful effort to be withheld. 'Let's see how you look at me tomorrow when the sheep shearing begins! I will be a fright from head to toe.'

He had a feeling she would look even more beautiful than she did in this moment. That must be what happened when one looked with the heart as well as the eyes. He had not allowed himself to look with the heart before and was glad of it.

How crushing would it have been to look at a lady with his heart only to have her gaze shift to Thomas, the Rivenhall heir? Crushing because looking with the heart felt like being in love. Looking with the heart also felt like looking at for ever.

He could not help but be afraid. He knew that Elizabeth liked him. She had only just said so. What she had not said was that she loved him.

The setting sun hovered a slice over the horizon when Elizabeth spotted William walking through the pasture towards the stream. After a day in the shearing shed, he was bound to be filthy and exhausted. Hungry, too. He had worked alongside the hired shearers, learning from them, laughing with them, as if he were one of their own. She admired his ability to put aside his position and be at ease with nearly everyone.

She also admired the way he looked pulling his sweat-stained, fuzz-embedded shirt off over his head while he walked. His weariness was evident. He would have to be exhausted after how hard he had worked all day. There was nothing she could do about how tired he was, but she could bring him something to eat.

She hurried back to the house. Once in the kitchen she put together a basket, then reached high in the pantry to the top shelf and withdrew a blanket. Penny offered to help, but Elizabeth refused. The cook was using every moment she had to teach the new kitchen help how to prepare for the guests who were coming from London next week.

While William might see this as a small, casual gathering, to everyone else at Wilton Farm it would be the grandest event to ever happen.

Going back out, she did not see William. He must already be at the stream washing up before coming into the house. She hoped he was not too weary to enjoy an alfresco dinner beside the water. The weather was warm and perfect for dining outdoors. Besides, having been too busy to spend time with him today, she'd missed him and could hardly wait to hear how his shearing experience had gone.

Coming to the streambank, she could not see him, but she could hear him clearly enough. He splashed and groaned, sighed and splashed again.

She spread the blanket and set out the food. Within

moments she heard his footsteps coming up the bank. He shook his head vigorously causing a spray of water to fly from his hair. There was a towel slung over his bare shoulder, but he had not used it yet. Droplets clung to his arms and chest.

His new, sturdy work trousers rode low on his hips. The waistband was damp and darker than the rest of the fabric. Apparently, he had not used the towel for anything but to toss it over his shoulder and look terribly seductive.

'Hello,' she said.

'Elizabeth?' He peered at her through dripping lashes. 'What are you doing here?'

'I have brought dinner.' She indicated the blanket she sat upon and, with a wave of her fingers, the food spread upon it.

'My angel,' he said with a great, relieved smile. 'I could eat anything but a sheep.' He sat down, leaned across the blanket and kissed her cheek. 'I apologise for not wearing my shirt, but it is drying out on a bush. I did not know you would be here.'

'I imagine I shall survive.' She tried not to smile, but really, what was there not to smile about? 'But you might not unless you eat.'

He picked up the end of a loaf of bread, nodded while claiming it was the best he'd ever tasted.

'How did you enjoy shearing sheep?'

'A little more than they enjoyed being sheared, I imagine.'

Oh, that grin, she adored it. She could look at it every day of her life. But wait—she truly could look at it every day of her life. This bare-chested, still-damp man was her husband. Her heart took a dizzy tumble imagining the possibilities. She thought about asking if he wished to get rid of the silly, imaginary line in front of their bedroom doors.

She could do so, he had left the decision on intimacy up to her. She nearly wished he had not. Her imagination was happily wondering what would happen if he forgot about food and lay her back on the blanket and kissed her and then… Well, never mind that…for now.

'There is dessert in the basket if you care for some.'

'With everything going on in the kitchen I'm surprised they have time to make us dessert.'

'They are practising the recipe so it will be perfect for your guests. Small pastries with strawberry cream which we reap the benefit of sampling.'

'Our guests,' he pointed out while reaching in the basket for a treat.

'You know them. I do not. I shall do my best, but really, I have no idea what to do with them.'

'It is a small group, eight in all, and we shall be informal.'

What was informal to William was probably the height of elegance to her. Truly, the thought of eight strangers to be entertained left her without an appetite. She reached for a pastry, none the less.

'I need for you to teach me how to behave as a lady.'

'You are a lady. Never believe otherwise.'

'What I mean is, I need to learn to behave in society. It is not the same thing as in Ambleside. I need to learn to live in both worlds.'

'For when we visit London?'

For all that she felt somewhat braver about the prospect, it was not likely to happen. She shook her head. 'For when London visits Ambleside.'

'You would never consider coming with me?'

'Only under dire circumstances…or if your brother or sister wed. Perhaps then, but I will hate it.'

'It isn't as awful as you think. Your aunt and uncle choose to live there.'

'I received a letter from them yesterday, did I mention it?'

'I do not recall that you did.'

'They are happy. They tell me how wonderful the city is. And yet I…' She shrugged.

'I will not force you to go to London, but if you change your mind, I will be there to keep you safe.'

'I know…but still, it remains that I will not know how to behave. What do London ladies do with their time?'

'They talk…but not of politics or things of that matter. But fashion, yes… Who is wearing what and where they wore it to. They read and discuss what is published in the gossip columns. They talk about children, of course.'

'Here in Ambleside, we also speak about children. But since I do not have any of them to discuss, I would need to talk about my lambs. That, I believe, would not be well received in a London drawing room.'

'It would be by Minerva. My sister is fascinated by everything.'

'But what else do they do?'

She might get by in society if she could simply keep active without having to carry on a conversation.

'They…' He looked puzzled for a moment. 'They attend balls and tea…they go to the opera…and sew.'

'Sew?'

'Yes, pretty flowers and such on handkerchiefs and linens.' He nodded, a piece of cheese poised in his fingers. 'That might be the one thing my sister has no interest in.'

Elizabeth had no great fondness for sewing, either, which was probably due to the fact that her sewing tended to involve mending, not creating pretty things. In her mind it was an apt illustration of the difference between Ambleside and London, between her humble self and a socialite.

'I will try my best to learn how to act, William. But in the end, I fear I will only embarrass you.'

He was reaching for another pastry, but stopped, clenching his fist. He shifted across the blanket until they sat hip to hip.

My goodness, but his bare skin smelled a far better treat than dessert.

'Do I embarrass you?' he asked.

'How could you? The situation is entirely different. People admire you. Your every little word has them nodding in agreement.'

'It is the way of things, I fear. The higher the position the more people think you know what you are speaking of. In London, it is my brother's words they hang on, not mine.'

'I sense that you and your brother are at odds. Have you always been like that?'

He shrugged. 'Not when we were young boys, but later. You see, in my eyes Thomas is the favoured child. Father makes no secret of how proud he is of him. As Thomas sees it, Mother was partial to me. She was not, but it is how he perceived it. Those resentments are between us, yet before we knew anything about titles and such we had grand adventures together. That is still there between us, I think, what we had as boys. I doubt that bond goes away no matter what comes later.'

'Perhaps you will find what that was again.'

'It is what I hope.'

'I think you are quite lucky. Growing up, I was not unhappy, yet seeing other children with their siblings... I would wonder what it would be like to always have someone of my own.'

'You do now. I am your own.'

Yes, indeed, he was. Sitting here looking at him with daylight faded to dark, stars and moon softly illuminating the pasture, she was awfully glad of it. What she needed was to be worthy of him in the eyes of his friends.

'If I am not to make you ashamed, you must teach me to be a lady and do it before our guests arrive.'

'As I said before, you are a lady. The finest one I know. I cannot teach you to be yourself and really, my dear, it is all you need.' He touched her cheek, then tapped the tip of her nose. 'Simply be yourself and all will be well.'

It would not be. He was looking at her through a filter of love—

What was that? A thought from her own mind only, but she had thought it for some reason. Now that she had thought it, and if it were true, it was more important than ever to make him proud. She was going to work very hard to become a lady worthy of him.

Chapter Thirteen

'Here they come!' The excitement she heard in William's voice was reflected in his broad grin. 'I'm only glad the weather is still pleasant and the roads from Windermere are not muddy.'

A situation he would not need to worry about if the rail spur cut through Ambleside. He did not say so, but it had to be on his mind.

Elizabeth refrained from pointing out that even if the road were muddy their new carriage, which William had sent to Windermere to collect the guests, would keep everyone comfortable. For all that she had disagreed with the purchase, she now saw that it had been a good one. Even practical in its way.

'How wonderful,' she said, meaning how wonderful for him...not for her.

She reminded herself that the Londoners would be here only two nights. That everything was prepared and in order. Rooms which had never been used were now clean and ready to welcome William's...no...their London guests.

Penny, at least, seemed in her glory. She was anxious to show off her skills to the wealthy and influential. Perhaps if Elizabeth were as skilled, she would look forward to it as well. In spite of her husband's encouragement, his assurance that his friends would accept her, she was not at all certain.

Over the past week he had done what he could to teach her to act as a proper lady. How to greet and smile and portray graciousness, even when one did not feel it.

No doubt when she stood up at a spur meeting and heatedly expounded her opinions, she was not acting as a lady. Because she was not such a genteel creature, all she would be doing while the Londoners were here was playacting. What would be genuine was her sigh of relief when they boarded the carriage and went back to Windermere and then to London.

For William's sake, she would do her best. She would smile when greeting them when all she wanted to do was to run and hide. For all her nervousness, there was one thing which made her glad. William was anxious to share his new life with them and was proud to be doing it. If he had been ashamed, it would crush her. Believing him to be ashamed of Wilton Farm and, by extension, ashamed of her would be unbearable.

'Murray!' William escorted her down the steps, leading her to the people coming in through the gate. 'Lord and Lady Mees!'

It was as clear as the halfway-blue sky that he was pleased to have his friends here, that he was in no way embarrassed at the turn his life had taken.

As he introduced her around, there was really one thing on her mind: she truly loved this man.

Leading his friends into the dining room where luncheon was to be served, William had never been prouder of anyone in his life.

He knew Elizabeth was nervous to the bone and yet she sparkled. What he saw in her eyes whenever she looked at him was utter joy. Perhaps entertaining had been a latent desire of hers which now that it was fulfilled made her happy.

She must have been paying attention to his tutoring because when someone brought up a political issue, she neatly turned the conversation to embroidery. She told Lady Mees that she had never had the opportunity to learn, but would be grateful for any advice the matron could give her.

Elizabeth was being well received by everyone but Lady Justine Anderson. The fact that she was not was probably his fault. He had kissed her once, briefly, and months ago. It was before he kissed Penelope. Perhaps she had got wind of the moment with Penelope and she felt slighted.

He would rather not have invited her, but she was Lord Mees's niece and she lived with them and so he'd felt obligated. All of this had nothing to do with Elizabeth so he hoped Justine would get over it, that her somewhat dismissive attitude towards his wife would change.

The meal rivalled what was served in the best homes in London. He would be sure to give Penny and her new helper an increase in salary. The foreman and his new assistant, too, for all the extra work they had done to make the stable shine.

This was his home, every building and acre of pasture. He wanted his friends to see it the way he did... with pride.

While they ate, the conversation turned to Murray's marriage next year. There was much talk about how lucky Murray was to have attracted such a well-favoured and high-born fiancée.

'It is a shame she was not able to come with you,' Elizabeth said.

That was when the conversation came to a hideous halt. Justine's smile took an ugly turn.

'Perhaps values in your quaint town are not as they are in London and so you are not aware, but for us, an unmarried lady is not allowed to be alone with a gentleman, it would be talked about.'

The woman's quick, sidelong glance at him revealed quite a bit. He truly did regret his past behaviour. Not only because it had been an irresponsible, juvenile way to behave, but dangerous, too. Unless he read her wrong, and he did not believe he did, a second kiss with Justine would have landed him in a compromise and an unwanted marriage.

More than that, after kissing his wife, he now knew his past kisses had been shallower than a mud puddle in summer. Worthless…foolish was what they had been. He was grateful to his father for forcing him into a position to grow up.

'Justine,' he said, smiling to appear congenial when he was, in fact, quite angry at his rude guest, 'have you ever given thought to the idea that it is a silly and often-ignored rule?'

'No, I have not.' How had he ever found her sarcastic smile to be attractive?

'I suggest you do. Times and society are changing.'

'Oh, yes, indeed they are!' Lady Mees declared. 'Why, my niece in America goes about quite freely with her beau and they are not yet engaged. And besides, how could James's fiancée have been compromised when we all travelled here together?'

'Surely you are not comparing proper English society to crass American?' Justine's eyes widened, her expression genuinely appalled.

'The fact of the matter is,' Murray said, 'Lady Sarah had every intention of accompanying me, but then her sister gave birth to her first child, so she decided to remain in London.'

'Pay no attention to Justine, Elizabeth,' Candice Jones, the other lady in the group, leaned close to whisper, but he heard her clearly. 'She is miffed because William... Well, she— I am sorry, I should not have spoken.'

Oh, dash it. His past was nipping him in the behind and all he could do was sit here steeped in regret. Then the most amazing thing happened. His wife smiled, giving him a wink!

'I do not blame you a bit for holding out against change, Lady Justine,' she said. 'I am fighting against a certain change in Ambleside, so I quite understand.'

Elizabeth Grant was a lady, born to it or not. Being descended from a title could not make one so, not at heart where it counted.

'The rail spur.' It was a risky subject to bring up, but he wanted to draw Justine's attention away from Elizabeth. 'I was in favour of it, but now that we've purchased a carriage, it does not matter all that much.'

'I think it would be a crime to see this lovely area cut up by rails.' Lord Mees pounded his fist on the table to accent his point.

Elizabeth glanced between Lord Mees and him, her smile triumphant and the prettiest he had ever seen it.

* * *

The weather started off ideal for entertaining. For the better part of the day, it had been sunny and clear.

William gave their guests a tour about the farm, showing it off with obvious pride. He showed them everything from the stone patio to the burned lamb pen. Then he took the men to the pastures to see the newly sheared flocks.

While they were gone, Elizabeth spent time with the ladies, learning the fine art of embroidering a flower. She considered demonstrating how to mend a sock, but she thought better of it. She had already made one blunder at lunch yesterday, showing ignorance of travel customs. Truly, these women would be no better off for learning how to darn a sock. They had servants to see to that chore.

For the most part, spending the afternoon with the ladies while the men were out had gone better than she'd expected it to. The next time they visited, she would only dread it half as much.

Looking out the window, she noticed the afternoon growing dim.

'It looks like we will have a storm this afternoon.' Lady Mees declared, with a little clap of her fingers. 'I have heard they are more severe here in the north than they are in London.'

'I cannot judge since I have only been to London once as a child.' There would not be a *twice* and that was a fact, nearly one, anyway. 'But we do get a great deal of rain.'

Some time over the course of the day she had stopped thinking of these people as William's guests. They had become her guests…their guests. She found she liked them better than she'd expected to, felt more at ease than she had thought to.

With the exception of Justine, they were easy to get along with. That woman had an unfriendly demeanour which suggested she might pounce upon her hostess at any unguarded moment.

Which, as it turned out, was the next one.

'Did you know your husband is a popular man in London? He and I—'

'Justine! Have you lost your mind?' Candice declared, her expression horrified. 'Do you think that makes you special? Most of us spent a moment in— Oh, dear, again I have said too much. Please excuse me. Speaking out of turn is a great flaw of mine.'

'You young people,' Lady Mees said, laughing and shaking her head. 'You think you invented party mischief? Why, back in my day we got away with the same thing and, might I suggest, more?'

'I promise all it ever amounted to is harmless fun. Balls can be tedious sometimes, you see, and—' Candice cast a glance out the window at the darkening sky. 'But I do apologise if Justine's wagging tongue and my words upset you.'

Oddly enough, they had not. Had William not been who he was, he would not be here married to her.

'Do not take it to heart, ladies, I am aware of my husband's past, playful antics.' And past, they were. She believed him when he promised to be faithful. She would have said more in his defence, but the front door opened and the men hurried inside.

'The wind is up and I fear there is a blower on the way!' Lord Mees declared, his smile wide, expectant.

To prove his words, a gust of wind swept inside,

knocking over a vase of flowers. Luckily, James Murray caught it before it hit the floor.

Standing, she walked to William. 'The stable doors are closed tight?' she asked quietly.

Oscar had been banished to the barn until the guests went back to London. After one of Justine's gloves had disappeared and then been found chewed, there really had been no choice in the matter.

'I saw the new man closing up. But I hope we have good latches. That is a powerful wind.'

A great gust whooshed around the corners of the house, howling under the eaves as if to make the point.

'We are in for it now!' Lord Mees exclaimed gleefully.

'Oh, good!' Lady Mees answered. 'It makes everything inside extra snug and cosy.'

Justine grunted, cast a scathing look at William for no apparent reason. This would not do. The woman must be set straight. Snuggling under William's arm, she smiled at Justine, nodded and then did the boldest thing she had ever done...apart from wedding a stranger. She went up on her toes and kissed him near, but not quite on, his mouth.

It might not be acceptable in London for a lady to do so, but this was her home and William's. If she wished to show affection for her husband, she would do it.

'A kiss for courage, Lord Mees, is what I always say.'

Lord Mees crossed the room, grinning at his wife. 'Indeed...any port in a storm.'

After that, the evening went smoothly—for a time.

A lively game of charades was interrupted by insistent rapping on the front door. William opened it to the new man. The fellow fairly blew inside, rain dripping from the brim of his hat.

'We have a problem, Mr Grant. The latch blew off the stable door. Both Murray and small Oscar are missing.'

All eyes shifted to Murray, who had pushed suddenly to his feet. 'Murray the lamb…my namesake,' he explained.

Murray was the first one to dash out of the house. Elizabeth hurried out after him.

'Her gown!' she heard Justine gasp.

It was a beautiful garment not meant for the elements. A fact which did not prevent her from rushing headlong into the deluge. What did a dress matter when it came to the lives of Murray and Oscar? William dashed out only steps behind her.

Pointing, he indicated that Murray should search near the far stable, Elizabeth the closer one.

William ran into the worst of the storm, dashing across the meadow towards the rising stream. It was not likely that two small, frightened animals would go that far, but it could not be ruled out.

As it turned out, James Murray was the hero of the hour. He discovered the pair of wanderers huddled under a bush in the paddock only yards from the stable door. Dashing towards her with a lamb under one arm and a pup under the other, he gave them to her. Then he dashed across the pasture, giving a shrill whistle to William to let him know the crisis was over.

Or rather, it would be once the animals were cleaned and warmed up. She could only imagine what the visitors were thinking as she carried the dripping, muddy creatures through the house.

If Justine judged her for running outside, she would convict her of high treason against fabric as soon as she spotted mud smeared all over the fancy brocade bodice of the gown. Let her gasp at the horror if she wished to…and apparently she did because that was the sound which sputtered from her lips, but the little ones were shivering and the best place for them to be was near her heart.

Elizabeth sat down on the hearth, placed the lamb and pup close to the fire. They would need a bath and a brushing, but first they needed to be warmed.

The front door opened. William and Murray hurried inside, wind whipping at their clothes.

She could hear them speaking to the guests, but her attention was on warming the animals. It crossed her mind that she was being a bad hostess, ignoring them as she was, but she was a farmer before a lady. Her priority must be the welfare of these small creatures. When she glanced up, the only person in the room was William.

'Where is everyone?' She had been so caught up in what she was doing she hadn't noticed them leave.

'Gone up to their chambers.'

'Oh, dear. I should have bid them goodnight.' She stood up, carrying Murray and Oscar to the kitchen.

William set a large pot of water on the stove to warm, then gathered several clean rags and brought them to the sink.

'I am sorry, William, they will think I am a miserable hostess.'

He lifted the pot from the heat and set it in the sink. He took Murray, dipped the lamb in the water, then gently scrubbed mud from his fur.

'If they do, they are fools. But I do not believe they are… Well, one of them perhaps is.'

'Justine?'

'I feel I must explain…about her and the others…but really, I have no defence to offer.' He dried Murray with the towel and then put Oscar in the water. 'The fact is, I did kiss those women and it meant nothing to me.'

'You need not explain, it is all in the past.'

'You are wrong. I must explain it to you…and I must face what I did.'

'A youthful kiss is hardly something to—'

'I was thirty. It would be easier to excuse myself if that's all there was to it.' He dried Oscar while he spoke. 'I kissed women, even knowing it meant nothing. Not to them or to me.'

'If you mean to apologise to me for your behaviour before you met me, you need not do it. You had your life and I had mine.'

He set the pup on the floor where he shook off the excess water, then scampered happily about, the lamb leaping and bounding with him. William crossed his arms over his chest, leaned his hip against the counter and stared at the floor. 'It is more than that and goes deeper than an apology.'

She touched his arm. His gaze jerked up. It seemed that what he was trying to tell her came from the deepest part of his heart. Moisture lurked in the corners of his eyes. Suddenly he lurched away from the counter, wrapped his arms around her, bent his head to her shoulder, then stood, silently hugging her.

'Whatever it is,' she murmured, 'I forgive you even though there is no reason for you to need my forgiveness.'

'When I kissed those women, Justine…Candice and

some others… This is hard to explain, but I did it to keep from having to make a commitment to any one lady…and to guard my heart against falling in love.'

He took a deep breath, lifted his head and then cupped her face in his hands. 'When I wed you, I was still guarded. I never meant to let you in. But you need to understand. When I kiss you, it is not like it was then. When I kiss you it does mean something. I am inviting you…no, begging you to come into my heart.'

His hands smelled like soap…for some reason it was all she could think of…because what was he saying? What did he mean? Did she dare hope she understood the message in his eyes?

'When I kiss you, Elizabeth, it…you…mean everything to me. I told you that first time we kissed that it was my first.'

He dipped his head, his breath huffing heatedly on her mouth before he kissed her. She felt a tremor pass through his fingers.

'I haven't been in love before, but I am now.' He kissed her again, pressing her close and, she believed, inviting her into his heart. 'I love you.'

Tears sprang to her eyes. If this was not a miracle, she did not know what was. Her throat tightened, she felt tears dripping down her cheeks.

How had this incredible thing happened to her? In the beginning, all she'd needed was to keep her farm. Wedding William was the means to accomplish that.

But along the way the most amazing thing had happened to her: she'd fallen in love with her husband. Now it was all upside down. It was the man she wanted; the farm came second to him…far second. And, wonder of wonders, he loved her, too. In the face of this revelation, all she could do was blubber.

'Are you happy about it?' he asked. 'A little at least?'

She nodded as hard as she could. It was time for a declaration of her own…and she wanted to tell him she loved him, too, but— Why could she not stop weeping? She had heard of weeping fits and she was having one. Luckily, it was out of pure and utter joy.

'Well…' *Sniff.* 'I think that…' *Sniff, sob, sniff.* 'After they go home, we shall discuss removing those pesky lines in front of our bedroom doors.'

'Why?' Since he was grinning at her she felt he knew quite well why. He wanted to hear her say she loved him, too. He deserved to hear it.

Oh, but how was she to express something so wonderful in mere words? 'I love you, too.'

And there it was, a simple often-used phrase which expressed a miracle.

Chapter Fourteen

It was not an easy thing to get his wife alone so they might 'discuss' removing the line.

He smiled, thinking of how the discussion would go because it was not going to be with words. The life-altering words had been spoken last night. Today was the time for a life-altering act. Declarations of the heart would be made with kisses, touches and the union of their bodies which would seal the vow of a lifetime.

As soon as he could get her away, their marriage would be a true one. So far, the prospect did not seem close at hand.

To begin the day there had been breakfast with his friends and Justine. Then Mr Adams had wanted to walk about, assessing what damage the storm had done. Elizabeth had been called to the kitchen to discuss some urgent matter having to do with a marauding rodent. To the rest of the world, this was a perfectly ordinary day. No one but he and his wife understood that this was their wedding night…or day if he could manage it.

If wind had not blown the half-framed roof off the new carriage house…if a board had not ripped off the side of the hen house and the hens not scattered…if the stream swelling over its banks had not undermined the lower bridge that the sheep used to come and go from the pasture…life would be a delight…a pure wonder.

He ought to have whisked Elizabeth away to the master chamber last night, but with the guests still present, getting up at all odd hours to watch the storm, borrow a book from the library or make a trip to the kitchen for a snack and tea…well, dash it. When the time came, he wanted to be all husband, not distracted host.

Very soon, any moment now…or hour…things would settle at the farm. He and Elizabeth would have time to give themselves to each other without the world poking its busy nose into their business…no, make that their pleasure.

Even now, hours after he had done it, he could scarcely believe he had admitted his love. And to his astounding joy, Elizabeth had admitted the same to him…with a great deal of weeping which touched him down to his soul.

After years of going to lengths not to not fall in love, he had tripped headfirst into it. Elizabeth was no less than a miracle in his life. His heart was open, full of rejoicing. Hopefully, his bed would soon be full of rejoicing, too.

Listening to Penny's tale of woe over the bag of flour ruined by a wicked ugly rodent, Elizabeth wondered if her eyes were still puffy.

Probably they had been three hours ago when the people from London departed. She could only imagine what they thought about it. It must be evident that she had been crying. Hopefully, they did not blame it on William and believe she was devastated because he had once kissed Justine…and Candice.

In some way, the fact that he had kissed so many ladies and never felt anything for them…that his heart had surrendered for the first time when he kissed her… made her feel grand. She was going to feel a great deal grander as soon as the events of the morning settled.

It seemed as if seconds ticked by as slowly as budding flowers came to full bloom, slower even than a snail would creep through damp grass. Truthfully, the feeling that time was dragging had not so much to do with the clock as with expectation…delightful anticipation of what today would bring.

Having slept alone for all her life, she thought it was going to be marvellous to wake in the night and find a big, warm, protective man in her bed.

Tick tock…about a hundred years later, or as the clock claimed three in the afternoon, things finally settled down. This was the quiet part of the day when the animals napped and so did their caretakers.

On an ordinary day, Elizabeth would take a leisurely walk beside the stream, or sit with a cup of tea while watching small birds flit among the flowers and bees gathering pollen. Birds and bees…where was her husband, anyway?

He was not in the far stable. Not in the close one, either. He was not working on the new carriage house, nor was he repairing the hen house. Where could he be? Perhaps seeing to the damage done to the bridge.

If they did not find one another soon, the quiet, lazy

part of the afternoon would be over. Perhaps he was in the house, looking for her. She would go there.

Upon rounding the corner of the stable, she ran headlong into him. He was carrying a blanket. With a great grin, he wrapped it around her shoulders, drawing her close. She felt his heartbeat racing and hers keeping up.

'Come with me.' His voice, a low, masculine caress, wrapped her up as neatly as the blanket did.

'Where?'

'I found a spot by the stream. It is secluded. No one will be able to find us, I promise.' He bent his head to kiss her within the snug woollen folds.

'It is a lucky thing I found you when I did, then!' declared an intrusive voice from a few feet away.

William turned slowly, a frown pressing his brows low. 'Minerva?' He blinked as if he could not believe what he was seeing.

Elizabeth, too, could not grasp the fact that her sister-in-law stood only feet away, smiling and seeming oblivious to what she had interrupted.

'What are you doing here?' William's tone was harsher than usual. Who would not sound that way, having been dropped so suddenly from delight to frustration?

Elizabeth completely understood how he felt.

'Where else would I be when Father has confined me to Rivenhall?'

'At Rivenhall.'

'You have been my brother for all of my life. You must know that is the last place I wish to be.'

'Wish to be and ought to be are not the same thing.' William looked at Elizabeth in resignation, gave a great sigh, then shrugged. 'I suppose we ought to go to the house.'

'I am ever so anxious to see it again! And Murray. I hope the sweet lamb is well.'

'He is happily scampering around somewhere with my dog.'

'You have a dog, too? I envy you too much for words.' She glanced between Elizabeth and William. 'It is nearly like you have two children already.'

Not really, no. And if she and William could not find time to be alone, pets might be the only ones they would have.

Even sitting here at the dining table, watching his sister eat scone after scone, he could not believe she was here. Usually he would be delighted to see her— just not under these circumstances.

Minerva's timing could hardly be worse, or more frustrating. He ought to be secreted away at the stream with Elizabeth, not feeling irate by his sister's untimely 'visit'. He could scarcely believe she had managed to run away from home. It was a bold thing to do even for Minerva. Father and Thomas must be frantic with worry.

'Tell me again why you were confined to Rivenhall,' he said, because although she had told him once already he was having a hard time visualising the event.

She sighed through a mouthful of crumbs, then started again at the beginning. 'Father began to natter on about suitable matches for me. As if the choice were his and not mine!'

William would point out that it was, that Father might know best in the matter, but his observation would not be taken well. The proof of Father's wisdom was evident in how well it turned out in his own life. He had to bite back the observation because it might result in Minerva running away from Wilton Farm, too. At least for as long as she remained here, she was safe.

'I told him I would not have him making my choices. This was no longer the dark ages like it was when he and Mother wed and that my future was up to me to choose. When Father said I was too young to know what I wanted…well, I told him what I wanted.'

'To become a circus performer?' Elizabeth asked, although she had already heard it once, the same as he had.

Even for Minerva this was unbelievable.

'Yes! I would begin as an animal trainer. May I teach Murray to leap through a hoop while I am here? Not a burning hoop, no, that would never do.' She shook her head firmly. 'But, of course, I aspire to be a trapeze artist. To swing about as if I am flying.' Minerva shot him a severe frown. 'So, then, Father scoffed at my dream, right out loud and in front of Thomas, who you know is even stricter about proper conduct than Father is. So what, I ask you, was I to do?'

'Anything but what you did, I would imagine,' he logically pointed out.

'No one was hurt. People quite enjoyed my performance. Strangers walking by the yard stopped to applaud.'

'What, my dear sister, do you imagine they were applauding?'

'My skill on the swing. I attached it high in the tree so everyone could see. What else would they be clapping for?'

'A young woman swinging merrily about and showing her legs in public? I can only imagine how distraught Thomas was to come outside and discover what you were doing...and an audience of young men gawking at you.'

'Young men enjoy trapeze performances. There is nothing wrong with that.'

'Young men enjoy watching half-dressed young ladies.'

'Do not be a prude, William. I know that you—'

'I was a bad example to you and now greatly regret it.'

She waved her hand as if doing so might miraculously guide the conversation in another direction.

'My costume was the epitome of professionalism for a trapeze performer. And my legs were decently covered with tights. Besides, it was not my attire which got Father in such an uproar, it was the message I painted on the banner over the front door.'

'Did you think he would not be furious? You informed every passing gent, in the most colourful language, that you had no interest in marrying. You have been raised to one day be a gentleman's wife, Minerva. To run his household and see to his needs.'

'*Fopdoodle* is not such a wicked word and it is so old that no one would be truly shocked by it.'

'You insulted the very men who will be your suitors when you debut.'

'I do not wish to debut or to marry. Can you imagine anything more tedious than seeing to my husband's needs? The man will become a widower within a year because I will die of boredom.'

'Your sister has a point, William. She ought to have some choice in her future.'

'We did not and look how well it has turned out.'

'That is not quite true. We did have a choice and we chose each other.'

'That was different.' He smiled at his wife, but scowled at his sister. Minerva truly did not seem to have any inkling of how badly she'd behaved. 'Elizabeth, you did not swing from a tree in Ambleside while wearing—'

'Proper and respectable clothing for the job.' Minerva returned his look, glare for glare.

If Minerva thought the garment to be proper, it proved she had no common sense. There was only one place his sister ought to be and it was not here. Rather it was at home under Father's attentive eye.

In the past, he had been his sister's ally in nearly all things. No mischief had been too great for him not to secretly admire, even when she came sneaking into his club. However, a trapeze performance in front of Rivenhall? Even he knew this was not appropriate behaviour.

'You cannot remain here. I will take you back to London tomorrow.'

Minerva speared him with a gaze, cocking her head at him one way and then another. 'I do not know who you are, William Grant!'

No, nor did he. What he did know was that he felt quite good about it, that just perhaps he had become the man Father had sent him here to become. Bringing his sister home would gain his father's approval.

Elizabeth felt the bottom drop out of her belly. She set aside the scone which she had been about to take a nibble of. William was leaving…going to London. For how long?

'Well,' she said, floundering for a reason to get away so that she might gather her flyaway emotions. 'I will let the two of you chat.' She hurried out of the kitchen and then outside where she sat down on a porch chair.

Birds and bees continued to go about their business in the shrubbery while she wondered how she had come to the point where being separated from William seemed utterly overwhelming. Only weeks ago, she had been an independent person, quite content to be in her own company, or that of her lambs.

Perhaps it would be good for him to go away so that she could find that part of her again. Not go back to being that way completely. But life was bound to separate them from time to time, especially with his family living in London, so it would be good to be able to get along without his immediate presence every moment of the day.

She would need to, because the very last thing she wanted to do was—

'Come with me, Elizabeth.'

To London? He must know she would not.

William sat down in the chair beside her.

'Is your sister angry that we are not letting her stay?'

'Stunned more than anything. She cannot believe that I am taking Father's side in the matter.'

'But you must take his side. It is only right.'

'Yes, it is something I must do. But I do not wish to be away from you.'

Oh, dear, she did not wish it, either, but...go to London? The place she feared most in the world?

'You will have a grand time without me, William.' It ripped her heart to say those words because she greatly feared they were true. 'Surely you want to be reunited with all your friends.'

'Yes, I am anxious to see them…and anxious for them to meet you.'

She ought to go, of course. It was time and past that she put the fear of a city behind her.

'If you are worried about what will happen at Wilton Farm in your absence, you need not be. Our employees have been here for a long time. They are reliable.'

'It isn't that. I know they are. It is only… You know why I am afraid to set one toe in that city.'

'Do you trust me?'

'Of course, you know I do.'

'Then come with me. London is as familiar to me as my own back garden. I will not let anything happen to you. You might even find you like it if you give it a chance.'

That sounded all well and good. She did trust him. But it was not only the past she hesitated to face. He could not protect her from being a social outcast. For all that he was comfortable in society, she still was not. All but one of the people who had visited Wilton Farm had been cordial. But they had been her guests and might have been putting on a show of being polite.

In London it would be different. Her country ways would stand out in stark contrast to their proper manners. The saying that one could not make a silk purse out of a sow's ear would be on display for all to see. Yet William believed she was not a coward. She did not wish to be one, which meant she ought to accompany him…test the strength of her character.

One day, if they were fortunate, they would have children. She did not wish to hide away at the farm while they went to visit London with their father. She did not wish to be away from their father as it was. Not only that, if he were to be anyone's father and she were to be anyone's mother, they would need to be together.

'I see you struggling with it and I will not force you to come.' He stroked her hair where it fanned across her shoulder. 'But if you choose to come, I promise you will not be sorry.'

Oh, yes, she might. And yet she would despise herself if she remained behind seeking solace among her sheep. There had been a time when her animals could give her that, but no longer. Now that she was a married woman, the comfort of her small, sweet creatures would not suffice.

She wanted her husband. It was only right that she be where he was. More, it was only right that she be worthy of him...and that she conquer her fear of an incident that happened in her childhood.

'You are right, of course.'

If she did not go with him she would miss the smile he was giving her. She was not certain she could do without it any more.

'All right, then. I will come with you.' She smiled because by putting on a show of confidence, she might eventually come to feel that way.

'You won't be sorry.'

He leaned across the arms of their chairs, pressing his lips to hers. How could she possibly be sorry when he kissed her that way? What she would regret was remaining at Wilton Farm and missing the smell of him and the teasing lift of his smile. The light that ignited within her whenever she saw it.

'Just remember, in the unlikely event that I do misplace you, Father still rides in the park every morning.'

'London,' Elizabeth admitted while looking out the window of the elegantly appointed Rivenhall carriage which had been waiting for them at the train station when they arrived, 'is nothing like I remember it being.'

Nor did it inspire the terror she had always imagined she would feel seeing the crowds, the tangled streets and the...the inns.

'I imagine it is not,' William said, sitting beside her and giving her hand a squeeze. 'Things do loom larger when one is small.'

'To me—' Minerva declared, her hands crossed over her middle in a petulant gesture. She did not bother glancing out the window at the marvellous buildings they drove by, 'It is still as dull as always.'

Surely not! Elizabeth was overwhelmed by the elegance of the structures, amazed by the number of people leisurely walking past shops and restaurants. They looked as elegant as the buildings did, strolling and chatting in the late afternoon as if there were no chores to be completed before nightfall.

Ambleside felt further from London than the several hours it had taken to travel here by rail. At first, boarding the train felt like a betrayal of all she believed in. After a few hours, she'd freely admitted it was a comfortable and convenient way to travel...at least for those who travelled in first class the way they were doing.

'Dull?' William's brows rose high on his forehead. 'How can you say so? There is no more exciting city than London.'

'Where one may not swing in her own tree no matter how thrilling her performance might be.' She arched her brows back at her brother. 'But I suppose you are happy to be home, back with your friends and your club...which a young lady, facing certain doom from boredom, may not attend.'

Would William attend his club now that Elizabeth was with him in London? More, if she had not come, would he attend? Perhaps he would. For all she knew this would be a common thing for a gentleman to do... be expected of him, even.

There was quite a lot she needed to learn about his life here. She did not know William Grant of London, the sought-after society guest, the man who took great pleasure in the company of his peers. She only knew the man who knelt in the mud to free a stuck ewe, the one who raced into a burning stable to save the live-stock. The man who spent a night in the pasture making himself equal with the shepherds.

And also, the one who drove her to distraction by speaking in public against her cause...then later convinced her that she was the one in the wrong.

She only knew the man who was hers. But there was another William Grant, the one who belonged to this vast city. Somehow, she was going to have to reconcile that man with the one she had fallen in love with. She could only imagine there would be times, seeing him with his peers, when he would seem something of a stranger to her.

'Here we are,' Minerva said, her tone resigned. 'No doubt Father will banish me to my chamber for the rest of my dreary life.'

The carriage driver opened the door, helping Minerva down the steps. William got out next and helped Elizabeth down.

'Welcome to your London home, my dear,' he said.

Gazing at the elegant structure, she could not imagine she would ever feel as if it were home. It was charmingly pretty, with flowers and trees gracing the well-manicured grounds, but still, the mansion was huge.

It was clear by William's wide grin that he was comfortable here, proud to be showing off the place where he had grown up. Beyond a doubt, he was happy to be here. An odd sensation tickled her nerves. It was something akin jealously, but not quite. It was more like fear. What if William did not wish to return to Wilton Farm? What if, being at home among his own, he decided this was where he belonged?

Well, she could not dwell upon the thought, because Lord Rivenhall and Thomas rushed out the front door. Her father-in-law's gaze at his daughter was stormy, but when it shifted to Elizabeth all she saw was heartfelt welcome.

'My girl,' he declared, giving her a fatherly embrace. 'Welcome to Rivenhall.'

Thomas followed his father out of the grand entry doors of the mansion. After giving his sister's retreating figure a severe scowl, he turned his attention to Elizabeth.

'Welcome, Elizabeth… Sister,' he said warmly. This surprised her since in her mind William was the warmhearted brother and Thomas the reserved one. She was quite touched by the affection in his greeting. 'It is wonderful to have you here. I hope Minerva's surprise arrival was not too distressing.'

It was, but not in the way he imagined. She and William still had not found their time to come together. Minerva's arrival had been beyond untimely and frustrating. Perhaps tonight if William's quarters were isolated and they retired early...

'I hope you are not too weary from your travels.' Her father-in-law took her arm and led her towards the house. 'We have a longstanding engagement, a small gathering only, but I cannot cancel at this late hour. I fear we must carry on with it.'

Oh, my...apparently she was going to be tossed into society without a moment to catch her breath.

Seeing Elizabeth standing beside his chamber window gazing out at the lamplight illuminating the garden below, William had to catch his breath. It seemed beyond belief that he was a married man and his wife was here with him. Also, beyond belief that bad timing had struck again. Guests would soon be arriving and, as a dutiful son, he would be required to help keep them entertained.

'You need not come down,' he said. 'It has been a long day and if you wish to remain upstairs, everyone will understand.'

'I would rather be with you.' She smiled at him. He knew she was gathering her courage...putting on a brave face. 'I am anxious to take a walk in your garden. It looks so enchanting with lanterns to light the paths. I have never seen anything half as welcoming.'

'It is your garden now, too.'

She stared down at it in silence. He wished he knew what she was thinking.

'I imagine it is every bit as beautiful in the morning.'

He did not believe that was all of what she was thinking, but her thoughts were her own so he would not pry.

'We shall take a walk after breakfast, too. I want you to be happy here. It is a marvellous place to live.' Her lips pressed into a tight seam so he amended, 'Even better to visit.'

'I imagine you and your brother had grand times playing in the garden. It seems a good place for adventuring, having so many paths and alcoves.'

Going down the stairs into what she must consider the lion's den, he recounted some of the mischief he and Thomas used to get into along those paths and in those alcoves, back in the days when his brother still enjoyed mischief.

Chapter Fifteen

Sitting beside William at the long dining table, Elizabeth could not believe she had thought the eight guests she had hosted at Wilton Farm to be a large gathering. There were twenty people at this table and, she thought, it could easily accommodate ten more.

It felt odd beyond words to have butlers standing about the perimeter of the room for the sole purpose of attending to her dining needs. Truly, she had more in common with them than she did her fellow dinners.

Not so William. Clearly, he had everything in common with them. He smiled, laughed and was clearly happy to be home and in company. He might be home, comfortable among his own, but she felt like an imposter, stylish gown notwithstanding.

William was handsome and at ease in his gentleman's garb. While she hoped no one would engage her in conversation, her husband chatted happily with everyone. Each person addressing him seemed to have his full attention. He had a way of speaking to people which could not fail to make them feel special, their company appreciated.

From the first time she'd met him, he'd made her feel that way, too. Of course, he would have been trained to act gentlemanly from the time he was a tot.

She got a lump in her belly wondering if, being a naive country miss, she'd misunderstood his attention towards her. Because of his training he might have treated any woman he met beside the road the same way. But, no, just then he clasped her hand under the table, gave it a long slow squeeze. He did love her and she knew it. No matter what, she knew his heart.

What she must remember was that he was a man of two worlds. There was the world he was born into where he was friend and associate of all these elegant people. Then one he had chosen to have with her, which was humble and yet wonderful in its own way.

'How do you find life in the wilderness, William? I imagine you miss the company of society a great deal?' asked a lady on the opposite side of the flowery centrepiece.

Even though the way she uttered the word *wilderness* bordered on condescending, her question was an honest one. No doubt everyone at the table had been wondering the same thing.

'I find it to my liking.' He squeezed Elizabeth's hand again which she found reassuring. 'But you are correct, Penelope. I miss society a great deal. I can only hope you will come and visit my wife and me at Wilton Farm.'

'Is it true that you delivered a baby sheep and named it Murray? He says you did but I, for one, do not believe it. You, of all people, doing such a thing!'

'It is partly true. Elizabeth delivered the lamb, then

gave me the honour of naming him. So, I called him Murray.'

The story caused laughter to ripple from one end of the table to the other.

'Oh! Please tell us more outrageous stories!' Penelope exclaimed.

'Later, perhaps.' He stood up, bringing Elizabeth with him. 'Dinner is finished and I have promised Mrs Grant a stroll in the garden.'

'Oh, but the gentlemen are retiring to the library for cigars and port. Do you not wish to join them?' Penelope seemed surprised that he would break with what must be tradition among them. 'And surely your wife would enjoy time getting to know us.'

Please let William insist on the walk! Not that the ladies were not friendly, but she would not know what to say to them since they had extraordinarily little in common.

'A promise is a promise. But I'm certain we will have time to visit with you later on.' As it turned out, William spent a great deal of time visiting with them.

After strolling in the breathtakingly beautiful garden she, being weary to the bone from the day's events, went up to bed while William went downstairs to continue getting caught up with his friends.

The next morning Elizabeth stepped outside Rivenhall House wearing a gown which was meant to be worn specifically when one went out walking. She could not imagine anything more frivolous, but she was going out walking and did not wish to stand out by being dressed unsuitably.

Perhaps she ought to have told William she was

leaving the house, but he had been busy with one thing after another and so she had not. More than that, she wanted to take this walk alone.

Perhaps this was too much…and done too soon. Reasonably, she could excuse herself from it. But, no, too soon might always be too soon. This was something she must do if she were to have any chance of moving on from where she had been all these years.

If she intended to conquer her fear of the past and this place, she would need to do it alone. If William accompanied her, he would only attempt to distract her from her fear when what she needed was to face it straight on.

She did not have long to accomplish the task. In only an hour she was to be back at the house where someone would be waiting to make alterations for yet another ball gown.

Once outside the gate, she glanced about, spotting a park which was only a short distance down on the other side of the street. That was where she would take her battle. If this was the park her father-in-law rode in the mornings, it could not hurt to be in a place where he might find her if things went wrong. Although, this time she had no intention of becoming the target of an awful man, of becoming lost and terrified.

She would return home in an hour, a stronger and braver person. Perhaps she would even go shopping and purchase a new doll. She would take it home and place it on a shelf to remind herself that she was free of old fears.

To that end, she nodded at a couple walking in the opposite direction to her. They nodded back. Seeing a woman strolling past with a perambulator, she said,

'Hello.' The lady smiled and said 'hello' back to her. Such greetings were commonplace in Ambleside, so she felt a flush of reassurance.

Spotting a bench under a shady tree, she sat down to think…about her father and his disappearance. She had put off looking squarely at the matter for far too long, casting the blame on a wicked city. If she blamed London, she would not need to think about it too deeply. But here she was and would likely be again, often.

She closed her eyes and tried to picture her father, but of course, she could not. She had no memories of the man since she had been only a newborn when he vanished. Aunt Mary had always insisted that he did not simply choose to leave. He had been infatuated with his infant daughter and would not have done so.

It was time to put away the fear of what happened to him once and for all. She invited the possibilities into her mind so that she might face them…and then reject them for what had likely happened.

Had he been abducted by a murderous fog? Perhaps been devoured by rats the same has her doll had been? No, those had been a child's terror.

Although no more terrifying than imagining the river reaching up to snatch him while he walked along…as if it were a living, frightful being. More than likely, he had been the man pulled from the Thames. Her aunt and uncle believed it.

He might have encountered a thief, fought the villain and lost the battle. Or it might be as tragic as losing his balance and falling into the river to drown. Both of those made heartbreaking sense. It was time for her to look where she had not the courage to look before…to accept it as probable.

From a short distance away she heard a child giggling. Opening her eyes, she saw a tiny girl being tossed over her father's head and then caught securely in his arms.

She had missed a great deal with her father—she would always be sorry for it. But she did have wonderful memories of Uncle James tossing her in the air. In all, she had been blessed as a child.

Next she turned her attention to her own ordeal... to being lost overnight. Drawing on her courage, she summoned the most horrid of her fears. It had been by far the worst...more frightening even than the ugly, red-eyed rats had been.

This was the one she lived over and over again, whenever she thought of the cold terrifying alley she had hidden in. Unlike whispers in the fog, this one had happened, not been imagined. While she'd shivered behind a barrel, a shadow had loomed on the wall directly over her. She recalled how unnaturally cold it had seemed and how it robbed the little bit of light there had been in the alley. She'd curled into a ball, trying to make herself as small as she could. A man's harsh laugh had come from very nearby. Probably the awful man come back to snatch her. She shook so violently he must have heard her bones clacking. She had been in genuine danger in that moment.

She reminded herself that she was no longer behind that barrel, but on a park bench.

All at once a breeze shifted the tree branches, allowing sunshine to touch her shoulders. Hurtful images blew away. In a puff they seemed to simply vanish. She determined not to allow them to darken her mind again. If they came knocking, she would slam the door on their lying grins.

She might not ever love London, but neither would she fear it as she had. Some parts of the city were not as safe as this park was, she understood that. But she also understood that she was smart enough to avoid dangerous areas.

Smiling, she opened her eyes to see a man standing on the far side of the path, watching her. Rising from the bench, she crossed to him. It might not be proper to hug William right there for all to see, but she did it anyway and he hugged her back.

'What are you doing out here by yourself, Elizabeth?'

'I went looking for my courage.'

'I gather you found it?'

She nodded, knowing old fears had scuttled away. 'I will never know what happened to my father for certain. But I know what will never happen to me.' She felt confident in a way she never had. 'How did you know where to find me?'

'Minerva saw you go out. With the park only across the road, it stood to reason. Besides, I will always know where to find you.'

'How?'

'I will follow my heart.'

The next evening, William waited at the foot of the stairs for Elizabeth to come down. He had to admit to being excited to see her wearing her new ball gown. She was bound to be the most beautiful woman at Lady Merriweather's ball and there would be many ladies in attendance.

Although he had not been gone from London for long, it came as a surprise that life was so busy, far more hectic than he recalled. With social engagements backed end to end, there was barely time to change clothes between them.

Back at the farm life was also busy at times...not hectic, though. And there were quiet times in the afternoon and the evenings... Ah, the evenings were peaceful, and a person had time to sit and watch stars travel across the sky. Here in London, one was not likely to see a glittering display, even if one had the time to look for it.

Tonight would involve another social whirl. Word had spread that he had returned. His company was as much sought after as it was before he married. Last evening, Murray had whisked him away to their club. Elizabeth had not objected, but rather encouraged him to enjoy an evening with his friends, so he had gone.

For as much as he enjoyed the outing, his heart was not completely in it. Not being the same man who had left London several weeks ago, how could he enjoy his pursuits in the same way he had? The entire time, while laughing and telling stories with Murray and some others, he had been thinking of his wife.

Tonight's event was bound to be enjoyable if only because she would be with him. The anticipation of attending a ball had his toes tapping in his dancing shoes. He always felt at home among happy crowds.

He could not recall looking forward to one more than he did Lady Merriweather's, in part because he would be introducing Elizabeth to society. They were bound to adore her. Although he had yet to see her in the new gown, he had no doubt that his shepherdess would spar-kle. She would capture hearts and win friends.

Seconds later his wife hurried up the corridor, not down the stairs he had been staring at. Coming into the hall, she whirled about, smiling at him. Her gown, the same soft green as her eyes, floated about her ankles.

Flesh-and-bone Elizabeth put imagined Elizabeth to shame. When she walked towards him, she appeared to be drifting across the floor. He scarcely knew who she was with her hair done up in curls and the pearl comb he'd had delivered to her earlier in the day tucked behind her ear.

He had wanted to give the gift to her himself, but Thomas had invited him to ride in the park. He could not refuse since it had been a long time since he and his brother had done anything brotherly together.

The scent of the garden clung to her. She must have come in from outside.

'You look elegant, my dear.' He looked her over from her pretty, but apprehensive-looking smile to the slender nip of her waist where a swathe of ivory lace draped across her hips, then caught behind and flut-tered to the floor in waves.

She blushed. A flash of heat pulsed through his limbs. Just like that, attending the ball was not his first choice of a way to spend the evening. It was too late to cancel so he would make the best of things and then call it an early evening. As long as Elizabeth did not mind leaving early.

He hoped if she did not it would be because of the appreciative looks she was giving him while he posed playfully this way and that in his ball attire. Or she might not mind retiring early because, while she seemed to feel better about being in London, she still did not feel comfortable about her place in society.

All she needed was a bit of time to know she was accepted by his friends. To have fun, laugh and dance. He would lead by example, make a point of having a grand time. He would smile brighter and laugh more often in the hopes that she was seeing what a grand time he was having and then understand that what might appear to be extravagant fun was, in this world of society, both acceptable and required.

This would be a delightful night and, afterwards, back at home it would be exquisite.

Elizabeth returned Lady Merriweather's greeting, but clearly her hostess's attention was focused on William.

And why should the lady be different than anyone else? Everyone's attention was focused upon him. From the moment they entered the mansion, people had been nodding and smiling at him.

'You cannot imagine what a surprise it was to all of us to hear you had run off to…wherever it was you ran off to and got married.'

'To Ambleside,' William answered. 'Wilton Farm.'

'Well, dear boy, I can tell you, you have been greatly missed.' Lady Merriweather lowered her voice to a tone which might, or might not, be considered discreet. 'The alcoves have become positively dusty.'

'And they shall remain so, Lady Merriweather.' With a playful wink at the older woman, he whisked Elizabeth away.

'Do not take what she said to heart, my dear. It is

the way of some society matrons to be the slightest bit outspoken.'

'Outrageously outspoken,' she muttered. But perhaps their hostess did not mean anything by it, or she would not have said it for Elizabeth to hear.

He led her past groups of people caught up in cheerful conversation, towards a room where refreshments were being served.

She felt eyes shifting her way ever so subtly as she passed by on William's arm. Naturally they would be curious but still, it felt to Elizabeth as if she were the one being served on the buffet table. Refined manners prevented them from staring at her outright. Even so, she felt their interest like pinpricks on her back as she passed by.

A sow's ear trussed up in an elegant gown was what they had to be thinking. And if they were not, it was what she was thinking. She gripped her husband's hand, striving to present the sort of smile which came so naturally to him.

If she lived to be a hundred years old, she feared she would not fit in with them. For William's sake she must try. She loved him far too much to behave in any way which might cast shame upon him.

They sat on plush purple chairs. William ate heartily, clearly appreciating the food on his plate. She tried to look as if that was what she was doing, but all she accomplished was to chew the same bite over and over again.

When they were finished eating, William said the one thing she truly did not want to hear.

'Come, Elizabeth, let's dance.'

'Stomp about, you mean. No, I would rather not. But I would greatly enjoy seeing you dance.'

Hopefully her encouraging smile hid the fact that, in truth, she would hate it. To watch him whirl about the floor with a pretty young debutante in his arms? To see her laugh and gaze into his eyes would be unsettling. At the same time, she did not wish to deprive him of the pleasure he was accustomed to.

'I will remain with you.'

'I will feel awful if you do not enjoy yourself. For my peace of mind, you must dance. Truly, William, I will enjoy it nearly as much as if I were doing it myself. I shall tap my toe the entire time.'

She saw his hesitation, but more than that she saw his longing.

'If you are certain? I would not want you to miss the pleasure.'

'Pleasure for you.' She nodded and waved her hand in the direction of the dancers.

Standing, he kissed her cheek, then, grinning, went in search of a dance partner.

Oh, dear, the last thing she wished was to see him choose a lady to dance with. It might be as bad as watching him dance with her. Curious, in a rather distressing way, about what sort of lady appealed to him, she went to stand beside the door and watch.

Would she look anything like Elizabeth did or would she be different? William loved her, she knew that and did not fear his affections would stray…but still…he had not chosen her, not in the beginning at least.

So what sort of woman would he choose had he not been forced to wed her? This was a foolhardy thing to do. Truly, she was comparing each elegant lady who set herself in his path to herself. Comparing and falling short. How would she ever live up to the elegant company he was used to?

She watched him stroll about the ballroom, pausing to speak with a dark-haired beauty and then a willowy blonde woman. He spoke easily with everyone, both men and women.

It could not be denied that he seemed happy to be doing so... Truly, she thought he might be glowing with pleasure to be among proper company.

Who was this man she had married? A gentleman of society was who. She had warned herself to expect this. Somehow seeing him among his own, at ease and happy in their company...well, it confused her. Who was he really at the heart and core of him?

Much of her fear of coming to London had been that she would not fit in... It was a genuine concern. But now she realised there was more to it than she had realised. There was another fear which she had not paid proper attention to until this moment.

She ought to have. Her dread at not fitting in all of a sudden seemed not as worrisome as seeing how very well William did fit in. Had she ever seen him so joyful, so happy and at ease?

She searched her mind and, no...she had not. These were his people, his lifelong friends...and she was jealous of it.

Not jealous in the normal sense. She did not fear he would be unfaithful to her or that his affections would wander. His sense of honour would not allow it. He said he loved her and she believed him.

And, oh my, how she loved him!

But she was terribly jealous of the life he shared

with his peers, a life she might never truly be a part of. She was jealous on behalf of Wilton Farm...feared it would never truly be enough to make this society gentleman happy.

While she watched, wondering which young lady he would take in his arms and spin happily about the dance floor, Penelope hurried up to him. The socialite stood boldly in front of him. Why, she had the nerve to nod at the dance floor. Even Elizabeth knew that the gentleman was the one who did the asking. All right, then, she was also jealous in the traditional way.

William shook his head at which point Penelope nodded towards a curtained alcove. Elizabeth stood up, gasping at the outright nerve of the woman.

William stepped around her, laughing and making light of the flirtation as if it were a game he had played many times.

In the end, William did select a woman to dance with. She was very pretty, slightly plump and about seventy years of age. William's attitude towards her was as attentive as it was with the younger women. Her husband had a gift for making people feel at ease in his company. No doubt everyone he encountered believed him to be a dear friend.

Person after person sought his company. He seemed delighted to chat with each and every one of them. It was a skill, she imagined, which gentlemen learned from childhood. While she had been learning to care for livestock, he had been learning to socialise. Their childhoods had been worlds apart. She had a sinking feeling that their lives today might be as well.

She had begun to feel the difference in their stations back at Wilton Farm. But there it had not been so difficult to convince herself it did not matter greatly. Here in Lady Merriweather's ballroom, she could hardly continue to shove it to the back of her mind, to pretend the differences in their upbringings made no difference.

She feared it perhaps did matter.

She tried desperately to recall a time when, at Wilton Farm, he had looked so at ease and light-hearted. Tried and failed.

Right there on the spot, she nearly gasped in dismay at where her thoughts were leading. She ought to back away from the dark tunnel her mind suggested she dive headlong into. How could she help it, though, when nothing mattered more to her than William's happiness did?

And what was it that would make him happiest? To be here where he belonged, among his own? Or to be at Wilton Farm, which never been his first choice?

The thought was a prick to her heart and, once there, lodged like a thistle. With her he was making the best of what life had dealt him. But what if he did not need to make the best of things?

This life, lived among this bright and smiling company of his peers, might be what was best for him. She had to admit she had never seen him look as relaxed. He had not stopped smiling since they'd arrived.

His love for her might be the very thing standing in the way of what was best for him. She nearly broke down on the spot, imagining it might be true. Hands trembling, heart quaking, she needed to get away by herself to think this over. To try to convince herself that this was not right…that her love would be all he needed in order to be happy.

It was certainly true for her. His love mattered more

than air or food…or anything. Even her beloved Wilton Farm. Turning her back on the dance floor, she went out the wide doors which opened to the back garden.

With only a few people outside, she was likely to go unnoticed. The garden path, being dimly lit by gas lamps was a soothing, private place to walk and think.

She dreaded what her heart was telling her. That marriage to her might not be best for him. Luckily, or perhaps not luckily…their marriage had not gone so far that it could not be annulled. Truly…she had never considered such a horrid thing until now. Annulment? A knife ripping her soul would not hurt worse. The very word made her sick at heart.

Was she wrong to believe that love was enough to see them through anything? She might be. The more thought she gave it, the clearer it seemed that their worlds would never meld.

Yes, her thoughts might be slightly warped given they were coming to her through the spiralling tunnel of despair she had allowed herself to jump into, but that did not make them any less true. While her marriage could be legally abolished, rescinded and cancelled, her love for William would never be.

How had her life come to this? Only a short time ago she had been deliriously happy. Pain made her clutch her stomach. She nearly stumbled.

Hearing women's voices as she approached a concealed area of the garden, she whisked the quickly falling tears from her face. She turned as quietly as she could to walk back the way she had come.

'I was at Wilton Farm when it happened!'

What? That was Justine's voice. Were the women talking about her?

'You may be confident that the gossip is true. She did exactly what you have heard.'

The gossip? She had been in London only days and she was already the subject of gossip?

'She rushed outside when it was raining...and why? To find a couple of animals! Any woman of breeding would have thought first of her gown. It was an irresponsible thing to do.'

'I predict our William will never be happy with a low-born woman, not in the long run,' said a stranger's voice. 'Having grown up with him, we know it is true.'

Low-born...the word, spoken so causally by those refined lips, ripped her soul. She had been judged... convicted of having a common birth. No matter how refined an act she put on, that would not change.

'I see a separation in his future. Poor dear man.' Another voice plunged a dagger into her bleeding soul.

'I would not be so sure of it,' Justine added. 'Remember, I was their guest and I vow he is utterly taken with her. And really, she is a lovely person. I like her quite well, but the fact remains she will never be one of us.'

'I find it sad,' said the voice which had suggested a separation. 'Any fool can see he adores her. But what will William give up for that love? Everything he has ever known! Everything that has ever made him happy.'

She ought not to feel like dying on the spot, hearing what they said. Had she not been struggling over the same awful idea? These hidden gossips only confirmed what was already in her heart. What, she must ask herself, was she willing to give up for love? Could she sacrifice love for the sake of love?

It might take more courage than she had.

Chapter Sixteen

William had never been so weary of keeping up his end of a conversation. What was it he and his companions were even discussing? The aches and pains of growing older?

Then, Elizabeth came in from the garden, seeming to him like a breath of fresh evening air. However, she did not look like a breath of fresh air. She looked pale, her lips drawn tight as if she were in some sort of pain.

Excusing himself from the older gentlemen he had been chatting with, he hurried towards her.

'Are you well, my dear?'

'All of a sudden I feel ill.'

He clutched her hand, which did indeed feel clammy, peering into her eyes as if he might see the cause for it in them.

'I shall call for the carriage. We shall go home at once.'

'It is nothing serious, only an uneasy stomach. You must stay, I insist.'

'And send you home alone while you are ill? No.' He urged her towards the ballroom doors where it would be a short walk to the hall.

'William… I do not wish for you to see me…' She touched her stomach, frowning. 'I would perish of humiliation.'

'You will not perish, I promise.'

'I will, because if the only way I can get you to remain is for me to stay here with you, it is what I will do.' She nodded, her expression set and stubborn. He was certain she meant it. 'I fear the result will not be pretty if I stay. We will both perish of humiliation. Please, William, if you love me, put me in the carriage. Send me home alone.'

'Very well, but I do not like it.'

'Thank you. And I will take another chamber for the night. Do not look for me for I shall be fighting my misery. Do not look so worried. I shall be right as rain in the morning.'

He saw her to the carriage. When he helped her up the steps, she hugged his neck tight…told him she loved him and that he should have a marvellous time. He thought he felt her chest hitch. Something was not right.

'I will send for a doctor.'

'Do not waste his time. I promise I will be well in the morning…this sort of thing happens to women… monthly.'

Oh! Now he understood.

She kissed him, then ducked into the carriage. He closed the door after her, then watched while it rolled away down the street.

Going back inside, he glanced about, feeling rather bereft. Everything was as it always was. People laughed, they danced and conversed. Young men flirted with young women. He remembered how much fun that had been and not so long ago. Now he stood beside the garden doors, watching and feeling an outsider. The very things that used to give him the most joy now felt shallow.

What would he rather be doing, he had to ask himself...dancing with his wife to the strains of the orchestra, or running across the pasture with her in the moonlight? Dancing would be wonderful. He could not deny it. He had tried his best to look as if he were having the grandest time in order to convince her to join him.

Ah, but being alone with her at their own home, with the stars and the moon winking down? He would choose being home...at Wilton Farm.

Upon their first meeting Elizabeth had told him, 'Welcome Home.' At the time he had had grave doubts that a rural farm could ever take the place of London. He had to laugh at himself because, now, the opposite was true. London could not take the place of Wilton Farm. He missed his dog. He missed having small lambs nibbling on his trousers.

More than anything he missed his wife, even though she had only been gone an hour and was less than two miles from where he stood here beside the garden door...he wanted nothing more than to be with her.

Since he had agreed to give her time on her own, he would not go back on it. He would dance with widows and sympathise with the older gents' aches.

He would laugh, chat and smile, all the while knowing that he was no longer wholly one of them.

What he was, was a budding farmer and a husband. No ball he would ever attend would rival walking his own lush, green acres while holding the hand of his very own shepherdess.

As soon as she was able to travel, he was going to take her home.

At sunrise William was woken by rapid pounding on his chamber door. Elizabeth! Perhaps she had been sicker than she let on and someone had run to fetch him. He leapt from the bed, grabbed the doorknob and flung open the door.

'Father?' No one could glare quite like he did, nor shake his fist so fiercely. There was a scrap of paper gripped tight in his fist.

'What have you done now?'

'Leapt from my bed dreading some sort of disaster.' The sense of doom was not easing, but rather growing while he looked at his father's face. 'What is going on? Is it my wife?'

Father shoved the crumpled scrap of paper at him. 'I might ask you the same. This was delivered to me by our carriage driver, shoved under the door where I found it this morning.'

What on earth? What could it have to do with him?

'Who is it from?' he asked, then sat hard on the bed.

'I will meet you in the study after you finish reading it.'

Before he even unfolded it, he felt crushed by a sense of doom. The missive was addressed to his father and signed by Elizabeth. William had to read it three times before the words made sense in his stunned brain.

Elizabeth had changed her mind about the marriage...given him consent to seek an annulment. Oh, she had assured Father it was not his fault, but hers. She made certain to point out that he had done a marvellous job in learning to run the farm. In her opinion he had succeeded in what his father had sent him to do. He had grown to be a man he could take pride in. He ought to no longer be forced to live in exile from London.

Where was the chamber pot? He was about to be ill.

Elizabeth was giving him his freedom. She was also giving him Wilton Farm…until he sold it that he might take up his life in London as it had been. Why? This was all wrong! Something had happened to make her run away from him and he was going to find out what it was.

He charged down the stairs, bursting into the study. Thomas sat in his usual chair beside the desk, shooting him a sharper glare than Father was. For all he knew Mother was frowning down upon him as well. The irony of it was, he had not done anything to deserve it this time…at least as far as he knew he had not.

'The last thing she told me was that she loved me and would see me in the morning,' he blurted out. 'You tell me how what she wrote makes any sense.'

Minerva poked her head around the doorway, then strode into the study, wagging her head. 'If you had any sense you would know.'

'What do you know of this?' he asked more harshly than his sister deserved, but his nerves were drawn tighter than they had ever been.

She rolled her eyes. 'Any fool can see she loves you more than anything. She does not wish to stand in the way of your happiness.'

'What do you mean? Did she write you a letter, too? Did you read this this one?'

'No, but I do notice things.' She shook her head, her expression indicating she noticed he was a great dunce. 'Don't you see that she feels unworthy of you? I, for one, do not understand it. It is not as if you are Thomas, after all. But she loves you too much to keep you from the life she thinks you ought to have.'

'That is absurd!' He glanced at Father, then at Thomas. Surely they thought so, too. 'I would choose the life I have with her a hundred times over.'

'All is not lost, then,' Thomas said, looking relieved and giving him a smile. That was something, Thomas smiling at him, so perhaps all was not lost.

'Not if you can get back to the farm before she moves away,' Father pointed out.

Yes, that had been one more thing she said. That it would be better if they did not see one another again and so she was moving away from Ambleside. He had glanced over those words without letting them sink into his brain because there was only so much a man could take at one time. But she had claimed she would leave Ambleside with all haste.

By Minerva's logic this would mean she loved him, just as she claimed to when she had told him goodbye last night. All he needed to do was convince her that he loved her more than he loved anything that came before her. All he needed to do was something which might be impossible and he would need do it in a hurry. Since she was running away, it was not likely that she would leave word where he might find her.

'I will take the next train for home.'

'I shall call for the carriage to get you to the station.' Father lurched up from his chair, rushed forward and embraced him. 'I am sorry I mistrusted your redemption, Son.'

If he had been stunned by his wife's abandonment, he was flabbergasted at his father's expression of favour. Battling emotions nearly overwhelmed him. Joy and grief...which would be the one to overcome him, bring him to his knees?

Minerva cleared her throat. 'And I am sorry there will be no trains leaving London any time soon. The tracks are in utter ruin.'

Sudden dread came out on top of both joy and grief. He locked his knees and stared at his sister.

'What happened to the tracks?' This could not be true...and yet it was Minerva saying it, so it might be. 'How do you know?'

'Everyone knows. It was in this morning's paper. They were washed away in the storm last night only an hour after the last train left London. It was a lucky thing the timing was not such that the train derailed.'

'What storm?' Thomas asked. 'It rained in the night, but not torrentially.'

'Twenty miles north of city, it was. I am sorry, Brother, the tracks are unusable.'

'I will have the carriage readied for a long journey,' Father stated, yanking on the bell pull and shooting him a bolstering nod. 'It will be difficult travel but still, faster than waiting for the tracks to be repaired.'

'I shall go with you!' Minerva made a dash for the door as if she intended to run upstairs and pack a bag.

'No!' The shout came from all three men at the same time.

* * *

Elizabeth stared at the pretty gowns hanging in her wardrobe. What was she to do with them? Considering the staid, simple life she had set her course on, they would be useless. Have Penny sell them and give the money to charity, perhaps? Or have her keep the funds for the time she might be unemployed after William sold the farm?

An eternity of days had passed…three in all…since she'd run away from the man she loved. Each day was rainier and more miserable than the last. They blurred in her mind, one miserable hour morphing into another.

She touched the lovely satin of her pink ball gown. Perhaps she should keep it because… Never mind. All it would do was remind her of what could never be. What she had tossed away with her own hands. She had lied to William, wickedly betrayed him, but all for his own good, if indeed there was such a thing.

She had not even returned to Rivenhall as she told him she was doing. Knowing the last train of the evening would be soon departing the station, she had instructed the carriage driver to go directly there. On the way she wrote a letter to be delivered to Lord Rivenhall in the morning. By rights she ought to have written it to her husband, but she could not manage it.

A soft knock sounded on her chamber door.

'Elizabeth!' Penny cried. 'You must come down for dinner.'

She opened the door, feeling bad for the anxiety creasing the cook's face.

'I am not hungry.'

'Nevertheless, you shall eat. I will not watch you starve. There are people going without food because they have no choice about it. We have a pantry stocked with food. It would be insulting to them if you let it go to waste. Come now, your meal is growing cold.'

'Very well.' Although Penny's logic made little sense, Elizabeth would at least pretend to eat.

Following Penny down the corridor, she paused at the head of the stairs, thought of the self-imposed line on the floor which had never been erased, for all that they meant to do it.

It was for the best really…an annulment was easier than a divorce, she supposed. It would not be as ruinous for William's reputation. Wouldn't this be what people were expecting, anyway? That in the end she would not live up to society's, and therefore his, standards?

She stared at the food on her plate. If only her heart could become as cold as her meal. Right now, it ached beyond bearing. Oscar Two lay under the table, no doubt waiting for falling crumbs…and for attention. The poor pup looked bereft. It was her fault, so she gave him a finger full of meat pie.

'I imagine he will send for you to live in London with him,' she mumbled, sitting at the table and feeling her stomach churn. Glancing about to make sure Penny was not peeking around the dining-room door, she slipped him another bite. The puppy sat up, wagging his tail. If only a scrap of food would heal her heart.

If only thought after thought would stop crowding her mind. They bounced off each other so ferociously she could scarcely determine which were reasonable and which were absurd. She was fairly sure the thoughts where William came racing after her, telling her she had been wrong to go away and that he did not wish to live without her, were fantasy. Hearing his voice whispering in her ear that he loved their life at Wilton Farm and no other life would do was a dream that would never happen.

The fact was, after what she had done to him… blindsided him with lies and deception…he would probably be glad to be rid of her. Chances were other thoughts were more correct. Faces of the proper society ladies she had met flashed in her mind pounding with the sensation of a headache. Oh, yes…those appropriate women were grinning and eager to fill the space she'd left open for them.

Which one of them would he choose, in time? How much time? An hour or a year, it mattered little since she was going to be miserable for ever.

She ought to have fled to Liverpool by now…or somewhere in Scotland. Every time she thought of where to go, she rejected the place for some reason or another. Not that she could have gone anyway, not with the weather making such a mess of the roads.

Oscar pawed at her skirt, his tail making his entire body wag. If a bite to eat made such a difference, she ought to give it a try. At the least it would satisfy Penny. In a short time, between Elizabeth and the pup, the plate was swept clean.

Since she had managed to eat, perhaps she could manage to sleep. Going upstairs to her chamber, she hoped it would be a deep sleep so that dreams could not invade and leave her more broken than she now was.

It was past midnight when William finally arrived at the farm, both he and the driver exhausted. The fact that they had made it at all indicated a miracle. The roads were nearly impossible to navigate. The carriage had got stuck more than a few times. So had many others. He and his driver had been obliged to stop and aid other travellers in distress. The journey to Ambleside had been an agony of delay after delay and left his nerves stretched almost beyond bearing.

But thankfully he was now home and he blessed the mud gathering on his boots. Mr Adams emerged from the stable, hurried to take charge of the carriage and the animals. From him, he found out that Elizabeth was still here.

The relief rushing through his bones at the news could be greater. He ought to rush up the stairs right now and set matters straight, not wait until morning.

Instead, he went to the stable. There would be no lambs to keep him company, they were out in the pasture secure in the sheepfold with their mothers and the shepherds. He needed time alone to consider what was to be done. Not that he hadn't had too much time already to think on the journey home, as it was. Time to think and worry and grieve.

Now that he was back where he belonged, he hoped his emotions would settle so that the things which popped into his mind would not seem so grim.

While he had spent a great deal of time wondering what he had done to make his wife flee, he had spent more being heartsick over the way she had deceived him.

One moment she told him she loved him, kissed him as if she did. Then, in the next, she had closed the carriage door and rode away, apparently with no intention of seeing him again. According to his sister, Elizabeth had acted out of love. That she had put his happiness above all else. Possibly, but this did not feel like love. It felt like he had been forsaken.

If Elizabeth did love him, she might have spoken to him about what was troubling her. He had believed that they were close enough that she could tell him anything. In his opinion, love did not walk away. Love faced troubles and grew stronger for having done so.

There was one thing he did know. Nothing would be resolved by storming upstairs and waking her.

Since he was already dirty from the trip, and restless, he might as well make use of his time by scrubbing the remaining smoke off the stable walls. His stable walls.

If, after he and his wife spoke, she still wished to end their marriage and go away, he would remain here. It was hard to know exactly when the change within him had shifted. When exactly he had changed from a man who loved society to one who loved his farm.

As far as he could tell it had not happened all at once, but gradually, day by day. Now Wilton Farm was dearer to him than London could ever be. The farm had given him purpose. He had learned to gather eggs and clean stalls. He knew what it was like to stay up all night beside a campfire and keep watch over his flocks.

Also, he had learned that a distant campfire did not equal a raging inferno…but if a raging inferno did happen, he knew he would face the flames to protect the stable and the animals within. Nothing that ever happened in a London ballroom could compare to it. With or without Elizabeth, this was where he belonged.

He took off his shirt, setting it on a post to dry out. Then he grabbed a bucket, filled it with water from the pump outside the door and began to scrub. And pray. Yes, he did belong here. But so did she. At the end of it...they belonged here together.

Something woke Elizabeth from the first sound sleep she'd had in days. Drumming rain could not be the culprit. She had slept through storms so often the sound was a comfort and not an alarm. Whatever the noise was it had not startled her to immediate wakefulness, but rather crept in, first by a vague thought which she had tried to ignore. The house was old and often made creaky noises in the night. Next her mind began to wander and then she decided she had to open her eyes.

Pushing up on the mattress, she sat still, blinking and cocking her head. For all that she wanted to hold on to a few more seconds of oblivion, something had awoken her and she should discover what it was. Perhaps Oscar had found some mischief to get into.

But wait...the noise came again. Cleary it was coming from outside the house. Shuffling to the window, she peered out. 'Oh, my word,' she grumbled.

Yellow light came from the stable windows. It was far too late for anyone to be up. Someone had to have carelessly left a lamp burning. If she did not wish to risk another fire, she would have to go put it out.

Not bothering to change out of her sleeping gown, she simply put on her coat. Since she was no longer a wealthy woman who could easily replace a pair of mud-ruined slippers, she went out of the house barefoot. The grass was wet, the mud cold and the stones slippery.

She walked slowly, taking one careful step at a time to keep from slipping. The trouble with going slow was that she was getting soaked. Even through her heavy coat she felt dampness creeping in.

Oh, my! Not only had someone left a lamp burning, he had left the stable unlocked. She would need to call a meeting of the staff in order to address the negligence.

Stepping inside, she spotted the lamp on top of a newly rebuilt worktable. She took a several steps towards it. A rustling noise came from one of the stalls. She spun towards it in time to see a head pop up, followed by a bare chest…then a muscular arm…and a large manly hand gripping a wet rag.

Watching water drip down William's wrist and dribble off of his elbow, she became tongue-tied and could not make a noise even if a rodent happened to dash across her bare foot.

'Elizabeth?'

She blinked, stared dumbly at him for the longest time.

'Yes, I…came to put out the lamp,' she finally managed to say. 'I did not realise… William, what are you doing here?'

'As you can see, I am scrubbing smoke from the stable walls.'

He dropped the rag, then strode out of the stall. He snatched his shirt from a post, shrugging his arms into the sleeves without buttoning it up. The fabric draped loosely over his chest in an intriguing but disturbing way…disturbing for a woman who was seeking an annulment, that was.

'But if you mean, why am I here… This is my home.'

That made no sense. She had released him from the agreement they made in the beginning, back when they had been foisted upon one another.

'Yes, but did you not read what I wrote to your father?' He need not be saddled with her any longer. 'You are free of all this.'

'Your coat is soaked through. Take it off before you begin to shiver.'

As if looking at him was not already making her shiver.

Without expression, he turned away, went to the stove and knelt to kindle a fire. What was he thinking? Whatever it was, he hid his emotion well.

She removed her coat, setting it on the post where his shirt had hung.

Rising, he turned to look at her. For an instant, his expression warmed, his eyes flared. Before she could wonder what was behind it, his lips pressed to a tight seam. She was not used to seeing him look so serious.

He pointed to a stool beside the stove. 'You should sit down and dry out.'

Oh, my word… She only now noticed how wet her nightgown had got. The way the fabric stuck to her body, knowing her form was not at all hidden from his gaze…well, it did nothing to encourage her envisaged annulment.

If he was moved by what her gown exposed, it did not show. Except for that brief flare of interest, he showed no expression whatsoever.

Evidently, the letter she had written had brought about what she intended. His sober demeanour told her what he was not saying aloud. In spite of the fact that he had come home, he no longer wished to be married to her. It could not be clearer that he hadn't come back seeking her love the way she had foolishly dreamed he might.

But why would he?

No…her treachery, her utter duplicity, had freed him of his misguided love for her. If her heart was breaking, shattering about her toes like glass shards, it was her own fault. She wanted to die. Sitting here on the stool, seeing him look at her with no apparent feeling…surely her heart would shrivel and stop beating. One could not hurt so desperately and still go on breathing.

'You will be happier this way,' she managed to murmur.

'Why would you think so?' He began to fasten the buttons on his shirt. 'I was under the impression we were doing rather well.' With a deep, defeated-sounding sigh, he crouched in front of the stool. He looked her hard in the eye. There would be no escaping whatever he meant to say to her. What she had done to him had consequences and it was now time to face them.

Would she be able to cling to the story she convinced herself was true? That he would be better off without her?

'I was also under the impression that you loved me, Elizabeth. You did say so the last time we parted.'

She stared at her lap, at her hands folded tight. She clasped them hard to keep him from seeing how her fingers trembled. Face to face she could not tell him she did not.

He touched her chin, lifting her face. His fingers also trembled. 'Was it a lie?' He turned his gaze away, staring at the wall he had been scrubbing. 'Was it all a lie?'

'No…none of it was a lie.'

He must have been holding his breath because it left

him in a rush. He squeezed his eyes closed. When he looked back at her moisture glistened in the corners.

'Why, then, do you wish to end our marriage? The truth, Elizabeth. I deserve that much.'

'Yes…you do. If I were not a coward, I would have told you straight away.' That statement was probably the truest she had ever made.

'You are probably the least cowardly person I have ever met. Now, talk to me. Surely you know you can.'

It would be easier to do had she not begun to cry. She had never been a weeper before, only since William Grant had ridden into her life on his citified horse.

'It is because I do love you that I did what I did.' She sniffled unattractively. 'Don't you see? I will never fit into your life…no matter how I dress or how I act, I will never be accepted into society. Society is what you love and I will not keep you from it.'

'Ask yourself this, then. If it is true that I want a life in London, why am I here and not there?'

He arched his brows and his smile ticked up. Only halfway and only in one corner, but it was there and she had never been so happy to see anything in her life.

'Why am I scrubbing smoke off walls when I could be waylaying some forward debutante behind a curtain?'

'I do not know,' fibbed the coward in her.

'But you do know.'

She bent her head to his shoulder, burying her face in his neck. She wound her arms about his chest and squeezed. 'Yes, I do know… It is because you love me, but—'

'But nothing. This is where I want to be. Even if you go away, I will remain here.'

His arms came slowly around her back. His palms pressed her skin, feeling hot even through the clammy nightgown.

'Elizabeth.' His breath stirred her hair. 'I love you. Surely you must know I want a life with you more than I want a life in society.'

'But you looked so happy to be at the ball.' She drew back to see what was in his eyes. Oh…my… 'I thought… and then I overheard those women in the garden and they said what I already knew, that I would never be one of them… Well, I wanted you to always be as happy as you looked then.'

'Oh, I see.' He laughed quietly while whisking the tears away from her eyes and cheeks. 'Some of what you saw was true, but most of it was acting… I put on a bit of a show so that you would see how much fun a ball could be if you gave it a chance. I wanted to you know how grand an evening in society could be.'

He hugged her to him tight and then set her back at arm's length, giving her a look which she could not glance away from.

'But once you went back to Rivenhall—or I believed you had—I took a hard look at it all. Nothing was as bright and glittering as I had once believed it to be. I understood, more than ever, where I belonged. All I wanted was for you to feel well enough to travel so I could bring you home.'

'And then I ran away without even telling you why. Oh, William…how can you not hate me?'

'Can a person hate his own heart? You are my heart, Elizabeth. Never doubt it.'

'But how can you believe me now after what—'

He touched her lips with his finger, shook his head.

'None of that. If my sister is to be believed and I am certain she is, it was all my fault to begin with. I should have made certain you knew how much I love you, that no place—not London, not Wilton Farm—will ever be dearer to me than you are. If it is your wish that we never visit London again, that is how it will be.'

'I only want you, no matter where it is. If you wish to visit London, or even live there, we will.' She cupped his face in her hands, felt the bristle of his unshaved beard scrape her fingertips. She inhaled the scent of his skin, so flushed and…if it was possible to smell heat, she did, and it came from every pore of his strong, manly body. 'I have made my peace with the city. And now I will make my peace with you, if you will have me.'

'I'll have you. My dear wife, never think I did not want you…that I will not always want you.' He would, rather like a spark seeking dry kindling. The stable was about to be set afire with his wanting her. This was one blaze he would cherish for ever.

His attention shifted to the clean pile of straw he had only just laid in the new stall. His expectation had been to sleep in it alone and grieving. He nodded his head in the direction of the inviting, if scratchy, heap of a bed.

'We can go inside if you would rather,' he suggested, desperately hoping she would not rather.

She shook her head. A lock of dark hair stuck to her face where there had been tears seconds ago.

'Shall I get a blanket?'

'No. Things have come between us and this moment too many times already. I will not have a blanket do it now.'

'Good, then.'

He scooped her up, carried her into the stall and lay her down on the fresh, clean-smelling straw. They had waited too long as it was. So much grief might have been avoided had they put this moment of their marriage before any other consideration.

He had been waiting for the perfect moment and situation. As it turned out, a pile of straw and rain beating down on the stable roof was it. All that had ever really been needed was the two of them, with the promise of for ever reflected in one another's eyes.

'William,' she sighed, reaching up for him. Bristly-looking straw cradled her, looking as if it tickled her neck and the backs of her knees where her gown rode high enough to expose them. 'I do love you.'

And right there he saw it, the miracle of for ever glistening in her eyes. Now, he would show her for ever, this time with his touch…with his kiss.

Pressing one finger to her lips, he slowly drew it down her throat, stopping to feel the quick thrum of her pulse. He kissed her there, heard her sigh again.

Then he trailed his finger, making little circles on her skin, to the spot where her heart pattered. He kissed her there, too, felt her quick intake of breath.

'Your nightgown is wet,' he murmured.

'Your shirt is buttoned,' she answered.

'We ought to do something to remedy the problem.'

And so he began. And then she did.

'Welcome home,' she repeated what she had told him that first day, but this time her smile overflowed in love.

'You are my home, Elizabeth Grant.'

'It is what I meant.'

Home in her heart. It was where he was always meant to be.

'What do you say? It is time to cross that line we drew, get good and rid of it,' he murmured.

He could not prove it was so, but he was pretty sure she crossed it a heartbeat ahead of him.

Epilogue

'If Father comes for me, you must tell him I am not receiving.'

Elizabeth sat on a chair, watching Minerva try to arrange three lambs into a single line. At three weeks old, the small creatures had no interest in learning tricks, only bounding and leaping. Truthfully, Elizabeth did not believe they ever would be. They were sheep and not terribly trainable.

For some reason Minerva was convinced the animals would be her path to joining a circus where she could eventually learn the skill of swinging from the ceiling.

'I cannot do that, Minerva,' Elizabeth answered. 'There is no such thing as "not receiving" at the farm. If you wish to hide from your problems, you have chosen the wrong place.'

Casting Elizabeth a grin, Minerva ran to the gate to snatch a lamb which was making a break for freedom.

'I imagine I am safe for the moment.' She shaded her face with her hand, peering up at Elizabeth. 'Father will take some time getting here. He had important guests to entertain and cannot possibly leave them simply to fetch me home.'

Elizabeth heard the front door open and close at the same time her sister-in-law disappeared around a hedge, chasing the quick little lamb.

'I would not be so sure,' William said, coming on to the porch. 'There is a carriage out on the road. It appears to be coming this way.'

'Coward,' she accused. 'You waited inside and let me deal with her.'

'There is no dealing with my sister. Not when she has her mind set.'

'I heard that!' Minerva emerged from behind the shrub, the lamb cradled in her arms, leaves and twigs stuck every which way in her hair. 'I do have my mind set. Father must accept that I am free to choose my own calling in life.'

As it turned out, it was not Lord Rivenhall who stepped out of the carriage, but Thomas.

After greetings and hugs were exchanged, her brother-in-law turned a severe look on his sister.

'Be ready to travel home tomorrow.'

Miranda stooped, picking up a lamb in each of her arms.

'I shall willingly go with you tomorrow,' she said.

'You will?' Thomas and William asked in unison.

'Yes, Thomas, as long as you teach these two to jump through this hoop by then.' She waggled the hoop hanging in the crook of her arm.

A discussion, or rather a dispute, erupted between Minerva and Thomas.

'Shall we take a walk? I feel I shall burst if I do not get away from the house.'

William stood back, giving her a long glance from head to toe. It settled on her middle. 'I believe you will burst if you attempt to go down the steps.'

'And whose fault is that?'

'All mine, my dear. I take full credit for your fragile state.' After a year, his grin still went to her heart and melted it.

'You may make it up to me by taking me for a short walk to the stream.'

'I imagine you do wish to get away from it all… or rather all of them, for a few moments. How many guests do we have at the house? I have lost count.'

'Murray and his bride.' She ticked them off on her fingers. 'Penny's cousin and mother, now Thomas… and Minerva who is not so much a guest as a truant.'

'I thought this was the wilderness.' He kissed her cheek, then led her slowly out of the yard. 'I will take you as far as the carriage house and not a step further.'

'It used to be. It seems that half of London misses you enough to travel north for a visit.'

'We ought to have my sister spread a rumour that we have set sail for India.'

'No one will believe it…not with the babies due so soon.'

'You keep saying babies. How can you be so sure of it?'

'They make me sure. There are far too many limbs stretching and rolling in there for it to be only one.'

She grabbed his hand, placed it on her belly. 'You see? Clearly there are two small bottoms bumping against your palm.'

'Perhaps, but you aren't frightened if there are two of them? I am.'

'Don't be silly. We have four arms between us. And do not forget our fancy carriage. You did purchase it in anticipation of keeping them safe while we travel.'

'How are you feeling? Have we walked too far?'

Her back was somewhat achy, but it had been all morning. What she needed was a good stretch. 'I will do. You may carry me home if it comes to it.'

'Comes to what?' The alarm widening his eyes made her laugh.

'Comes to me giving birth on the way to the carriage house.'

He took her elbow. 'We are going back now.'

'I was jesting, William. I meant if I grew weary of walking on my own...which I am not.

But then again, perhaps—'

'Hello!' came a shout.

Looking out at the meadow, she saw a man and woman walking hand in hand.

'Samuel and Lilly,' she said. Samuel had waited less than three months after she wed William to marry another neighbour. They did look quite happy. Her former suitor smiled at his wife in a way he had never smiled at Elizabeth.

She glanced at William waving and returning the greeting. Every time she saw her neighbour, she was grateful to have married William. Had she settled for Samuel she would never have known true love. No... and neither would Samuel.

'I bring news!' Samuel exclaimed when he was still several yards away.

Elizabeth pressed her hand against her belly. It had

grown as hard as a stone. It had been doing something like it on and off for the past two weeks. This was different, though, more intense…and crampy.

The sensation went away as quickly as it came so she focused her attention on Samuel's news.

'We came as soon as we heard!' Samuel's grin was as wide as she had ever seen it. 'I knew you would want to hear it right off.'

William was giving her an odd, speculative look.

'The rail spur is not coming here! The railway has abandoned the idea for good and all,' Lilly announced.

'That is splendid news,' William said.

With the splendid news delivered, her neighbours walked back across the meadow, their arms twined about each other.

'Who are you?' she asked under her breath.

'We have too many visitors as it is. I do not wish to make it easier for them to get here.'

'My word, but you have changed.'

He laughed, casting her big, roundish body a glance. 'You have changed more.'

'The one thing about the spur is that it might be easier for someone else…say a doctor, to get here.'

'Why are you breathing funnily, Elizabeth?' His stare shifted between her face and her belly.

'I believe there are two sweet souls about to join our family.'

'How "about"?'

'Quite soon, I think.'

He scooped her up in his arms. It was a lucky thing he was strong…stronger even than when he had first become a farmer.

'I can still walk,' she pointed out.

'I do not doubt it, but I am not sure I can, not without an urgent purpose to carry me forward.'

'Very well.' She snuggled into his shoulder, smiling. 'I could get used to this.'

Then he stopped halfway to the house and kissed her. 'I thought I should do this while there is still time. Two babies, you really think so?'

'Yes…and look, William! Another carriage just pulled into the yard. I believe my aunt and uncle have arrived just in time.'

'Heaven help us,' he muttered.

To her way of thinking, Heaven already had, time and time over. Blessings fell around them in the form of laughing voices in the yard, of small sheep bleating and Oscar barking at the new arrivals.

'Welcome home,' William said and she knew he was speaking to their children.

* * * * *

*If you enjoyed this story,
why not check out these other great reads
by Carol Arens?*

The Making of Baron Haversmere
The Viscount's Yuletide Bride
To Wed a Wallflower
'A Kiss Under the Mistletoe' *in*
A Victorian Family Christmas
The Viscount's Christmas Proposal